"I need to leave Carter's.

"If I stay here," Rachel continued, "I'm going to spend my time filing papers for my uncle and eventually living with fourteen cats. I want a life."

Ryker had left Carter's; he'd searched for a life. It hadn't worked out well.

"How do you think I can help you with that?" He kept his distance, as if she could weave a spell on him if he got too close.

"I want you to help me become more like you."

Ryker hadn't felt a sense of danger like this since he'd been deployed.

"You don't want to be like me."

But if he said no, she was going to ask someone else. What would that guy do? The thought of someone hurting her, taking advantage of her, bothered Ryker. She thought being nice was a bad thing. She was wrong.

Dear Reader,

I've so looked forward to writing this book. This second book in the Cupid's Crossing series gives Rachel from *A Valentine's Proposal* her chance at romance.

I identify with Rachel—I grew up a good girl and have that people-pleasing gene. Also, my husband picked me up for our first date on a motorcycle, and later in life I learned to drive one. I also had an accident on a bike, but fortunately, I only suffered a skinned knee and a broken ankle bone.

Like Ryker, alcoholism has been a factor in my family, and I've personally seen some of the fallout. I know it's not a rare phenomenon: AA currently counts more than two million members worldwide. I apologize for any errors in misrepresentation, since I've written from my own perspective.

I hope you enjoy Rachel and Ryker's story.

Kim

HEARTWARMING

A Fourth of July Proposal

—

Kim Findlay

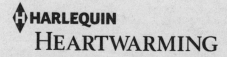
HARLEQUIN
HEARTWARMING

HARLEQUIN®
HEARTWARMING™

Recycling programs
for this product may
not exist in your area.

ISBN-13: 978-1-335-17992-0

A Fourth of July Proposal

Copyright © 2021 by Kim Findlay

This edition published by arrangement with Harlequin Books S.A.

For questions and comments about the quality of this book,
please contact us at CustomerService@Harlequin.com.

Harlequin Enterprises ULC
22 Adelaide St. West, 40th Floor
Toronto, Ontario M5H 4E3, Canada
www.Harlequin.com

Printed in U.S.A.

Kim Findlay is a Canadian who fled the cold to live on a sailboat in the Caribbean and write romance novels. She shares the boat with her husband and the world's cutest spaniel. Bucket list accomplished! Her first Harlequin Heartwarming novel, *Crossing the Goal Line*, came about from the Heartwarming Blitz, and she's never looked back. Keep up with Kim, including her sailing adventures, at kimfindlay.ca.

Books by Kim Findlay

Harlequin Heartwarming

A Hockey Romance

Crossing the Goal Line
Her Family's Defender

Cupid's Crossing

A Valentine's Proposal

Visit the Author Profile page
at Harlequin.com for more titles.

To Ritchard, for encouraging me to take chances

CHAPTER ONE

Nice.

Nice nice nice nice nice.

Rachel Lowther had had *nice* up to her eyeteeth. The next time anyone mentioned how nice she was she was going to scream. Or swear. Or punch.

She stiffened when she heard someone enter the parsonage kitchen behind her. The church management team meeting was wrapping up, but Rachel didn't want to talk to anyone. That was why she'd hidden herself in the dishwater.

A teacup was offered to her.

"You're such a nice girl, Rachel. Now that Cupid's Crossing is a Center for Romance, we'll have to find you a nice boy!"

Rachel ground down on her teeth, hard enough to remove enamel, fists clenched to keep herself from doing any of those things she'd threatened as Mavis Grisham, who was about eight hundred years old and eighty pounds when soaking wet, patted her arm.

Cannot scream at Mavis. She gave me peppermints in church when I was a kid...

Rachel almost trembled from forcing the muscles of her face to smile as she grabbed the empty teacup from Mavis's hands and placed it in the sink. Mavis shuffled her way out of the kitchen, having done her part to help out.

It was more than most of the committee members did.

Rachel was tempted to smash the cup. She could see it: the pink roses breaking into bits of china as the sound reverberated around the kitchen. Everyone would rush in to see what had happened as Rachel stood there, shaking with frustration.

Instead, she ran more soap and water as she considered just how wrong Mavis's statement was. How did she count the ways?

Rachel wasn't a girl. She was twenty-nine. That meant she'd be thirty on her next birthday.

Thirty!

And she might be nice, but she didn't want to be.

Nice was dependable. Reliable. Nonthreatening. Noninteresting.

Nice was boring. And Rachel was so tired of being boring.

The town had recently changed its name

from Carter's Crossing to Cupid's Crossing. Abigail Carter, who basically ran the town, had had to close the lumber mill. Now she was making the place into a Center for Romance, trying to keep the town economically viable. Rachel couldn't complain about the name.

Even though she kind of wanted to mock it.

Her best friends had gotten engaged in the past few months, so apparently, Cupid was here.

But Cupid wasn't interested in Rachel any more than any other man in town.

How long had it been since she'd been on a real date? The last one had been with Nelson Carter, local veterinarian and lifelong friend. They'd gone to a concert together, but driven in separate cars, and his grandmother had sat between them. They'd never been more than friends, backup dates for each other when they were in the lurch.

Not that she had her lurch date anymore. Nelson was engaged. To the event planner who was making this town into a Center for Romance. At least someone was finding love in Cupid's Crossing.

Her friends Jaycee and Dave were getting married. They'd had their engagement party on Valentine's Day, another Cupid's Crossing romantic success story.

Not her. Nope.

Yes, she'd gone out on some dates. Real dates. But they'd been a long time ago and they'd been…nice. And boring. Even the kissing.

She was too nice to be a good kisser, apparently.

Rachel sighed in the now-empty kitchen. Her anger evaporated, and she sagged.

The best kiss Rachel had had in her life had been back in high school.

It was the most interesting event that had happened in her life, which was sad on so many levels she didn't want to count anymore.

She'd been tutoring the baddest boy in school. And, of course, she'd had a crush on him. She was a walking cliché.

He'd kissed her, once. And that kiss had been so amazing that he'd never returned to tutoring. He'd dropped out of school, gotten into trouble and left town to sign up for the military.

For all that he'd had the failing grades, while Rachel had straight As, he'd been the smart one. He'd left Carter's Crossing and found a life for himself.

Presumably. He'd never come back.

Rachel relaxed the hands that had come perilously close to crushing the pink roses on the teacup again. She drew a long breath.

"There you are, m'dear." Rachel's father, widower, minister and clueless as to how she really felt, patted her on the shoulder. His eyes were smiling behind his glasses. He ran his hand over his bald head and sighed happily. "Everyone's finally gone. You're such a help. I don't know what we'd do without you."

Hands buried in soapy water, Rachel forced another smile. "It's not a big deal." Just part of being nice.

"I hope you don't mind—I told Stanley you could represent us on this new committee."

Rachel froze up, hands still wrapped around that stupid teacup.

"What committee?" She couldn't make her voice sound happy. She was tired of being roped in to all-around drudgery. Tired of letting people do that to her. She already spent too much time taking care of Uncle Stanley.

"Now that things are underway with this Romance program, the town has a lot to do to get ready. You can represent the ecclesiastic and legal needs. Your uncle will help you with any legal issues, of course. Since you're working for him, you're already on top of most of those, and I can help you with anything related to the churches in town. It works out very well. Oh, here's my cup."

He set it on the counter beside her. He was proud of how helpful he was.

Rachel closed her eyes and counted to ten. Then twenty. She was at a hundred when she opened them again and by then her father was gone.

She placed the pink rosy teacup in the drying rack. She wiped off her hands on a tea towel. When she walked back into the living room, there were bits of paper and some hidden plates scattered around. None of the food was left over: she baked a mean cake.

No, she baked a *nice* cake.

She went through the motions of cleaning up, returning furniture to where it belonged, her father long gone to his study. He'd never think of offering further assistance. Her mother had always taken care of that, and Rachel had stepped into that role after she died.

When the cleanup was finally done, she headed upstairs. She'd slept in this same room her entire life. The same *nice* room.

Rachel sat on her *nice* bed.

And wrestled with some non-nice thoughts.

She needed to do something. And it would need to be big.

Despite what Mavis suggested, single men weren't coming to the new Center of Romance.

The people coming to Cupid's Crossing were couples. People already together, already in love or falling in love. People were coming for romantic weekends, to propose, to celebrate anniversaries.

Not to find nice girls.

No, if Rachel was going to find what she wanted from life, she needed to become less nice, less boring, and she was going to have to leave Cupid's Crossing.

Sometime between washing the teacups and now, she'd made her decision. She was not going to stay here in Carter's or Cupid's Crossing. She wasn't going to be nice. She was going to find a life for herself, instead of a life helping everyone else because she was *nice*.

Her father would be shocked. There would be fallout at the law office. But it was time to screw up some backbone before she found herself looking at sixty instead of thirty, still not having lived.

She paused as the thought settled in her mind.

She was going to have to leave.

It was a scary thought. She'd lived her whole life here. All her friends and family were here.

But if she didn't leave, she was absolutely

going to become the town spinster, helping everyone else, then going home to her cats.

She was going to become a cat lady. And she didn't even like cats.

Her mind was grappling with those two conclusions. She had to become less boring, and she needed to leave.

That was a much bigger decision than anything the leadership team had come up with tonight.

My name is Ryker, and I'm an alcoholic.

It wasn't the first time he'd said the words. Sure wouldn't be the last. But they hadn't felt this heavy since the first few times he'd forced the words out of his mouth.

Because this time he was back in his hometown. The place he'd escaped fourteen years ago. The place where he was the local screwup, the kid most likely to fail. That was what he'd been escaping from fourteen years ago.

But here he was, back in Carter's Crossing. They'd been right, all those years ago.

The second A in AA was Anonymous, but in a town this size, there was no anonymity. He recognized most of the people sitting in the church basement with him. If they hadn't placed him before, as soon as they heard his name, he'd seen the recognition on their faces.

Son of the town drunk, back and hitting up an AA meeting first thing. Last thing he'd done before leaving fourteen years ago was wrap a car around a tree while drunk.

Not much changed.

Ryker sat back and let the meeting do its work, focusing on what he had to do to get through the next day without drinking. One day at a time.

One of the familiar faces came to shake his hand after the meeting was over.

"Ryker. It's nice to see you again."

Ryker returned the handshake with a firm grip. "Mr. G."

The name slipped back easily. Mr. G, or Mr. Gifford, had taught computer sciences at the local high school. It was one of the few classes Ryker didn't skip.

Well, not as often as the others.

"Want to grab a coffee and catch up?" Mr. G was smiling at him, as if he was happy to see Ryker back.

If Ryker was honest, he'd have to say no, he didn't want to catch up. But he hadn't wanted to come back here to Carter's Crossing in the first place. He couldn't cut himself off, not if he was going to get through this without losing his sobriety. There was a lot he'd do to hang on to that two-years-sober pin.

He was going to accept help.

He nodded and followed his former teacher out of the church basement. He kept his head down, eyes on the ground in front of him. It was hard to be invisible when you were over six feet tall, wearing motorcycle leathers, but he'd do his best.

The diner was around the corner from the church. Same as it had been fourteen years ago. Walking in the door was like revisiting seventeen again.

Ryker didn't want to be seventeen again. He didn't want to revisit a youth he'd wasted. He was pretty sure his sponsor would tell him that meant he should.

Somehow, life had come down to doing all the things he didn't want to. It had been easier in the air force. At least, at first.

He followed Mr. G into the diner, sliding into the seat opposite him in a booth at the back. He glanced around. It hadn't changed from what he remembered. The vinyl was the same faded red, but since the seat wasn't ripped, it must have been updated at some point. The pictures, the light fixtures, the counter and stools, all looked the same.

It even smelled the same.

A tired-looking woman brought them menus and a coffeepot.

"Hey, Brian." She shot a curious look at Ryker. "Anything to eat?"

Mr. G, Brian, shook his head. "Just coffee, thanks."

She set down the menus, flipped over the cups and filled them with practiced pours. Then she picked up the menus and walked away.

Mr. G and Ryker opened creamers and poured sugar into their cups. Ryker caught the smile on his teacher's face before he shot another wary glance around the diner and focused his gaze down.

"I owe you an apology, Ryker."

Ryker's head shot up. "What?"

Mr. G sighed. "I wasn't in a good place, back when you were in my classes. I've been sober for fourteen years now, but that's not really a good excuse. I knew things were bad at home for you and your siblings, but I wasn't paying attention."

Ryker stared into the man's eyes. They were serious.

"That wasn't your job." Ryker hadn't expected help from the teachers at school. He hadn't expected help from anyone.

Mr. G shook his head.

"This is a small town. Everyone knew what

your dad was like. We should have done something—*I* should have done something."

Ryker felt a lump in his throat. He wasn't used to handling concern. Whatever he'd expected from this return to his roots, it hadn't been this.

"I appreciate the thought, sir, but I'm not sure what anyone could have done."

Mr. G grimaced. "I'm not sure, either, but it's one of my many regrets. I wanted to get that off my chest. And to ask if there's anything I can do to help now."

For the past few years, since leaving the air force, Ryker had been living in a big city, a place where it was easy to be lost in the crowd. Not here, though. Everyone would soon know exactly why he was back.

Ryker didn't want to ask for help. But trying to do everything on his own was what led him to needing AA. He'd had to ask for help then. And, with his sponsor miles away, he needed someone here and now.

Mr. G was offering, and he couldn't afford to refuse.

"I went to the house. Thought I could stay there while I sorted things out. But I can't."

Mr. G didn't have to ask what house, or what he was sorting out, or why he couldn't stay there. The whole town would know that his father had fallen and been taken to a nursing home in an ambulance. They wouldn't be shocked: he was the guy who'd been hurt operating machinery at the mill while drunk. He'd spent the rest of his life abusing Abigail Carter for firing him, his kids for being underfoot, and alcohol to deal with life. And now, Dad wasn't going back to the family house. Not anymore.

The house was a flotsam of empty and full whiskey bottles, dirty dishes and garbage. He'd taken one step into the building and had to leave, immediately.

His father wasn't taking his sobriety away from him.

"I booked a room at the motel in Oak Hill, but I need to find another place to stay."

It was still hard to ask for help. But easier to ask someone from AA. They'd understand, in a way nonalcoholics couldn't.

Mr. G had narrowed his eyes, an assessing look on his face.

"I might have a possibility. What exactly are your plans?"

Ryker took a long swallow of his coffee. His plans were fluid.

"Someone needs to get the house ready to sell. I'm the only one willing or able to do it.

Not sure how long that will take, and I'm not sure what I'm doing after."

Of his six siblings, he was the only one not in prison and also willing to return to Carter's Crossing.

Mr. G nodded. "Are you good with your hands?"

Ryker stared at his fingers, wrapped around his coffee cup. His hands he was good with. It was always his brain that had been the problem.

He stretched the aforementioned hands out. "I can do some repairs. Not sure what all the place needs, but I hope it's stuff I can handle."

"Are you looking for work, too?"

He shrugged. "Maybe. Depends on how long I'm here, how much the place needs."

When he was drinking, he'd never had enough money. Now he mostly stayed in, and had some cash saved up. He also worked for himself, projects he could do anywhere he could plug his laptop into the internet.

He could do that here once he found a place to stay. Money wouldn't be a problem, not for a while.

Mr. G tapped on his mug. "The mill closed down a few years ago, so those jobs are gone, but Abigail Carter has a new business she's working on. There might be something for you, depending on what you can do."

Ryker didn't think Abigail Carter would want to hire him for much. Especially not the one thing he'd learned to do for himself.

"Computers." Ryker was amused by the look of surprise on his former computer teacher's face.

And then a smile. "You mean you learned something from my classes?"

"A bit. It was the most interesting class I had in school. I got to work on that while I was in the air force."

"Hardware or software?"

"I know a bit about the hardware, but I mostly worked with programming."

"I'm going to introduce you to Mariah. And then I'll speak to Benny," Mr. G said. "I think we can help each other out."

RACHEL WAS THE first to arrive at the diner for the regular Tuesday night meeting with her friends Mariah and Jaycee. Which was normal. She wasn't the one with a fiancé to distract her.

The three of them had started meeting like this in the winter when they were planning Jaycee and Dave's engagement party. Jaycee had gone a little crazy over that party, but everything had worked out beautifully. Trust Mariah for that.

Since Tuesday nights were the guys' nights to hang out at the Goat and Barley playing darts, the three of them kept meeting on Tuesdays. Mariah was a wedding and event planner who'd come to Carter's Crossing last fall to set the town up as a romance center, and sometimes they'd talk about that. Mariah was a bottomless well when it came to ideas. Since the town mill had been closed, they were desperate for new revenue, and the Cupid's Crossing idea showed a lot of promise.

Rachel and Jaycee had grown up in Carter's Crossing together. So sometimes she and Jaycee amused Mariah by telling her stories of small-town life, especially if the stories embarrassed Nelson, Mariah's fiancé. Nelson, Rachel's former lurch date.

Rachel was taking her turn to talk to the two women tonight. She wanted to tell them about her need to leave.

They'd be surprised, but Mariah had come to Carter's—no, *Cupid's* Crossing from Richmond, Virginia, and had planned to move to New York City. She understood the allure of bigger places. Now that Mariah was engaged to Nelson, Rachel thought Mariah had changed her mind and was going to stay here, but Rachel wasn't.

Maybe they could help her with her other plan to become less nice, less boring. They were both anything but boring. Jaycee had gone a bit overboard on the drama before the engagement party, and Mariah had grown up traveling the world on a sailboat.

Rachel had no intention of changing her basic self, but she needed to find new interests, new hobbies, new something. Jaycee had problems because her future mother-in-law didn't like her. Rachel didn't think anyone didn't like her.

How bland must she be if she couldn't offend *anyone*?

Her friends could help if she could convince them she meant it. Everyone thought they knew her, and then they overlooked her. They didn't take her seriously. She was serious about this. Nervous, but serious.

Jaycee was the next to arrive. They hugged, and Jaycee pulled off her coat.

"Where's Mariah? I've got news, and I'm going to need both of you."

Rachel blinked, then sat down. Okay, her news could wait. She hadn't made any kind of plan yet.

Their waitress brought over Jaycee's coffee. Rachel had given their usual orders when she arrived.

"This is crazy. You know, sometimes life throws a curveball, just when you think you've got it all worked out. Crazy, right?"

Rachel nodded, but she didn't know. Her life didn't have curveballs. It didn't have fastballs. It had soft lobs, and she missed those anyway.

The bell over the door tinkled as Mariah came in. Her cheeks were a little pink: Mariah had grown up in warm climates and still found the New York State weather cold.

"When does spring finally get here?" Mariah unwound her scarf. "Does this place ever warm up?"

Rachel grabbed Mariah's coat as it slipped off her shoulders and folded it onto the empty chair.

"Stop complaining, girl. I have news!" Jaycee was bouncing in her seat.

Another cup of coffee arrived. Mariah poured cream in and took a sip. "Okay, what's the big news?"

"I'm getting married!"

Rachel and Mariah exchanged a glance. Since Jaycee had received an engagement ring at Christmas and the town had hosted a party to celebrate her engagement on Valentine's Day, this wasn't really news.

Rachel had to wonder if Jaycee didn't understand the definition of a curveball.

She grabbed Jaycee's left hand. "Oooh, look, a ring!" she teased, showing it to Mariah.

Jaycee rolled her eyes. "No, I mean I'm getting *married*. This summer."

"You've set a date?" Rachel's mouth dropped open.

"That soon?" Mariah looked shocked.

Mariah had spent years as a wedding planner. Obviously, she was used to a longer time line for weddings. Yeah, it didn't take forever to plan a wedding in Carter's Crossing.

Jaycee nodded, and then shook her head, looking slightly confused.

"That soon, but we don't have an exact date."

"Explain!"

Jaycee took a breath. "Dave's sister, Denise, is pregnant. With twins. She's due this fall. His parents have decided to move to Florida to be near their grandbabies."

Rachel didn't ask why they weren't staying here to wait for Dave and Jaycee's future kids. Jaycee's MIL-to-be wasn't her biggest fan and had only stopped subtly putting Jaycee down when Dave threatened to cut her out of his life.

Jaycee sighed. "I know they'd talked about moving south, but I'm pretty sure Monster-in-Law will use this as an excuse to miss our wedding. And that will bother Dave. So we're going to get married before they leave.

"That is, if you two can help. I know I'm asking a lot, but, Mariah, if anyone knows how to do this, it's you. And you're my best friend, Rach. I want you two to help me pull this off and to be my bridesmaids. Can you?"

The normally confident Jaycee had a worried look, one that only showed when she was dealing with Dave's mother.

Rachel made a quick decision. She could wait to leave until after Jaycee's wedding. She needed time to find a job and a place to stay. She could set the fall as her moving deadline.

She echoed Mariah's "Absolutely." She might be tired of being nice, but she would never be too self-absorbed to not be a good friend. And maybe she felt just a little relieved that she didn't have to do anything yet.

RYKER PUT HIS FOOT down on the ground, letting the bike go silent. He looked at the two-story building.

Mr. G drove into the parking lot behind him.

Ryker lifted a leg over the bike to dismount, and then hauled the bike back on its kickstand. He pulled off his helmet and hung it on the bike handlebars.

Mr. G got out of his truck and came to stand by Ryker.

"This is it."

The parking lot wasn't large, maybe big enough for ten cars. The building was two stories, a work/business space on the main floor and possible housing overhead. It had signage over the door and front window. Gifford's Repairs.

There was a garage to the side. One car was in the paved lot in front of the building. Ryker could remember, long ago, when the store had been a video rental outlet. Someone had tried to start a bakery after that. He had been caught shoplifting candy from it when it was a convenience store and he'd been a kid.

A hungry, troublemaking kid.

"My son, Benny, was in a car crash after you'd left."

Ryker winced. It had been a miracle that he hadn't hurt or killed someone when he'd crashed a car, drunk as a skunk.

Mr. G's eyes widened. "This was bad weather, Ryker, not drink. Black ice. But Benny is in a wheelchair now. We helped him set this up so he'd have his own place. He's always been good with his hands.

"There's lots of things that need fixing, appliances, et cetera. Folks around here can't afford to replace their stuff when it breaks. He's been able to make his own living and has an apartment on the main floor along with the shop. All wheelchair accessible.

"Upstairs is empty. No one has been interested in renting it. It's a place you could stay, if you want.

"Benny's been trying to help people with computer problems, but that's not his thing. I know a bit, but it's all theory, and I'm retired now, and I'd like to not be working anymore. I thought maybe the two of you could work something out. You could help him with the computers people want fixed, and live upstairs.

"Don't tell Benny, but I like the idea of someone being around. I worry."

Ryker glanced at his former teacher. It wasn't hard to see that he cared and worried about his son. Ryker remembered Benny as a troublemaker, not at Ryker's level, but still his dad cared and worried about him.

Ryker had no idea what that was like.

Mr. G nodded at the door. "Wanna take a look?"

Ryker glanced up. There was a lot of space on the second floor—more than he'd need. This was on the bad side of town—everything this side of the train tracks to the mill had been the poorer, working-class section of Carter's

Crossing. This was where Ryker fit in. He didn't need a lot of comfort or anything fancy.

It wasn't far from his dad's home. It would be cheap, and he could do some work on the side, make a bit of money. He wasn't sure he'd be welcomed anywhere else in town.

He nodded and followed Mr. G into the shop.

RACHEL CHECKED THAT the coffeemaker was prepped for another pot of coffee. There were two carafes of the stuff already in the next room, but all the meetings at the church required a lot of coffee. People who were volunteering their time believed they were entitled to beverages in return. And cookies.

Taking care of the coffee and setting up wasn't "officially" required of Rachel. But this meeting was in the hall of her dad's church, so she had come to make sure everything was ready to go, just like she did for everything else that went on here. Tomorrow night she'd set up for AA and Al-Anon, which rotated among the local churches. Then Friday—was there another meeting Friday? They started to run together in her head.

At least, for this one event, it had been nice that Mariah had been here with her, helping get everything ready and thanking Rachel for her work. Mariah, at least, didn't consider this to be Rachel's default responsibility.

Mariah was obviously new in town.

With a quick glance, Rachel saw that it was five minutes after the hour so everyone should be here. She gave one last glare at the coffeemaker, since it was old and temperamental, and crossed the hall to the meeting room. Most of the seats were taken, and she didn't need to look around to know who was there. Mariah gave her a nod and then stood up to get things started while Rachel slid to the back corner where she'd set out her own notepad.

A longtime veteran of meetings, she wanted to be at the back of the room, where no one would pay attention to her. She had a habit of doodling to pass the time and didn't always want curious eyes watching what she drew.

Lately, her doodles had become less *nice*, which might have caused heart palpitations among longtime residents of Carter's Crossing. Her brain had begun to generate caricatures of some of the more long-winded speakers being attacked by zombies. Or clowns. She ended up shredding a lot of notepaper, but it was a fair exchange for her sanity.

Mariah thanked everyone for coming.

"I appreciate that you've all given some of your time to help plan and execute the vision to make Cupid's Crossing a Center for Romance. Our Valentine's Day events were a success, because everyone in town pulled together to make them so."

Mariah had a ring on the all-important finger of her left hand from one of those events, so she'd certainly rate them a success.

But to be fair, and Rachel usually was, Mariah had worked hard at planning all three events, and they'd been great.

Rachel scribbled out her doodle of a diamond ring and paid attention to Mariah again.

"We received excellent publicity. But now we need to build on that to make this town a destination people consider when they're planning romantic events. We have the video and photos to show what we can do. We'll soon have the first bed-and-breakfasts ready to go. The renovation of the mill is underway. I've drawn up a list of attractions and points of interest in the area and spoken to the people involved there."

Rachel knew the places involved. She and Jaycee had helped Mariah create her list.

"We're not totally up to speed, but we're ready to bring in our first visitors. And to do so, we have to let the world know what we've got, and that we're open for business. For that, we need an online presence."

For most people in Carter's Crossing, their only online presence was in the yellow pages. There was no website for Carter's Crossing, and that had to change. Rachel knew Mariah had been speaking to people back in the city to work on a website for the town under the new name of Cupid's Crossing.

"We're very fortunate that I've found someone local to help with this, since the project is meant to promote local business. We have an excellent website developer in town, at least temporarily. Some of you may remember Ryker—"

Rachel's head snapped up so quickly she almost heard it crack. She followed the turn of heads to see where everyone was staring and for the first time noticed the man in the opposite corner.

CHAPTER TWO

RYKER WAS NOT a common name. But was this…? Yes, it was.

Fourteen years was a long time. Ryker had changed, enough that Rachel wouldn't have recognized him at first glance. But once she'd looked, she could see it was him.

He hadn't raised his head as Mariah spoke about his experience with website design, but Rachel had known that jaw, that inky black hair. The stubble was new, as was the larger body build. But he'd starred in enough of her vain dreams over the years that she knew it was him.

She wondered if he still had those silvery gray eyes. Once, they'd looked at her as if she'd been pretty, interesting. Bad-boy Ryker, looking at ordinary Rachel like that, had made her dizzy, giddy. He'd kissed her, and she'd almost passed out from the excitement of it all.

Then he'd stopped coming to tutoring and stopped coming to school. After his car accident he'd enlisted in the air force, and then he'd stopped coming to Carter's Crossing at all.

Until now.

There was a moment of silence as everyone came to terms with the reappearance of Ryker Slade. Rachel's eyes widened as she remembered that his dad had been taken to a home. That must be why he was back.

Well, of course it was. Did she think he'd come back to see her?

He lifted his head, and his gaze circled the table, finally touching hers. Rachel felt that same giddiness, same dizziness. He looked down at the table again, and there it was, the same disappointment as before.

Rachel rolled her eyes at herself. Some things never changed.

She sighed quietly. She had to get out of this town, and she had to change. Maybe, if she wasn't leaving for a while, she needed to start changing now.

Rachel didn't pay attention to the rest of the meeting. She'd talked over all this with Mariah, so knew what was planned. Except for the Ryker-back-in-town-designing-websites part, which really would have been nice to be prepared for. Of course, Mariah had no idea that Ryker had played any kind of role in Rachel's life.

No one knew. Not even Ryker.

When she found herself starting to doodle his name, she quickly scratched it out and turned to a fresh page.

Mariah continued the discussion about future plans for Cupid's Crossing, leading people to agree with her ideas with admirable diplomacy. Rachel didn't think of this town as a place Cupid was going to be comfortable in. Setting aside her own pathetic romantic history here, it was hard to picture the infantile archer enjoying winters, falls or even springs in New York State. It was a little too cold to be naked most of the year.

No, if Cupid was going to fit in here, he'd need to wear more clothing. She quickly sketched what she envisioned. Flannel, perhaps, and a pair of jeans. Boots, and a bit of scruff on that rounded face…

For fun, she added an ax, instead of a bow and arrow, and imagined the god of love chopping down trees. Wiping sweat off his brow after some hard work. Tapping maple syrup from a tree.

Maybe he'd sit up on a branch, with his bow and arrow, waiting for someone to wander by. He might fall asleep before that happened.

Suddenly, Rachel realized the meeting was over. She looked up anxiously, but no one had noticed that she'd zoned out. Mavis had stopped to talk to Mariah, and the others were gathering their stuff and heading out of the room.

Rachel wasn't in a rush. She still had to clean up. And right now she didn't want to have to say anything to Ryker.

It was stupid, but she hadn't seen him since their last tutoring session, the time he'd kissed her. She had no idea what to say to him.

Hey, Ryker, sorry that kiss was so bad for you that you had to leave town. It's the best I've ever had, but...

Not that a bad kiss from her was the reason he'd left. Obviously, it wasn't a big deal for anyone but her. Still, it was better that she just didn't try to speak to him. Not till she had time to get her wayward thoughts under control.

She used her arms to cover her notepad, pretending to be busy gathering her pens. She watched the doorway out of the corner of her eye, counting heads leaving the room, waiting for Ryker to exit.

She wondered how long he was going to be around, and if she could manage to avoid him for the whole time he was here. She could make it a game…

Mariah escaped from Mavis and came her

way. Rachel leaned back, relieved to not be in danger of looking at Ryker.

Mariah had a glow about her, one she'd had ever since Valentine's Day when Nelson had proposed to her, followed by Mariah proposing to Nelson. She'd said no, then he'd said yes, and then they'd gone through a staged proposal, one of the events that would be on the town website.

The two of them argued whenever they weren't kissing. Rachel would have gone crazy living like that, but it worked for them. Rachel couldn't help but be happy for her friends, but they did make her feel like a third wheel. Or fifth, if Jaycee and Dave were around.

Not on purpose, but how long could she be the only unattached member of the group before things started to get weird?

"Rachel, I have to run. I don't want to leave you to clean up on your...what's that?"

Rachel's arms were no longer covering her notebook, and Mariah was staring at Rachel's sketch of a warmly attired Cupid, dozing in a tree while a couple walked underneath the branch he was perched on.

"Ah, sorry. I was just doodling. I already knew what you were—"

Rachel was afraid that Mariah would be

upset to know how little she had been listening. Not the case. Mariah tapped the doodle.

"That is awesome. I had no idea you were so talented. Do you draw a lot? Why didn't you say anything? We could use that." Mariah sounded excited.

Rachel squinted at her Cupid. Was he really that interesting?

"Still drawing?"

A shiver ran down Rachel's spine. The voice had changed in fourteen years, grown deeper, but Rachel would have known it anywhere.

Ryker. Her notebooks had been covered in doodles in high school. When she'd been his tutor.

"What do you think, Ryker? We could use this on our website, couldn't we? I love this, the Cupid, but made specific for Cupid's Crossing. Grown up, dressed like a lumberjack, hot…"

Rachel could still feel Ryker behind her. Speaking of hot… She wanted Mariah to stop talking. She wanted her to leave. She was having problems catching her breath and didn't think she could have spoken intelligible words if her life had depended on it.

"We'd want some color. You can do that, can't you, Rachel?"

Rachel was gripping her pen so tightly she was afraid she might break it. The silence was becoming awkward. She nodded, hoping it would be enough to get the others to leave.

Mariah spoke again. "I'm getting ideas—I'll email them to the two of you."

Gaah! It was bad enough that Ryker was here, but now she'd have his email.

"Ryker, let Rachel know what you'd like. Rachel, that is really awesome. We can pay you for this stuff, if you don't mind doing a few pictures for us. It's the perfect vibe that we're looking for. I gotta run now—are you okay to clean up? I'm sorry to leave you."

Rachel nodded again and lifted her head to give Mariah a smile. Mariah was already heading out, so if Rachel's expression looked like a deranged clown ready to terrify some children, Mariah didn't notice or say anything.

Rachel carefully closed her notebook, waiting to hear Ryker step away. She shoved her notes, pens, pencils and notebook into her bag. She finally heard Ryker's footsteps, but instead of heading to the door and leaving—*he was supposed to be leaving!*—he moved to the table where the coffee was.

Really? It was 9:00 p.m. Hadn't everyone had enough caffeine for one evening?

She heard a rattle and looked up. He was gathering up the coffee carafes and extra cups. Her eyes widened. For a moment she

watched his movements, smooth and controlled. Then her mental freak-out about seeing
Ryker again settled enough that she realized
he was cleaning up.

"You don't have to do that!"

He turned to her. "It's okay. I'm happy to
help."

Rachel put her bag down. She closed her
eyes and took a deep breath. This was silly.

Someone was helping her clean up, and she
was acting like an idiot because she'd had a
crush on this guy back in high school. Fourteen years ago. She had to get over this.

"Thank you." She began piling up the dishes
left on the table.

Ryker followed her into the church kitchen.
Rachel's stomach was doing a shimmy. She
tried to suck it in, make it settle down.

Rachel pulled down the door of the dish-
washer, and let Ryker stack the dishes inside.
She ran water in the sink. Ryker headed out
again and came in with more of the dishes that
had been left behind.

"Do I need to stack the chairs?"

His voice got the shimmies going again.
Gaah!

Rachel had no idea where Ryker had learned
the church cleanup routine. He'd never crossed

the threshold of a church here in Carter's Crossing while he'd lived here.

"That would be great, thanks."

Rachel could wrap up the debris from a meeting in her sleep. She finished in the kitchen and turned off the lights. She went back to the meeting room, where Ryker had finished up everything.

"Anything else?"

Rachel shook her head. "This is great. Thanks, Ryker."

Why couldn't she think of something to say beyond "Thanks" and "This is great"? Saying his name for the first time in fourteen years gave her chills. Chills and shimmies. Could she not act like a normal person, for once?

Rachel grabbed her jacket and bag. She flicked off the lights, and Ryker followed her up the stairs, and to the door of the church. She was aware of every step he took, as if the air between them vibrated with each movement he made. She opened the door and he stepped out, waiting while she locked up.

She prepared herself to say a polite, but distant, goodbye. How hard could this be? She'd done this all her life. *Good night and thank you, Ryker—*

"I have some ideas for the website, places

where those Cupids might fit in. Are you good to meet up and discuss it?"

Rachel felt her brain frying again and looked at the ground. "Um…"

Yeah, she was totally acting normal.

"I'm tied up tomorrow night, but maybe Friday?"

Rachel imagined how her fifteen-year-old self would have responded to Ryker's asking to meet her on a Friday night.

Twenty-nine-year-old Rachel was equally tongue-tied. And embarrassed. The silence stretched.

"If you don't want to do this, I understand."

The tone in his voice was wry.

Rachel looked up into those gray eyes. They were guarded, his hands in his pockets. What did he understand?

"You can work with Mariah, and she can send me what she wants me to use."

Rachel was still grappling with what Ryker meant.

"Good night, Rachel. It was good to see you again."

He turned to go, and she finally got it. He didn't think she wanted anything to do with him. He'd had a bad reputation, back before he'd left Carter's Crossing.

Even if she'd been worried about his reputation, a meeting in the diner with Ryker Slade wouldn't harm her. And she'd never want to make him think she was like everyone else, expecting the worst of him. Suddenly, the words burst out.

"No, Ryker, that's not it."

He turned back to her, standing at the bottom of the steps.

Rachel shook her head. "This took me by surprise. It's not you, I promise. It's—"

He waited.

How did she explain? Could she say it out loud, finally?

"It's just…" She sighed. "No one knows this."

"You don't have to tell me."

"I was planning to tell Jaycee, but she's getting married, and Mariah…"

Ryker still waited. None of this mattered to him. She had to stop babbling. It was stupid: she either couldn't speak or couldn't stop around this man.

"I'm leaving. Leaving Carter's. I just don't want to make more commitments when I'm going to have to pass it all on anyway."

She felt his gaze on her face, assessing her words.

"When are you going?"

"Not till late summer at earliest. I'm in Jaycee's wedding. I've just been feeling…stifled. Smothered. I need to do something for me."

She hadn't articulated this to anyone else, but Ryker didn't appear surprised.

"That seems fair. Should I tell Mariah it's not a go?"

Rachel leaned against the door.

"No. I'll do this—the drawings. As long as I'm here. I might want that extra money when I go."

"Would you rather work directly with Mariah?"

Rachel ran her gaze over his face, noting the changes fourteen years had made. There wasn't much to see as far as expression went. Ryker had never been easy to read, at least not for her.

"I don't mind working with you, Ryker. I promise, it's just been a weird time for me. I can meet you Friday. When and where?"

RYKER WATCHED RACHEL cross the lawn to the parsonage next door. She must live at home still. He wondered if she'd married, and split up, or never left home. He'd been cut off from Carter's since he left and had no idea what had happened to people here in the past fourteen years.

He had left everything related to the town

behind him, and rarely thought about the place or its residents since he left.

There were exceptions. When he'd been through bad times. Rough times. The kind of times that you thought might be your last times.

He'd thought of Rachel at times like that.

He hadn't joined the air force for noble reasons. He'd been given the option of enlisting, or jail. Life in the air force had been a job, for the most part. One that taught him to grow up. Be a "man." He'd had to straighten up and having a purpose had been good. But when the bad times had hit, he'd remembered Rachel. People like Rachel were the people that made what he did in uniform worthwhile.

With the reputation his family had, not many people in the town had been kind. Rachel had been. She'd tutored him, for a bit. She'd been a friend to his sister Jess.

Not many people had wanted to hang out with any of the Slades.

He turned to walk back to his new, temporary home.

He'd thought that Rachel might be worried that his reputation still carried here, and that people would talk about her if she hung out with him. It made him all too aware that the Slade family reputation wasn't just something he would need to deal with while he was physically here, but that it might jeopardize the sale of the house.

He couldn't change what decades of bad Slade behavior had done to influence how the town thought of his family.

Maybe, if he kept his nose down, worked hard on the house and helped on this website, someone would be willing to make an offer. He and his siblings would need that equity to keep the old man in the home.

He didn't want to dwell on that, when thoughts of the house and the ghosts that haunted him there made him want to find a bottle. He needed to focus on something else.

Rachel's drawing had given him some ideas for the town website, so he'd work on that till he could fall asleep. Help get Rachel a bit of money to leave town with. A bit of payback for what she'd done for Jess and him. Something nice from a Slade.

THURSDAY NIGHT WAS the familiar routine of AA in a church basement. A different church tonight than on Tuesday, since they rotated them through the little town.

He'd been in meetings in many places. There was a sameness to them. The faces might change, but the stories had a common thread.

Even the physical details of the meetings themselves: stacking plastic chairs, uncomfortable for long sits. Bad coffee, with powdered creamer. The smell of cigarette smoke.

Didn't matter what the people looked like: expensive suits, or tattered sweats, everyone had the same problem. Ryker had been tied up with work and came just in time to slip into the church before the meeting started. And for the second night in a row, he ran into Rachel in the church basement.

She didn't notice him. She was hovering in the hallway.

It had been obvious last night that she took care of the mundane details for the church events. It was her father's church, so it was probably expected that she'd step up. He wondered if it bothered her. If it was part of the reason she was leaving.

The way she was hovering, though…that wasn't about making sure there was enough sugar and cookies on the table. He knew that hover. She was debating going into the meeting.

Not much surprised him anymore, but this did. He knew there were no stereotypes when it came to alcoholics. Anyone anywhere could need one of these meetings. But he'd never thought of Rachel like that.

Him? Probably predestined. Rachel?

But as the meeting started, while he stood there like an idiot and watched Rachel hover, he realized she was at the door to the Al-Anon meeting, the one for friends and relatives of alcoholics, not the one for alcoholics like him.

So not Rachel having a problem. Would it be…her father?

No wonder she was hovering. That would certainly cause a reaction. Yeah, anonymous was in the name, but not in this town.

Ryker cleared his throat. Rachel jumped, and looked around with a guilty expression.

"Ryker." Her voice was low and soft, quiet. "Um, am I in your way?"

He shook his head. His meeting was the next room down.

"I'm off to the other group. Are you going in?"

Her mouth twisted. "I can't, really."

He wanted to ask her if it was her father. What it was like for her, living at home, with an alcoholic. Was her dad like his? But he was making assumptions. Anyone who saw her in the meeting would do the same. That was exactly why she was hovering, not going in. He wanted to help.

Asking if her father was a closet alcoholic was not going to help.

"If you need someone to talk, I'm here."

He probably wasn't qualified to help with whatever her problem was, but he wanted to. Rachel had helped him, unknowingly. She helped a lot of people. And he didn't think many people helped her.

They certainly hadn't last night.

She blinked, startled by the offer. "Uh, thanks. I guess I'll see you tomorrow?"

He watched her for a moment. Saw her bite her lip, look all around the hallway, just not at him.

He wasn't helping, standing here and watching her. He nodded and passed by her to attend his own meeting. The one he needed, since he still had to clean up the home he'd grown up in, and that was going to take a lot out of him.

He refused to give up two years of sobriety to that.

RACHEL TOLD HERSELF she was an idiot.

It wasn't the first time.

Seriously, though, spending any time with Ryker was just stupid.

It was obviously stupid because she was standing here, in front of her closet, trying to find the right outfit to impress the man for a meeting about the town website. It had been fourteen years, yet she was responding like she was still that fifteen-year-old girl, crushing on the school bad boy, reading more into every interaction than had existed.

It was *so* stupid. He'd already seen her Wednesday, at the town meeting, and last night, at the church, and a change of clothes was not going to change his impression of her. She had a pretty good idea what the women he'd have dates with would look like, and none of them would have a closet of clothes like hers.

Her clothes were all too *nice*. Why was she obsessing over this? It was a stupid infatuation, reigniting from her high school crush, and just as silly. Back in high school, Rachel hadn't known Ryker. She'd built up an imaginary character based on his face and his reputation and the fact that he'd spoken to her.

Now she was almost thirty, and getting giddy and overcome by the admittedly good looks of a person she knew even less than she had back in high school. It was pathetic; that was what it was.

She was in the middle of a group of friends who were all coupled up, in a town that was going to extort the romance out of everything they could. Ryker just happened to have re-appeared now, when all this was conspiring against her. If there was anything to prove that she needed to get away and find a bigger place to live, this was it.

Well, that and the limits of her closet.

Meanwhile, she needed to find something to wear. Something nice. Something to wear to the town diner, where she'd have most of anything she wore hidden under the table, unseen, so she could meet Ryker, discuss what silly pictures they wanted from her and try hard not to act completely idiotically in front of him.

Rachel sighed. Nothing new was going to spontaneously appear in her closet. She grabbed her jeans, the newest ones, and a button-up shirt and a pullover. She grimaced at her reflection. Navy was boring. But anytime she went shopping, she couldn't decide what colors other than the safe neutrals looked good on her.

She had tried to find clothes that were more…well, not sexy, but closer to that than her normal choices. She'd never been able to decide if she'd crossed over the line, the line that the pastor's daughter shouldn't cross.

So neutrals, safe, nonsexy clothes, took up all her closet.

Angry with herself, she turned away, grabbed her bag with her notepad and pencils and pens in it, and stomped to the door.

"I'm heading out, Dad." She called down the hall to the study, where her father spent most of his time when at home, head lost in a book or discussing theological topics online.

"Okay, Rachel. Do we have a meeting tomorrow?"

"Yes, Dad. Bazaar meeting in the morning, and the interfaith lunch."

Her father stepped into the hallway. "That's right. What would I do without you?"

Rachel's smile froze. She didn't know what he would do, either. But she wasn't sure it was fair to expect her to be his support.

She had her own life.

Guilt leaped up and shook a finger at her. Her dad had no one else. He would do anything for her—if he thought of it.

After her mother died, stepping up, helping out, had been her instinctive response. She'd assumed that if she was good, did the right things, then eventually, somehow, she'd get her own dreams fulfilled, and in some vague, fuzzy way, her father would be taken care of.

But it wasn't happening. And as much as she loved her father, as much as she wanted to do the right thing, she was finding it more and more difficult.

There was this thing, bubbling up underneath the surface, a cauldron of resentment. Her father had fallen in love with her mother, had a family and a job he loved.

Why couldn't Rachel have that, too? Why couldn't he see that she had needs and wants, as well? Why did he think it was perfectly okay for her to do nothing but take care of him and then, while at work, take care of Uncle Stanley, as well? She'd almost gone into the Al-Anon meeting last night just because she was running out of ideas about how to deal with her uncle.

She could almost feel those manacles holding her here.

"Are you off to see Jaycee?" he asked, oblivious to her inner struggle.

"It's a meeting about the town website." She didn't tell him she was meeting with Ryker. She wasn't exactly sure why.

"Oh, very good, very good. So pleased that this town is embracing possibility again."

Fine. Great. The town could have possibilities but what about Rachel? Was she some Jane Austen parson's daughter, destined to take care of the parsonage for the rest of her life?

"Gotta go, Dad." She turned to leave, afraid that this anger, these rebellious thoughts, were going to explode soon.

Her father wasn't cruel. He was just oblivious. He had the welfare of the town in his care, and somehow never saw her as anything but an extension of himself. He didn't *listen* to her, even when she'd told him about her uncle.

Nothing was going to change unless he did, or she did.

He wasn't changing. So maybe she… But a look at the time warned her she needed to get going before Ryker thought she'd chickened out.

She pulled on her jacket and boots: March hadn't given way to spring yet but was hanging on to winter cold and snow. She stomped down the steps to the sidewalk, turning to downtown and the diner.

She hoped she wouldn't make a fool of herself in front of Ryker, but she was such a mess of conflicted feelings right now that anything was possible.

She had to get away.

RYKER CAUGHT THE glances of people as they passed by. He was leaning against the brick wall of the building next to the diner, waiting for Rachel. He'd arrived early but hadn't wanted to head in alone.

The glances he caught were nervous, wary. He knew his appearance unsettled some people.

He'd gotten out of the habit of making himself look ordinary and harmless. He was a big guy; he had tattoos and was wearing his leather jacket, since he hadn't brought much with him. His hair was long and his five-o'clock shadow scruffy.

He ran his hand over his chin. Maybe he could have shaved, at least. And he should probably get a haircut. It just hadn't been a priority.

He'd spent time in places where looking scary had been an asset. He should get over that mind-set if he was going to spend time back here in Carter's Crossing.

If was the key.

He needed to clean up the family home, arrange to get it listed for sale. He wasn't sure how long that would take.

And once the house was sold, there wasn't much point in staying in Carter's Crossing. Or Cupid's Crossing, either.

No one here was going to welcome back a member of his family. They'd be happy to see the Slades gone for good.

He didn't blame them.

He didn't know if the people passing by recognized him, but if they did, they didn't greet him. It would be best if he got himself together well enough to clear up the mess his father had left behind, and then move on.

He had to admit, the website he was working on for the town was a fun project. Mariah was giving him a lot of leeway, but then, she didn't know him the way the rest of the town did. He'd stay while he got that underway, and while he made sure his grip on sobriety was up to a visit down memory lane, and maybe he could keep up the work on the website after he left. Very little of what he did best needed to be done in person.

"Ryker?"

He recognized Rachel's voice, the only person other than Mr. G who'd welcomed him here in Carter's. Rachel had always been much too nice for her own good.

He turned. She was bundled up. Ryker tended to ignore the cold, but her cheeks were pink, and the tip of her nose red. She was biting her bottom lip, looking nervous.

Maybe this was a bad idea. Word would be spreading that one of the Slades was back in town, and it wouldn't do her reputation any good to be seen with him.

But Rachel was already halfway through the door of the diner, so he turned to follow her.

The diner felt much the same as two days ago. But this time people looked at him and paused.

Word had definitely gotten around.

Rachel didn't respond to the stares. She slid

into an empty booth and opened the buttons on her coat. Ryker took off his jacket and sat in the seat across from her, dropping his jacket down beside him.

The same waitress as last time came to pour coffee.

"Rachel." She nodded at his companion. "Ryker Slade." Her voice cooled several degrees as she stated his name.

He didn't recognize her, but she knew his story.

Rachel ignored the byplay. Was she oblivious or deliberately avoiding it?

Rachel flipped her cup over. "Can we have menus, Jean?" She shoved the cup toward Jean, waiting for a pour from the coffee carafe.

"Did you want coffee, Ryker?"

Ryker met the death glare in the waitress's eyes and nodded, flipping over his own cup. Then he withdrew his hand, just in case.

He didn't remember this woman, but it would have been easy enough for his father or siblings to have caused her pain.

His family was good at that. He'd lost touch, after he'd been overseas. The twins, the oldest of his siblings, were in prison. Ethan and the girls had been gone for years. His father would have spent the past years venting all his anger on the people he'd find here when he no longer had his family to use as punching bags.

The town might just throw a party when they were finally gone.

Jean's lips tightened to the point of disappearing as she poured the hot liquid. Ryker slid over to make sure he was out of range of an accidental spill on his lap. She strode away, with another glare at Ryker.

Rachel's gaze followed Jean's back.

She turned to him with a frown. "Do you get that a lot?"

It was tempting to play dumb and ask what, but Rachel wasn't going to let it go; he could see that in her tense expression.

"Couple of times. People who've figured out who I am. Word is spreading."

Rachel shook her head. "That's not fair."

"Rachel." He waited to make sure she was listening. To him, Jean's reaction was natural and expected.

"I was trouble when I left here. I'd just wrapped a car around a tree while driving drunk. My whole family was a bunch of hellions. No one should be happy to find another Slade in town."

She squinted at him.

"Then why did you come back?"

CHAPTER THREE

WHY HAD HE come back? Good question.

"Someone has to sell the house, now that Dad's in a home."

"Why you?" Rachel was leaning forward, hands clenched tightly around her coffee cup. She looked prepared to do battle.

"The twins are in prison. Ethan is overseas. The girls are all…gone. California, Australia…" And no one knew where Jessie had ended up. For practical purposes, they were all on their own. He hoped they didn't hate him for leaving.

Her lips pursed. "You were the only one who would."

"Basically."

"Is it going to take a long time? Since you're doing the website, are you planning to stay for a while?"

Ryker didn't know the answer to that himself.

"The first day I was back, I ran into Mr. G. From high school?"

Rachel nodded. He was pretty sure she understood where he'd met him.

"He apologized."

Ryker was still surprised by that. Must be why he was telling Rachel, who couldn't have any interest.

Jean slapped menus down in front of them.

"Thanks, Jean," Rachel said, gently rebuking the woman. Ryker heard Jean sniff, but she didn't glare at him. She didn't look at him at all.

Ryker scanned the menu, checking prices. The selection was much what it had been when he'd left, but prices were higher. He needed to take the time to get groceries, since eating out wasn't a pleasant option. He'd use the local store: motorcycles were not designed for hauling large quantities of shopping.

Rachel barely glanced at her menu before closing it.

"Why did Mr. G apologize?"

"He thought he should have done something about Dad. And what was going on at our place."

Ryker closed his menu. "Probably because of that, Mr. G said his son had a place I could stay, and Benny could use some help working on computers at his shop. He set up a meeting with Mariah. I have somewhere to live and some work till I get the house done."

Jean came back and took their orders. The pinched look on her face made him wonder if he was doing this for nothing.

Ryker didn't want to talk about himself anymore.

"What have I missed while I've been gone?"

Rachel lined up her cutlery and her napkin. "Not a lot. The Carters had to close the mill, for financial reasons. That's why Mariah came here. She and Abigail are working to make Carter's Crossing into a romance center they'll call Cupid's Crossing."

"And you drew the Cupid because of that."

Rachel shot him a small smile. "My mind was wandering, since Mariah had already talked about the meeting with me. I knew what was going on. Except for you."

Rachel stopped. Ryker wanted to ask her what she'd thought when she found him at that meeting.

She hadn't shot him any evil looks. But she hadn't looked comfortable with him, either. He didn't believe it was because she didn't want more commitments before she left. Rachel was the kind of person to say something nice in any situation, rather than an uncomfortable truth.

He wondered again why she was leaving. He had no good reason to ask.

He was curious about her, though. He'd have expected her to be married, maybe have kids… be living more of that ideal life she'd always had.

"What have you been doing these past fourteen years?"

Rachel twisted her cup. "Not much. I'm a paralegal for my uncle—I don't know if you remember him. He's a lawyer, the only one in town now."

The Slades hadn't ever required the services of Rachel's uncle. If anyone in their family needed a lawyer, it would be a public defender. Rachel's uncle took care of the legal needs of ordinary families. Wills, real estate, that kind of thing.

Ryker might consult him once the family home was ready for sale. If things went well.

"Are you married?"

Rachel looked up at him. "No." The corner of her mouth pulled down.

"Divorced?"

She shook her head. "No. I told you, not much has happened."

She didn't sound happy about that. Maybe that was why she was leaving.

"What about you? What have you been up to?"

Ryker took a breath. He didn't want to share with Rachel much of what he'd done; it wasn't a pretty tale. But he could wrap it up in one sentence, and while it might not tell the whole story, it would tell enough.

"Two tours, two divorces, two years sober."

He watched her face. She bit her lip, but then they were interrupted by Jean, returning with their food.

Jean left, and he determined to change the subject. He didn't want to dwell on his past or think about what he still had to do at the house. His future was uncertain. There was a reason he wasn't a sociable guy: there wasn't a lot about himself he wanted to talk about. Especially not with Rachel, who'd always made him believe he had possibilities.

"I've been thinking about your Cupid." They'd picked up their utensils, ready to eat. The website was a safe topic of conversation. And it was the reason they were meeting, after all.

"Here's what I came up with."

RACHEL LET RYKER lead their talk to Cupid. She'd always liked to doodle, and while she'd never have expected anyone to want her sketches on a website, drawing was more interesting than most of the jobs she did around town.

It was better to get off personal topics with Ryker. That short summary of his life for the past fourteen years had hurt her.

There was so much pain in those seven words, not much of an improvement over the tough times he'd had here in Carter's. She had no personal experience with military life, but she read news articles and she had an imagination.

She'd been setting up for the weekly AA meetings at their church for years, and she'd heard stories, and gotten to know the people. No one came to those meetings without hurting. Hurting badly.

Ryker's divorces were another matter. Feeling sympathy for someone who'd gone through two divorces was basic human decency, but they elicited a different kind of reaction in her, as well. They made it clear to her that he'd never thought of that kiss they shared, or of her after he'd left. He'd been able to put Carter's behind him and go on with his life.

While Rachel was still here doing *nothing*.

She had to change that. Scary as it was.

She'd promised Jaycee to be in her wedding, and would help out, of course. She couldn't leave until after that event. But in the meantime, she would work on changing herself. If she could figure out how.

It was almost April, and she was probably here till September. She couldn't bear the thought of waiting, doing nothing, now that she'd finally worked up the nerve to leave. She was afraid of letting that dream die, and finding herself, next March, in the same place. Only she'd be helping plan Mariah's wedding, and maybe a baby shower for Jaycee.

They'd move on with their lives, and she'd be stuck.

She couldn't let that happen. She had to do something between now and September to start changing nice Rachel into interesting Rachel. She just wished there was someone she could ask for help, someone who wouldn't be rushing to assure her she was fine as she was.

She didn't need patronizing. She needed a kick in the butt.

But for now she let Ryker explain what he wanted to do on the town's website. She made notes about the Cupid drawings he thought he could use and offered a couple of suggestions herself. The whole time she reminded herself that feeling anything about Ryker was silly. There was no change she could make that would attract his attention.

She didn't know this man. Most of what she thought she knew had been about Ryker the boy, what she'd made up in her head when she was a kid. It was time to put those ideas away.

She should just draw some stupid Cupids and wrap it up. Then be done. For once, put what she wanted and needed first.

Their dinners were finished about the same time the website conversation ended. Rachel told herself that it wasn't a date, and that now that their business was done, it was time to leave.

Ryker wanted to pay, but Mariah had told Rachel that the committee would cover the meal. Ryker's lips compressed, but he let her take the bill to the cash register.

Jean sniffed. Rachel wondered if it would have been wiser to let Ryker pay as he'd asked. It wasn't a lot, but she could see Jean putting the worst possible spin on this. The poor man was being labeled a freeloader, just because of his last name.

"I need the receipt, Jean. Mariah is going to reimburse us for this, since it's for town business."

Jean narrowed her eyes. But she carefully totaled up a receipt and passed it to Rachel, watching her fold it into her wallet.

Ryker held the door for her as she stepped out.

"Were you afraid Jean would think you were my sugar mama?" he asked, amusement running under the words. Amusement and... resignation?

Rachel bit back some very un-nice comments. "It's not fair that she just assumes the worst."

"You think getting that receipt is going to change her mind?"

It wouldn't, Rachel knew. Not totally. But maybe it was a start.

"Does it bother you?" She'd told herself not to get involved. She could email her drawings to Ryker after this, and they didn't need to meet up again. That would be smarter.

But this judgment Jean, and others, were passing was unfair. Rachel didn't know Ryker, not really. But he'd served two tours in the military, which should earn him some respect. And he said he'd been sober for two years. That was also an accomplishment.

Ryker had done stupid things, bad things, before he left. But he'd also had a horrible home life. His sister Jess had been in Rachel's class. Rachel had tried to befriend her. She knew more about how bad things had been in the Slade home than anyone like Jean could imagine.

Ryker just shrugged. "No point."

"It bothers me." Rachel had a strong sense of right and wrong.

She caught a small smile. "Don't sweat it, Rachel. Nothing you can do."

Ryker fell into step beside her as she headed home. He was wrong. There was a lot she could do. People didn't notice what she did, and often overlooked her, but she'd been able to quietly deal with things behind the scenes. Her father and her uncle often were given credit for Rachel's ideas. Rachel had been raised to be modest, so she hadn't pushed herself forward, but she had some influence in this town.

There was no reason she should try to influence people about Ryker, but that didn't mean she wasn't tempted.

And that was an excellent reason not to do so. Especially when he wasn't staying, and she was leaving.

She turned the corner to head up to Church Street. Ryker kept pace beside her.

"If you're staying at Benny's, this is the wrong way."

"I'll make sure you get home."

"What do you think could possibly happen to me in Carter's Crossing?"

He shrugged and kept walking beside her.

"If you were the person Jean thought you

were, you wouldn't be walking me home. Not unless you were going to mug me."

She glanced at Ryker and found a mocking expression on his face.

"What?"

"I'm sure Jean could think of some other reasons to walk you home that weren't quite… respectable."

Rachel felt her cheeks flush. She hadn't thought of anything like that. There was no way Ryker had, either. Not about her. Why would he?

He'd been who knows how many places in the past fourteen years. She'd been nowhere.

It was too bad she couldn't borrow some of what he'd experienced. She'd like to know more, be more interesting. She could trade him some of her pristine reputation.

She didn't want people to look at her like they did at Ryker. She didn't want to go that far. But she wanted to be interesting. To maybe have a few secrets in her past.

She sneaked another look at Ryker.

He was staring ahead of them, appearing to have forgotten Rachel. His jaw was set, his face…sad? No, *bleak* was the word that sprang to mind.

He had secrets. He had stories. They weren't

pretty ones, she could tell, and she wasn't stupid enough to wish to go through what he had.

But he'd tried things. Risked things. Whereas her life had been lived on the surface, with no surprises, he'd hit the depths.

He might have hit the heights, too. If so, he'd paid. Did he think it had been worth it?

He wasn't stuck in this town, having never truly lived. She didn't want to hit bottom and fail twice at marriage, but she wanted to do something, risk something.

She could only imagine what it must have been like, two weddings, two times stepping out to have that special someone, to build a future. He'd served his country, probably risked his life for others.

Rachel had put out chairs in the basement and baked cakes.

What a waste of a life.

She was going to have spent thirty years not really living. She wasn't going to waste another thirty years like that.

Ryker stopped, and she realized they were at the gate to the parsonage.

"Thanks for walking me home." She was glad it was dark. She had no idea what she looked like, with these thoughts rushing through her head.

"Good night, Rachel." Ryker nodded and

turned to head back to what had always been known as the wrong side of town.

Rachel's fists were clenched in her pockets. She wanted to yell after Ryker, but she didn't know what she'd say.

She wanted change. And this time, she was ready to do something about it.

RYKER CAME DOWN the stairs to the main floor. He'd worked on the town website after he'd walked Rachel home. This morning he'd brought home some groceries. He was, temporarily, at least, settled.

He didn't know for how long. He couldn't put off clearing up at the house. Once he'd gotten rid of the alcohol and garbage, he hoped it wouldn't take long to get it ready to sell. Then he'd be free to go. A new place, where he didn't bear the reputation of his past, and his family's, appealed. There had been glances his way at the store, and on the street. In this town, his last name came with a bad reputation.

That was a burden he hadn't carried for fourteen years.

"Hey, Benny." His new boss/landlord was sitting at a bench, tools meticulously placed close at hand. He had something scattered in pieces around him.

Benny lifted his head. "Ryker. Glad to see you."

"Brought you a coffee."

"Thanks. You didn't have to."

"You've provided me with enough." Ryker set it down near Benny's left hand.

"You ready to work?"

Ryker leaned against the counter that ran across the front of the open space. There was room for customers to drop off their broken items. Ryker saw a lawn mower resting against the wall. People were preparing for spring. He jerked his head at the lawn mower.

"Want me to bring that back for you?"

"Sure," Benny said. "But that's not what I was referring to."

Benny wheeled around to a table on the other side of the room. Ryker saw three laptops stacked up.

"Computer problems?"

Benny sighed. "Not exactly. The one on top needs to be cleaned up. There are enough viruses on that one that it won't even start now. The others are for websites."

Ryker frowned. "I don't need any machine but my own to set up websites."

"You know that, and I know that, but..." Benny ran a hand through his hair. "I tried to explain, I promise, but in the end, it was just easier to take the machines. Maybe you want to, I don't know, do a quick cleanup on them anyway."

Ryker looked at the laptops. They were older. They might need more than a cleanup.

"Did you get the passwords?"

Benny coughed. "They don't have any."

Ryker sighed. He'd need to explain security to these people. "So what's this about websites?"

"It's the Cupid thing."

"I'm already doing the town website."

Benny nodded. "These two are a couple of the seniors who are going to open bed-and-breakfasts. They need a website to take bookings. And it needs to tie in to the town website."

Ryker stared at the laptops while he considered.

Mariah had mentioned something about connecting other local businesses, but she hadn't indicated that it would be immediately. They hadn't gone into the details of how that connection would be set up.

Seniors who brought in their computers, expecting to pick them up with a website ready to go obviously had no idea what was involved. They'd need photos, descriptions...not anything he could create out of thin air.

The town website was a project that could keep him busy and keep him in cash while he took care of the family home.

Two bed-and-breakfast websites would extend that for a short time. *If* he wanted to take it on. But it wasn't going to be as simple. Mariah knew what she wanted and understood what was involved. Dealing with these seniors was going to be a whole lot different.

He was going to have to provide a short class in design for them as he worked on their sites. Explain it in a way they could understand. He wasn't sure he wanted to make that kind of investment, not here in Carter's Crossing.

No, Cupid's Crossing. It would take a while to get used to that name.

"You okay?" Benny asked.

Ryker nodded. "Not sure I signed up for this."

Benny laughed. "Yeah. It's a project for sure. Are you ready for the bad news?"

Ryker turned to him. "This was the good news?"

Benny was serious now. "There were more people needing websites. They didn't all bring laptops, but they thought I was doing the work. When I told them that was your baby, well…"

Ryker's lips tightened. Yeah, he could imagine some of the reactions.

He hadn't wanted to come back here. Carter's Crossing was full of bad memories.

He didn't need to get involved in a town that didn't want him.

"Hey," Benny said. "There are judgmental people here, like everywhere. But you've changed, and they'll see that." He shot a glance down at his chair. "I didn't have the best reputation, but I turned it around."

"How do you know I've changed?"

Benny rolled his eyes. "You've been here, how many days? You haven't had a drink, you've gone nowhere but to AA and town meetings, and haven't ravished anybody, or opened a hellmouth. Honestly, it's been a little disappointing."

Ryker had to hold back a laugh, and he didn't laugh much anymore.

"I'll be sure to schedule an orgy."

"Okay, but it has to be at my place. I can't get upstairs." Benny grinned back.

"Noted."

After a pause, Ryker picked up the three laptops. "Need anything?" he asked.

Benny wheeled back to his bench. "I'm good. Dad's picking me up for dinner. Want to come with us?"

"No, thanks," Ryker said. Benny merely nodded, already immersing himself in his work.

Ryker climbed back upstairs.

He wasn't sure what to do about these additional websites, but he'd take a look at the computers. He was surprised at the implied trust leaving them here indicated. Maybe Rachel and the Giffords weren't the only ones who thought he'd changed.

IT WAS GIRLS' NIGHT again. Rachel was ready for wedding preparations. She was curious about what Mariah would come up with. She couldn't remember a wedding here in Carter's—Cupid's Crossing that had been professionally planned.

Mariah sat down across from Jaycee and dropped a binder and notebook on the table. From what Rachel could see, it looked like Mariah had made a start. But that wasn't what Mariah wanted to talk about.

"Jaycee, I'll get to the wedding stuff. But first, can you guys tell me about the Slades?"

Rachel almost swallowed her tongue. What was Mariah doing?

"Why do you want to know about the Slades?" Jaycee asked.

Mariah was agitated. "I thought I'd found the perfect solution for the town website. Brian Gifford told me about this guy, his former student, Ryker Slade, who'd just come back to town, and that he designs websites. I looked up some of his work. He's good."

Rachel almost smiled, but Ryker's success had no connection to her. Still, she was glad to know he was doing well.

"He's someone from the town, does good work and should know this place, right? But I've had a lot of blowback from people warning me about him and worried what he'll do.

"First of all, do they think I'm stupid? The guy has a good reputation and does good work, or I wouldn't consider hiring him.

"He's a veteran, and he's a local. Why are so many people afraid of him?"

Jaycee looked at Rachel. "Maybe you can explain it better, Rachel?"

Rachel hoped her face wasn't flushed.

"Ryker's dad…well, he's not a nice man." Wasn't that an understatement? The Slades had a place outside town, and his mother, she died when the kids were still pretty young. There were seven of them. Ryker's dad was injured at the mill, so he couldn't work. What he could do was drink.

"The kids sometimes showed up at school with bruises. And they didn't always show up. My dad went out there a couple of times, but it didn't go well.

"The kids got into trouble. I don't think any

of the boys finished high school, at least not here."

Mariah narrowed her eyes. "Sounds like maybe the people in town could have done a bit more to help the family. I mean, if the man was hurting his kids—"

Rachel nodded. "People are more aware now. And yes, we probably should have."

Rachel had tried, in her own way. She tutored Ryker and befriended his sister. It hadn't been enough, and it hadn't done any real good.

"So the dad was a drunk."

"Not just a drunk." Jaycee leaned forward. "He was mean and would get in fights. If he was mad at you, he would do stuff. Nothing you could prove, but burned-down sheds, cars broken into, things like that. He hasn't been able to do anything lately, 'cause he can't get around much anymore, but he was awful. He went into a home recently, right, Rachel?"

Rachel nodded. "A month ago."

Jaycee shivered. "I don't envy the people taking care of him in the home."

Mariah tapped her pen on the table.

"Okay, Mr. Slade senior was bad news. Why are people so upset with Ryker?"

Jaycee and Mariah were waiting for Rachel to explain.

"Ryker got in an accident, drove a car into

a tree. He was seventeen. He was drunk. It wasn't his car."

Rachel had been devastated when she heard the news.

"When he could leave the hospital, he was given a choice. Instead of being arrested, he joined the air force. This is the first he's been back since."

Mariah was still tapping her pen.

"So has he changed, or is he still trouble? Should I cut him off this project?"

"No," Rachel blurted.

Mariah asked, "No, he hasn't changed, or no, I shouldn't cut him off?"

It was stupid, but Rachel didn't want him to leave. And he had changed. He shouldn't be chased away by his past, and by what his dad had done.

"He's changed."

"That's right, you met with him. You're sure he's changed?"

Rachel hoped her heated cheeks weren't obvious.

"Yeah, we met up to talk about those Cupids."

Jaycee looked puzzled, so they explained about Rachel's sketches.

"And, well, there's stuff I can't share with

you," Rachel said. AA was supposed to be anonymous, after all, and she never divulged the information she had access to from her work or helping her dad.

Jaycee understood. "I know, confidential stuff from the church and the law office. Okay, if you can vouch for him, I think we should give him a chance."

Jaycee hadn't grown up in a perfect home, so she had sympathy for anyone who had to prove themselves. Her future mother-in-law was biased against her because of her upbringing.

Mariah gave a nod. "That's what I thought. His reputation for web design is excellent. I reached out to some of his clients, and they're pleased with his work. I'm not going to lose a good asset because of some misplaced prejudice. I'll talk to Abigail. See what we can do about that.

"Okay, now let's get to what Jaycee wants to hear. The summer wedding. I've got some ideas. And Abigail thinks the Romance Committee might get behind this. Do you mind if we make a big deal of your wedding, Jaycee?"

Jaycee's face split in a smile. "Not at all. What are you thinking?"

Rachel readied herself to listen and provide

the appropriate responses, but the conversation with Mariah had given her an idea. Maybe she could help Ryker and herself at the same time.

CHAPTER FOUR

RACHEL WALKED HOME. She didn't have an escort this time and felt safer without Ryker's disturbing presence. And it gave her time to work out this idea.

Part of her mind was stuck on Ryker. It wasn't right that he wasn't getting a fair shot here. Sure, he'd had problems growing up. But Mariah had made a good point. Carter's hadn't done much for the Slade kids.

Ryker was stuck with the reputation he'd had when he left. Never mind that he'd served two tours. He could have chosen to try to fight an arrest back then. He could have followed the path his older twin brothers had.

She understood, in a weird way. She was stuck with a reputation, as well. He was the bad boy; she was the good girl. She didn't want to have that label when she left.

Was she going to be able to be a different person in a different place? It would be easier to stick with her same routines and habits when she no longer had the comfort of familiar work and friends. But if she did that, there was almost no point in leaving.

It would be good to change things up before she left.

Ryker had told her he was two years sober. It could help him hang on to his sobriety if the town would support him a bit.

She stopped at the gate to the parsonage.

If her plan worked, maybe she could do that. Help people to see that he wasn't like his dad and his brothers. It was easier for people to keep the same image of him that they'd had for years. That didn't take any effort.

They should make an effort. They needed to think.

She had already done that with Jean, on a small scale, when she'd made it clear that Ryker wasn't getting a free meal for nothing. Maybe she could do more of that kind of thing. If Ryker wanted it. Surely, he didn't want people glaring at him, misjudging him for however long he was here?

And maybe…maybe she could ask him to help her change?

Her whole body flushed at the thought. She still had this stupid crush, and spending time with Ryker wouldn't help.

Or would it? She'd made up his character in her head. She didn't really know him.

He'd been divorced twice. That meant he had some problems with relationships. Maybe, spending time with him, she'd find out what it was that ended those marriages. Things that would kill this crush.

And she could shed some of her nice reputation. The guy with those tattoos and the leather jacket? Yeah, he knew about not caving in to other people's expectations.

Was she being stupid?

Maybe. But it might be a way to deal with this seething unrest that was building up inside. Before she wrapped a car around a tree.

Was she bold enough to try?

MARIAH SENT AN EMAIL to both Ryker and Rachel, and Rachel sent back some sketches. And, in an email that did not cc Mariah, she asked Ryker if they could meet and talk.

Ryker had managed to clean up the one laptop and explained to the owner about cookies and viruses and was confidently expecting to see the machine back for another cleaning before long. He'd checked out the other two, run some scans and then paused.

If he agreed to set up their websites, he was committing to stay for a while. He wasn't sure yet that he wanted to do that.

He'd intended to get in and out as quickly

as he could. Most of his memories of Carter's were not good. Especially the ones tied to the house he was supposed to prepare for sale.

Somehow, over the week or so he'd been here, he'd remembered other, more pleasant things.

As the snow was finally overcome by the rising temperatures, signs of life were springing up. There was a smell he remembered as spring in the air. In the city, with so many competing and conflicting aromas, he'd forgotten what that was like.

He didn't go out much in Carter's and didn't like the reaction he often got when he did, but it was quiet, and sometimes even relaxing here. As long as he didn't think about the house, he was more at peace than he'd been for a while.

Benny was a good guy. Whatever had made him act out, years ago when Ryker was still around, that was long gone. He'd been through some bad stuff but had a better attitude about it than Ryker did, and Ryker hadn't lost use of his legs.

Ryker didn't have a place to go back to whenever he did leave Carter's Crossing. Before he'd come here, his landlord had wanted the apartment he rented for a kid who was boomeranging back home. Ryker could find another place, but he didn't have one ready right now. He freelanced, so could do most of any work that came in right here, from his laptop.

He was in limbo, for the moment. His sponsor was back home, but Mr. G had stepped into that role.

Maybe he should take some time here, take his time with the house. If he could stay mostly inside, where he didn't interact with the general population of Carter's Crossing, that would be great.

Maybe he needed this time to figure out what he was going to do with himself now. After two years of sobriety, he was finally in a headspace where he could trust his decisions. Maybe, then, people might be able to trust him, as well.

Rather than make that call right now, he agreed to talk with Rachel. She offered to pick him up. It was still cold to be driving around on the bike.

He was curious what she wanted to talk about, but knew he'd soon find out. He didn't spend much time thinking about it, as he waited by the bottom of the stairs to his new place. Patience was possibly his one virtue.

She stopped her car in front of the repair shop, and he opened the passenger door and slid in.

Rachel gave him a nervous smile. "Hey,

Ryker. Are you okay if we go someplace private?"

Ryker paused. With many women, he'd know what that meant. With Rachel? He had no idea.

"Or not. I mean, I didn't want to talk at the diner, but I'm not trying to kidnap you." She drew in a deep breath. "I'm a little nervous. I thought we could go out to Nelson's farm. He and Mariah are busy today, so we'll be alone. It's nice out there."

He could see the tension in her grip on the wheel. He couldn't imagine what was making Rachel so nervous, but he wasn't afraid of her. If she felt better talking at some farm, he could live with that.

"Where is Nelson's farm?" He knew the Carter family—everyone in town did. But they hadn't had a farm property that he'd ever heard of.

"It's the old Abbott place."

The Abbotts had moved away before Ryker was born. The place had been falling to pieces.

But he knew where it was. "That should be fine."

Rachel nodded. "Good."

She shifted the car into gear, checked over her shoulder and her mirrors and pulled out onto the road. They drove past the mill, the one

Abigail Carter had closed, where he saw signs of construction, then on out to the highway.

"Nelson Carter bought the Abbott place?" Ryker was long away from news of Carter's Crossing.

"When he moved back, yeah. He has rescue horses out there."

That sounded like the town golden boy, Nelson Carter.

"Where did he move back from?"

"He went to school in California, then was down near Richmond, working in a veterinary practice that specialized in horses. After his wedding fiasco, he moved back here, opened his own practice and bought this place."

Ryker didn't pay much attention to the professional part of Nelson's history. It was a given that a Carter would be successful.

"What happened at his wedding?" This was the interesting part.

Rachel fidgeted in her seat. "I don't gossip."

"Is it a secret?"

She sighed. "Not really."

"Did it involve you?"

She turned her head, startled. "Me? No, of course not."

She turned back to the road, her cheeks flushed.

"I always thought you and he might end up

together." They'd spent a lot of time with each other, back in high school, as he remembered.

For some reason, that made her jaw clench.

"Nelson and I have no romantic interest in each other. He was engaged to someone in Richmond, and she didn't show up to the wedding. Her dad was one of the partners at his practice, and it got really messy. So he came back here."

Rachel gripped her mouth tightly shut, so Ryker knew he wasn't going to hear any more.

"And there's still nothing between you and Nelson?" Was that why she was so upset?

"No. Nelson and I are just friends. We've always been friends. People can stop thinking there's anything more. He's engaged to Mariah now anyway."

Ryker digested that information. Mariah had been wearing a ring, but he hadn't wondered where it came from. Mariah was pretty, but he hadn't been interested. He had a spectacularly bad history with relationships, so had cut that idea out of his plans.

He did wonder how Rachel really felt about Nelson, and Nelson engaged to Mariah. She was obviously close enough to Nelson to be comfortable at his place when he wasn't there.

If she did care about Nelson, that might explain why she wanted to leave town. Couldn't fault her for that. In Ryker's opinion, Rachel's kindness would be a bigger asset in a relationship than Mariah's more obvious beauty, or planning abilities, but he wasn't Nelson.

After two failed marriages, he had a better idea of the traits that would make a relationship last. Not that anyone was asking him.

Rachel pulled into the driveway to the Abbotts' old place.

The house was still falling down, while the barn looked well maintained.

"Does Nelson live here?" Would Nelson live in the barn? Because no one was living in that house.

Rachel laughed, some of the tension gone now that they had arrived.

"No, he has an apartment over the carriage house at Abigail's. He didn't like the idea of his grandmother living alone there."

"None of the other Carters are still here?"

Ryker hadn't paid any attention to Carter's Crossing after he'd left. He'd wanted to forget his past, and he'd severed all ties to the town. Back now, after all these years, it was easy to assume things were the same. It might look like nothing changed, but apparently, some things did.

"No. Everyone else moved away. Nelson's the only one who's come back."

Ryker felt an eyebrow lift. That surprised him. There had been a lot of Carters, and they seemed to have it good here. But he'd grown up in a run-down house, outside town, with an alcoholic abusive father, little food and less money. He didn't know anything about the world the Carters lived in.

Rachel braked near the barn and turned off the car. Ryker saw five horses in the field.

She undid her seat belt and opened the door. "We can go in the barn if it gets cold. But it's quiet out here. It's a good place to think."

Ryker nodded and followed her to the fence. The five horses turned to watch them, and then started over. Rachel reached into her pocket and pulled out some carrots.

"You come here a lot?"

She shrugged. "Not a lot, but enough."

She propped her arms on the fence and waited while the horses approached. One hung back, but the others all pushed their heads toward her, eager for the carrots.

Ryker didn't know horses, but even so, these weren't pretty. They mostly looked old and the worse for wear. They wouldn't have a lot of homes queueing up to take them, if Nelson decided to close the farm down.

Ryker had always been resentful of the town boys, the ones with money and nice homes.

But Nelson was doing something good. Maybe he'd lost some of that entitled confidence he'd worn when he was in high school.

With the carrots gone, the horses started to wander away. Rachel turned around, arms still propped behind her on the top of the fence. Her gaze was focused inward, and she drew a breath.

She was finally ready to get to whatever she needed to say, out here where there was no one else around.

Ryker had no clue. He couldn't begin to imagine what Rachel wanted to talk about. He shoved his hands in his pockets and waited.

She met his gaze, then dropped her own to look at the ground in front of her. Her foot was tapping.

"I should have asked you this first. How long are you staying in Carter's—I mean Cupid's Crossing?"

Every time Ryker heard the name *Cupid's Crossing* he wanted to ask if the speaker was serious. It was a stupid name. He got the connection with the romance business the town was trying to generate. He was doing the website for it, after all. But he was glad he never had to tell anyone in his unit he was from a place called Cupid's Crossing.

Rachel's toe started to dig into the slushy snow in front of her.

"I haven't decided yet."

He wasn't sure what she wanted, but he wasn't making promises.

"But you're here long enough to do the town website. And to get your home ready to sell."

House, not home. It hadn't been a home for a long time.

He shrugged. "I can do the website remotely. I don't have to be here for that."

"How long will it take to get the house ready?"

He gazed out over the pasture. There were two answers to that question. The actual hours it would take to do the physical work. And then, the added time for him to deal with the parts of the job that weren't physical, that involved memories and emotions. He didn't know how long that part would take.

He glanced back at Rachel, who was watching him.

"I don't know."

She kept watching him. "Would you like me to help?"

He took a step back. He had no idea why she would want to involve herself in cleaning up the mess in the house, but it was a terrible idea. Probably enough gossip had spread around town after they'd had to send an ambulance to get his father out of there, but he had no desire for more talk about how his father had let things go.

"Only if it would help. I've done this kind of thing before, helped when someone had to go into a home. It can be a difficult thing. What to keep, what to get rid of, what there isn't room for..."

For some people, that would be the problem. Not for him. As far as he was concerned, everything was going to the dump. There was nothing there he was interested in keeping. And he didn't care if his father wanted anything. The old man had never cared about what his kids wanted.

Rachel took another long breath and closed her eyes. "Not to push, but everyone knows things were bad at your place. And I don't know your story, but the fact that you're going to AA makes me think that maybe there are things in that house that could be a problem for you. I'm just saying, if I can help, I'd be happy to.

"Because there's something I want you to do for me."

RYKER INTENDED TO say no. It was hard to ask for help. He'd worked on it in AA. He'd had to admit sobriety wasn't something he could handle on his own.

Having Rachel go through the dump he'd grown up in was too much.

He knew the kind of home that Rachel had been raised in. The kind where parents cared. They came to school events. They noticed if you skipped school. They made sure you had food, and clothes and a clean, safe place.

She had probably seen some of the other side thanks to her father's job. But that didn't mean he wanted her to see how bad it had been in his place. He didn't need more pity. Especially not from her.

There'd been a time, back in high school, when she'd looked at him as if he was someone, as if he wasn't a troublemaking kid on the fast track to failure. She'd almost made him believe he could be different.

Time had proven otherwise. And he needed to guard against her insidious optimism.

He didn't want Rachel to see the place. But he didn't say so. Not when she wanted something.

What could she want from him?

His assets were few. He traveled light. He'd learned to hurt people and defend himself in the air force, but that wasn't anything he connected with Rachel. Was she secretly being threatened?

He could work with computers. Did she want a website?

She was waiting for him to respond.

"What do you want me to do for you, Rachel?"

If she wanted a website, they didn't need to come somewhere private to talk. That left his skills from when he'd been enlisted. He had hoped he'd put his violent days behind him. If someone was hurting Rachel, though…

Rachel stared at the horses, not him.

"I need to leave Carter's. If I stay here, I'm going to spend my time filing papers for my uncle, organizing my father's life and eventually living with fourteen cats. I want a life."

Ryker had left Carter's, and he'd searched for a life. It hadn't worked out well. Rachel had better odds in her favor, but that didn't mean she'd find what she was looking for. The problem with leaving to change things was that you were the same person when you arrived at the new place. Your problems tended to piggyback along with you.

As if she'd heard him, she continued on.

"If I leave, I think it will be easier to set better boundaries and find things *I* want to do. I need to say no to people, and it's hard to do that with people who gave you peppermints in church. But I also need to change myself, or I'll keep doing the same things in a new place.

"I'm a boring person, with no backbone. I can't leave until after Jaycee's wedding this summer, and I can't do everything at once, but for these next few months, I want to start changing. That's what I want your help with."

Ryker could have been relieved that she didn't want him to be her bodyguard, or some kind of superhero from a movie, but this didn't sound a whole lot better.

"How do you think I can help you with that?" He kept his distance, as if she could weave a spell on him if he got too close.

She looked at him then. Her brown eyes were intent, her cheeks flushed from the cold or embarrassment. The tension in her shoulders and the grip of her hands on the fence showed she wasn't at ease.

"Ryker, you've lived about three times more of a life than I have. You're not boring, and you're not nice. I'm both.

"You can shake off what people think about you, while I'm a chronic people pleaser.

"I'm about to turn thirty, and I'm tired of wasting my life. I want you to help me become more like you."

Ryker hadn't felt a sense of danger like this

since he'd been deployed. He could feel the hairs on the back of his neck rising, and his fists were clenching in his pockets.

"You don't want to be like me." He didn't want anyone to be like him. He hated to think of what Rachel would have to go through to get anywhere close to what he was like.

She sighed. "I don't want to be exactly like you, and I couldn't be. But I want to move closer to your side of the scale."

He didn't know what scale she was using, but she was better off staying where she was.

"There's nothing wrong with you, Rachel."

"Come on, Ryker. Look at me."

He was. Whenever he found himself in a situation where he felt in danger, he looked carefully. He'd never thought of Rachel as dangerous, but something was going on with her. He hadn't succeeded in his marriages, but he'd learned the signs of trouble.

"What's wrong with how you look, Rachel?" She was wearing a blue scarf, jeans, below-the-hip-length coat, sensible boots for coming to a farm and warm hat and gloves. Her face was bare of makeup, again, appropriate for a farm. "You look…nice."

"Aaargh!" It wasn't loud, but it was a scream. Not a shock that he wasn't married anymore.

Even if he didn't say much, he managed to say the wrong thing.

Rachel marched up to him, and he had to force himself to hold his ground. Her eyes were flashing, and her cheeks were definitely heated. She looked much better than nice. *Angry* worked for her.

"I. Don't. Want. To. Look. Nice."

He made a mental note to never tell a woman she looked nice again. He couldn't remember if he had with either of his wives, but if it set Rachel off, it must be bad.

She stretched out her arms. "Look at me!"

He was looking at her. He didn't fear that she would hurt him, not physically, but he had no idea what was coming.

"Did your wives, or anyone you dated, look like this?"

No. No, they had not. Girls who looked like Rachel never came into his orbit.

"That's not something you should be upset about."

"Aaargh!" Rachel didn't like that comment any better. "I know, I'm not a sexpot."

He blinked. Sexpot?

"I'm not going to walk down the street and find men with their tongues hanging out no matter what I wear. But I want to look…at least, a little bit, sexy."

Ryker banished some very inappropriate images his brain threw up at the idea of Rachel dressing sexy.

She didn't think she was sexy? Attractive?

He hadn't kissed her in high school, torpedoing his tutoring opportunity, because he thought she was unattractive.

"Rachel, I'm not someone who can do a makeover."

"That's not what I want." She blew out a breath. "But you can tell me what a man finds attractive."

CHAPTER FIVE

RYKER HAD NO IDEA how to deal with this. He thought Rachel was attractive the way she was. He did understand what she meant, though.

She wasn't loud and flashy. She didn't make the most of her best attributes with tight clothing and makeup. She was understated, which he had thought was an indication of the fact that she wasn't needy or desperate for attention. He liked that.

He could imagine, though, what guys from his unit would think if she was at one of the bars they'd hung out at. They'd have passed her over, might even have made rude, derogatory comments. They'd have liked the flashy and obvious.

Not that he could judge. His wives had been flashy and obvious.

Of course, those guys weren't looking for anything serious. Rachel didn't look like a good-time girl. She looked like a longtime girl.

Maybe that wasn't appealing to the guys she was interested in.

Those guys were stupid.

So was Ryker, so far, judging by the way she'd responded to his comments.

"Attractiveness is subjective, Rachel."

"Well, be subjective."

His sense of self-preservation was still on high alert. He didn't see any way this was going to go somewhere good.

"I don't understand what you want from me."

"Think of an attractive woman. You're out somewhere, and you see someone who grabs your attention. Someone you want to get to know better. What does she look like? Not her body or face, but what is she wearing?"

"Uh, clothes?"

Rachel glared at him. She wasn't going to let this go.

"Well, I guess it's good she's not naked. But what color? Is she wearing a dress or pants? High heels or boots?"

"A dress. Red. High heels." Sure, it was a stereotype, but yeah, if he saw someone like that he'd notice. He wouldn't go chat her up, not now, but he would have.

Rachel looked down at herself and sighed. He blinked. She was wearing blue jeans and boots. Nothing like he'd described. He hadn't done well.

"And that tells me I'm doing this wrong."

"Rachel, you asked about when I go out. I don't go out now, so that's what I would have looked for before. And you, if you were going out, you wouldn't wear what you've got on now, either—"

He broke off. Maybe she did. Maybe he'd shoved his big feet even farther into his mouth.

"You're right." She sighed. "But I don't have a red dress. I don't have anything red."

"It doesn't have to be red—"

Rachel rolled her eyes. "I get that, Ryker. But even the dresses I have… This imaginary dress you see on this woman— does it go down past her knees? How low is the neckline? Does it have long sleeves?"

Ryker had lost all grasp on the imaginary dress. He had a picture of Rachel going shopping for a red dress, short, tight, neckline cut down to her belly button…and part of him was ready to imagine that. But he couldn't imagine Rachel enjoying herself wearing something like that or the type of attention she'd got.

"Rachel, don't worry about some stupid thing I said. You don't want to wear something that makes you uncomfortable. Before you worry about what some stranger thinks, you should be happy with what *you* feel about it."

Rachel shook her head at him. "Do you think

your imaginary woman in heels was comfortable? Women sacrifice comfort to look good."

Ryker shrugged. "I don't think I can help you with this."

She set her jaw. "I think you can."

"I can't tell you what to wear."

"You can tell me what not to wear. And you can tell me some of the things you did with women you dated. Things that are interesting."

Oh no. No way. That was not a conversational trail he was going to follow, no way, no how.

"Rachel, I think you have a weird idea of what my life's been like."

"It hasn't been as boring as mine."

He snorted. "Rachel, I've been divorced, twice. I'm not really an expert on what you want."

Rachel stilled. She almost visibly deflated in front of him.

"I'm sorry, Ryker. You're right. I shouldn't be asking you to revisit painful parts of your past. I thought… I thought maybe I could help you lose some of your bad reputation and you could help me lose some of my good reputation."

She must have caught the horrified expression on his face. "No, I wasn't going to ask you to make me become a floozy—"

He held back a grin at the word *floozy*, relieved that she'd reconsidered. Though the thought of not having most of the people he met give him "that" look was a nice feeling.

"Just to be a little more fun. A little stronger, more self-confident. I'll still help you with your dad's place if you want, but I'm not going to ask you to repay me for that. I'll find someone else who can help me with this."

Rachel turned back to the horses, obviously embarrassed at the whole conversation. She looked smaller, where for a few moments, when she'd been standing up to him, she'd looked bigger, stronger.

That was what she wanted. To be more. More confident, more willing to take what she wanted. She deserved that.

Now she probably thought she was hopeless, thanks to his ineptitude. Either that, or she was going to ask someone else.

That thought made the hair on his neck stand up again. Who would she ask? What would that guy do? Would it be someone she could trust?

If she was looking for a bad boy, she probably shouldn't. She might be approaching thirty, but she was sheltered. Innocent. An easy mark.

The thought of someone hurting her, taking advantage of her, bothered him. She thought being nice was a bad thing, a handicap. She was wrong about that.

Maybe he could do this. Maybe he could help her take a few steps onto the wild side, but not enough to hurt her or compromise what she might want to do in the future.

He could always say no to anything too outrageous.

He didn't want her to come to the house. But maybe helping her would change the minds of some of the people in this town. Maybe he could get rid of the house, and someone would tear it down, renovate it—so it was no longer the place in his nightmares.

He'd never really found a place to put down roots. He'd learned to travel light and only rely on himself.

But he had a history in this town, and not all the memories were bad. It would be nice if, should he decide to stay for a bit, he could set up websites for people without them assuming he was going to rob them blind.

He had no idea how she could erase what people remembered about him and his family, but it would keep her distracted from taking too long a walk on the wild side.

"Okay, Rachel."

She turned to look at him, all spark gone. "Okay?"

"Okay, I'll help you and you can help me. Though I don't know what you think I can do, and I have no idea how you're going to undo my reputation here in Carter's Crossing."

A smile grew, bringing out a dimple in her left cheek.

"Really?"

The spark was coming back. That felt good, despite his reservations.

She held out her hand. He pulled out his own hand and shook hers.

"Deal," she said.

He had a deep gut feeling that he was going to regret this.

RACHEL HAD TOLD RYKER to come to the church Saturday morning at six.

"Is that too early?"

She saw a corner of his mouth quirk up in a grin. "I think I can handle it. We had to keep early hours in the air force."

Right. Well, he should be good to go at six, then.

For Rachel, it was a bit of a struggle. She had to be at the law offices for 9:00 a.m. weekday mornings, and up for church on Sundays, so Saturdays were her day to sleep in. Supposedly. Too often there were events like this, the spring bazaar, that ate up her free morning. It was a fundraiser for the church, and heaven knew they needed funds, but each year it seemed there were more things left on Rachel's shoulders as the older members of the congregation had to give up their responsibilities.

This year, though, she was making some changes. Well, two. It was a start. First, she asked Ryker to come help.

Ryker's family had never attended any church in town. If they had, they might have been offered some assistance, either food or clothing. But Mr. Slade had been the least churchy person in the whole environs of Carter's Crossing, and none of his kids had ever defied him to come to church.

There was a lot of physical work that had to be done to set up the bazaar, and every year Rachel had done more of it herself, concerned that her elderly assistants would keel over in a heart attack.

She deserved help with this. Somehow, everyone just assumed she could handle it all. She hadn't asked anyone if they thought enlisting Ryker to help was a good idea. She'd just done it. If she was left with the work, she was going to get the help she needed.

Even Nelson and Dave, her friends, never thought to offer to help, and were always busy.

Ryker's showing up to help with the bazaar would definitely make people think twice about what kind of man he'd grown into. And as a bonus, Rachel would have less of the heavy lifting to do. It was a win-win.

The second change she'd made was in her appearance. Previously, she'd always helped with setup in her oldest jeans and a baggy sweatshirt, things that could get ripped and dirty. Then she'd change into a skirt for the bazaar itself.

This year she wasn't going to wear a skirt the way her mother always had, and her grand-mother, and probably her ancestors for fifty generations or more. No one wore a skirt on Saturdays except for the seniors who, admit-tedly, made up the core of the bazaar crowd. Lately, though, even some of them had been arriving in pants. It was a small step, but Ra-chel was going to attend the bazaar in pants. She was going to hear about this, she was cer-tain.

This time she wasn't going to care.

She'd also bought new clothes. Something red.

Her mother had been big on dressing mod-estly, and even after she died, Rachel had followed her guidelines. At first, it seemed dis-loyal to change drastically, and then, it was expected. Her father thought she was a model of modesty and decorum.

Well, models of modesty and decorum weren't getting a lot of dates here. And she wanted a family, a home, someone who loved and wanted her.

It wasn't like she hadn't thought about this before. It had always been a struggle, though. How much did she change? Where was that line that went too far? How did you ask your friends to help you push your personal limits without sounding like you thought they might have crossed that line? Rachel had always accepted that her line was different from everyone else's.

But talking with Ryker, even though it hadn't been completely productive, had given her an idea. He'd mentioned being comfortable with what you wore.

But she'd noted his expression when he talked about a red dress. Red was not a color she had in her wardrobe. But now she decided she wanted something in red. If that was the color a guy thought of first, then darn it, she was going to get something red.

Not a dress. But she'd gone online and looked for a red top.

She'd found something she liked, something

that had a pattern with a lot of red, something she thought looked pretty, had a lower neckline than she was used to—though compared to others she'd seen, still safely on the side of modest—and sleeveless. She'd ordered a red cardigan, too—not the usual warm, chunky ones she wore, but something light. Something that wouldn't hide every bit of her figure underneath. And she got it in a smaller size than usual.

Then, throwing caution to the winds, she'd ordered the jeans that the model wore in the photograph with the red top.

She'd asked for rush delivery.

The clothes were more fitted than she was used to. But she was comfortable enough in them. She felt good. Maybe even pretty.

It wasn't a big thing, but it was a thing. One tiny step out of her rut.

She hoped she was confident enough to handle it if anyone complained.

A check of the time told her she needed to get herself over to the church. No more time to primp. She shoved her phone into her pocket, picked up her lists, since many of her volunteers used cell phones only as phones, and therefore did not get emails, and headed out the door.

GETTING UP EARLY wasn't a problem for Ryker, though it was nice of Rachel to consider that. He wasn't sure exactly what she wanted him to do at the church, so he'd worn nicer jeans and a button-down shirt. Both dark blue. Nothing to stand out. Nothing to make people nervous.

He'd walked over to the church. People were waiting outside, so he stood back by the sidewalk. He didn't recognize most of the people, though some faces looked vaguely familiar. A lot of glances were cast his way. He crossed his arms and leaned against the fence, debating how long he needed to stay before he could leave in good conscience.

He wanted to help Rachel help him, open up some options, but he wasn't staying here like a zoo exhibit forever. None of these seniors would be prospective buyers for the house. He wasn't sure exactly how Rachel thought setting up the bazaar would help.

Then the door of the parsonage opened, and Rachel came out.

She came at a trot, and the people gathered turned to her. They'd been waiting for her, as well.

He wondered if they appreciated that she was willing to take charge of this event or if they took her for granted.

Then he noticed she was wearing red. And

looking good. Somehow different and better in that bit of red.

Not fire-engine, attention-seeking red, but still, red. Since he clearly recalled their conversation, he wondered if the red was for him.

No, not for him. She wouldn't do that. But maybe, because of him? Was this Rachel walking on the wild side?

If it was, he suspected there might be monks with a wilder side than Rachel had.

Ryker hung back, content to watch, while everyone gathered around Rachel, waiting for her to tell them what to do. He saw her glance around, and then smile when she saw him at the gate.

He felt that smile. It sent warmth through him that had nothing to do with the spring sun.

Was it a smile of relief? Had she wondered if he'd show?

He wasn't the punk he'd been before. He kept his word.

Rachel motioned him over.

"We've got some muscles for the heavy lifting today, everyone. I don't know if you remember Ryker Slade, but he's volunteered to help us."

More glances his way. Surprise, suspicion, relief. Mostly surprise.

"The tables for the tearoom were set up last

night, so the tea committee can go in and get started there. Andy and Ryker can help us move the outside tables out here, then the rummage people can get those ready to go. Mavis, you know where the cash box is."

She continued to organize, assigning people jobs for a bake sale, a garden sale and a craft table. Once most of the crowd had headed to their posts, she walked over to the church door, a couple of elderly men on her tail.

"Coming, Ryker?" she asked with a glance over her shoulder.

He nodded and pushed himself off the fence. One of the elderly gentlemen looked up at him.

"Didn't you join the air force, way back?"

Ryker didn't remember the face, but he was sure his story had made the rounds.

He nodded.

The man straightened. "I served in 'Nam."

The elderly veteran looked like a loaded rifle and pack would knock him over now, but Ryker respected what he would have been through.

"Are you out now?" the man continued.

"Yes, sir," he responded. The guy deserved respect.

"Thanks for helping us." He gave Ryker a nod.

And the way he said it, Ryker knew that this

guy wasn't going to check that Ryker hadn't stolen something. They shared a bond and mutual respect. Ryker stood a little straighter, felt a little less out of place.

But he hoped this guy wasn't going to lift anything heavy.

There were tables to be carried outside and gazebos to cover them. Chairs for volunteers to sit on.

Rachel got her elderly helpers to take out the chairs and the tent covers for the gazebo frames. Then she grabbed the end of a table and waited for Ryker to pick up the other.

"Do you carry these on your own?" The old guys wouldn't be able to lift much.

"I could get my dad to help, but it takes forever to pull him away."

Ryker picked up most of the weight of the table.

"You need more help. These guys—they're willing, but they're pretty old." He glanced around to make sure neither was close enough to hear him.

She shot him a smile. "That's why I asked you to come."

"What would you have done if I wasn't here? Or told you no?"

She was backing up the staircase with one

end of the table, so that he could bear most of the weight.

"If I'd had to, I could have asked Nelson or Dave, but they're usually busy."

Ryker helped her maneuver the table out the door and down the front steps to the lawn. There the elderly gentlemen were waiting to unfold the legs and position it properly.

Ryker followed her back into the building.

"Everyone assumed you'd take care of it."

She stiffened, pausing in her step for a moment, then nodded.

Ryker hadn't seen Nelson Carter or his buddy Dave since he'd dropped out of high school, but he wanted to find them and ask them what their problem was. They'd been friends of Rachel's back in school, kids from the nice homes. Didn't they notice Rachel, see all she did?

No wonder she wanted to leave.

Ryker spent the next two hours helping set up the spring bazaar. He'd never gone to one while growing up and wasn't sure he'd even heard of them. He had no idea how much revenue the event might generate, but could it possibly earn enough to make up for the effort involved?

The opening was at eight, and by then, everything was good to go. Tables were under canvas roofs and covered in an assortment of foods and merchandise. Inside, the tearoom tables were set with dainty cups and fancy tablecloths.

Ryker found Rachel, as he'd been doing all morning.

Her hair was a little mussed, and her cheeks touched with pink, but it looked like everything was ready. Mavis Grisham, at the table by the sidewalk, gestured that the first people could make their way in, so better or worse, it was on.

"Anything else?" He'd been asking her that for the past two hours.

She turned to him with a smile. "Everything is great. Thank you so much, Ryker."

She glanced around. Her crew was busy, but some of the newcomers, fresh in the gates, were shooting looks his way.

By now, the story of his return had made the rounds. He saw the glances, saw the recognition on some faces. And the expressions, none of which were happy.

The crew, though? He didn't think any of them were unhappy he was there. He'd worked hard enough to have built up a sweat.

She moved close to him and spoke, quietly enough to not be overheard.

"I think you might have changed some minds here. And these people all talk."

She stepped back, and he was tempted to follow. Bad idea, he told himself.

"I apologize for doubting you." He shot her a glance. "But you took good advantage to work on my reputation."

She bit her lip. "I did appreciate the help. Are you feeling like I used you?"

He shook his head. "You needed the help, and I was glad to provide it. When do you have to close this place up?"

"Three is the stated wrap time. We'll be out of food and plantings by then, and it'll just be the jumble and craft tables with leftovers to pack up."

"Do all the tables need to go back inside?"

Rachel nodded. "But I won't ask you—"

"I'll be here." She opened her mouth as if to argue. "I wouldn't want anyone to say I shirked."

Rachel relaxed when she saw that he was smiling.

He didn't have a lot to do today. He probably should have made another attempt to do something out at the house, but helping Rachel had been a good excuse to procrastinate. It was a nice day, and he'd take the bike out, before coming back to help with cleanup.

Keeping busy was a good way to stay sober. The house could wait. But not for much longer. Seeing more of Rachel was just a bonus.

CHAPTER SIX

RACHEL WATCHED RYKER LEAVE. He'd been an incredible help. He was strong. He'd taken off his jacket as he worked up a sweat, and his biceps had bulged beneath his sleeves while he carried tables and chairs. As well as boxes full of the odds and ends that the bazaar always accumulated.

Rachel hadn't been able to spend all her time with Ryker as they were setting up. She was needed often, to answer questions, settle disagreements and assign tasks. While she'd moved from group to group, she'd overheard people talking about Ryker. Some were suspicious about his motives, and there'd been a lot of talk about what he'd been like in high school. But she'd also heard the appreciation for his help and a few comments about Ryker having served in the air force.

She didn't know if he would be able to overcome his reputation with everyone, but the people who hadn't been hurt by him or his family would be more likely to accept him now that they'd seen him in a helping role. It was a start.

She'd been busy throughout the bazaar, solving problems, helping out when people had lunch breaks, stealing time to eat some food herself. Her father had joined the volunteers not long after Ryker left, praising them for their help. He didn't say much to her.

She loved her town, knew and loved most of the residents, but they did take her for granted, especially her father. She was worried about what would happen when she left. Would anyone else find it worthwhile to take over the bazaar? It wasn't a big fundraiser anymore, but people who'd grown up with the event loved it. It gave many of the older members a sense of purpose that they lacked in their lives.

And her father? Her uncle?

She shook her head. She deserved her own life. She wanted a partner, a family, a life of her own. She'd done her part for this town, for this church.

She wasn't going to let herself feel guilty.

Just before three, she heard a loud engine. Loud and getting closer. Like everyone else, she turned and watched a motorcycle pull up in front of the church.

Motorcycles never came to her father's church.

The rider pulled off his helmet.

Ryker.

Rachel stared. She noted his hair was messed from the helmet. He was wearing that leather jacket, jeans and boots. The leather jacket wasn't an affectation, she realized. It was equipment, for the bike.

Ryker might look edgy, or a little threatening to the people watching. Rachel could sign off on that.

But right now her gaze was focused on the motorcycle.

Not many people drove motorcycles, not here in Carter's Crossing. Cupid's Crossing. Whatever. Nice people didn't, for sure.

Ryker looked dangerous and cool. Things Rachel wanted to add to her own reputation. Dangerous might be a stretch. But someone riding a motorcycle was interesting. Not bland.

She wanted to learn to ride the motorcycle. That was what she was going to ask Ryker to do for her.

In her mind, she was already flying down a road, covered in leather. Other people turned their heads when they saw her. No one knew it was her. No one said, "Oh, how *nice*." No, they envied her and maybe warned themselves to watch out for her.

She'd have to buy the right clothing to wear

on the bike. Helmet. Jacket. Gloves and boots. Those things? They'd be unlike anything she'd ever worn.

Yep. She was going to learn to ride a motorcycle, and when she moved to her new place, no one would think she was boring and nice.

RYKER WORKED just as hard at cleanup as he had in the morning setup.

They'd lost assistants. Somehow, things cropped up and people who were supposed to help had to leave. It happened every year, and Rachel was so grateful that Ryker was here.

The tearoom had already been tidied away, so they didn't need to do much in the kitchen. But the tables and chairs and covers all had to be brought back inside and packed away for the fall bazaar. The leftover merchandise was bundled up to be donated to a secondhand store.

Ryker did whatever she requested. He remembered where things came from and didn't ask her half the questions people normally did, the ones who did this twice a year. It made the tedious job of cleanup so much easier and quicker.

It was noticed. Rachel caught the glances, heard the comments. Ryker had changed part of his reputation today.

She felt warm and proud. Like he belonged to her, and these changes reflected on her.

She rolled her eyes. She needed to get a grip.

Once everything was done, and Mavis, the last volunteer, had gone home to take care of her dog, it was time for Rachel to talk to Ryker.

They were standing at the back door to the church. They'd both been through those doors more times than she could count today.

"Would you like some leftovers? There's a bunch in the fridge."

Ryker's shirt and jeans were smudged with dust. Rachel expected hers were, as well, but she didn't regret her choice of outfit. At least ten people had told her she looked good, and no one had made a negative comment—not that she'd heard, at least.

She decided she wasn't going to worry about things that she hadn't heard.

Ryker had picked up his jacket, prepared to leave. Rachel coveted that jacket. She was going to get one.

Did he have something planned this evening? A date? It was Saturday.

He watched her, something going on in his head, but all he asked was, "Sure?"

"It's the least I can do. You worked hard today."

He shrugged. And followed her into the kitchen.

She drew a breath. This was her chance. Her stomach was doing the shimmies again, but she couldn't stop to dwell on that. She was on a mission.

Rachel opened the fridge and leaned in to see what was left. Sandwiches from the tearoom. She grabbed those. The scones were all gone, but there were some tarts left. Probably from Mrs. Ellsby. She wasn't very good at pastry these days, but she wanted to help.

Bingo. The youth group had met last night, and there was leftover pizza. Hopefully, that would tide him over.

Ryker was moving around the kitchen, looking in cupboards. He found plates, cutlery and glasses. On his own, without asking.

Rachel reminded herself to focus.

There was lemonade in the fridge, as well. Their feast awaited.

Rachel distributed the food between two plates, making sure the largest and nicest portions were on the one that she passed to Ryker. There was no place to sit in the kitchen, and she didn't want to pull out any of the tables and chairs again.

Ryker understood without her explaining. He leaned against the counter, plate in hand.

"Thanks."

Rachel shook her head. "No, thank you. I wish I had something better to thank you with."

A small smile tugged up a corner of his mouth. His jaw was shadowed, though he'd been clean-shaven this morning.

And his hair, now that it was no longer mussed up from the helmet, was shorter. He'd gotten a haircut.

She dragged her attention back from his hair, which was all too close to those eyes…

"No thanks necessary. I need to thank you."

Rachel paused, a sandwich partway to her mouth.

"Thank me for making you lift and carry things?"

He shook his head.

"Part of this thing with the town website—locals are setting up websites as well for bed-and-breakfasts. Mariah wants everything linked together. But not everyone was…comfortable with me doing the work."

Small towns could have long memories.

"A couple of people today asked me about doing their websites."

Rachel opened her mouth to respond, but he shot her a grin, and that full smile—it transformed his face. The brooding, heavy expression was gone, and his eyes were bright. For a moment she even forgot to breathe.

She forced her mouth to close before she started drooling.

Ryker didn't appear to notice or was too used to this kind of response.

"Apparently, helping out with the bazaar has made them think I've changed. So thank you, for that."

Rachel looked down at her plate, trying to regain her composure. This was her chance. If she didn't look at Ryker, then maybe she could do this.

"I was hoping you might do something for me." She took a breath. "You did say you'd help me."

She bit her lip. Maybe this wasn't a good idea?

She remembered when Ryker pulled up to the church, a couple of hours ago. The motorcycle. The way people looked. The sound.

"Depends what it is." There was a note of caution in his voice. What did he think she'd ask?

Grabbing the bull by the horns, or the bike by the handlebars, Rachel blurted out, "I want you to teach me to drive a motorcycle."

RYKER HAD FINISHED the sandwiches quickly, each dainty square a bite for him. He'd been considering picking the pineapple off the piece of pizza when Rachel had asked for a favor.

He'd looked up and seen her cheeks pinken.

She had a smudge of dirt on her chin and one on her forehead where she'd brushed back her hair. That didn't matter.

She looked pretty, sweet, nice. She looked like someone who made the bad times worthwhile. She'd worked hard today, for very little appreciation from what he'd seen. He'd been ready to agree to anything she asked when his native caution stepped up.

Blind promises were not a smart idea. Especially when Rachel wanted to become less of a good girl. He had no idea what she might be asking for.

Then she'd come up with an idea he'd never considered.

I want you to teach me to drive a motorcycle.

Drive a motorcycle? Why would she want that?

Riding a motorcycle came with a fair amount of risk. He understood that, and was as careful as possible, but he knew all the time that the biggest danger came from other drivers, and that, he had no control over.

Maybe Rachel had been watching *Easy Rider* and thought riding a motorcycle would be cool. Maybe she liked the idea of dressing up in leather. Maybe she really wanted to drive a bike.

He held back the no that had been his first response. He couldn't picture Rachel on a motorcycle.

And that might be the real reason she wanted to do it.

He'd promised to help her, and she'd said she'd help him. She'd done her part, so he owed her. He just didn't know if she understood what she was getting into.

He'd been thinking too long. She looked up at him, disappointment on her face.

He blew a breath.

"Have you ever been on a motorcycle, Rachel?"

She shook her head.

"You might not like it."

"Do you?"

Yes, he did. Liked it enough to ride his bike up here in the cold and snow, so that he'd have it with him. It had been a good reason to join AA—if he lost his license, he couldn't ride. And with the danger inherent in riding a bike, he couldn't afford any distractions. Even in the bad days, he'd never driven his bike if he'd been drinking.

He'd learned his lesson, after wrapping a car around a tree when he was still a kid.

He'd done enough stupid things.

"Why don't I take you for a drive with me first, so you can see if you like it?"

Then he wondered if he'd been an idiot.

Her face lit up. "Would you? I'd love that."

He could see she thought so. Her eyes were sparkling, and she was bouncing on her toes.

Rachel had complained that her life was boring, and if the idea of a bike ride gave her that much anticipatory pleasure, it must be pretty dull.

"Tomorrow?" he asked. It meant postponing working on the house again, but he could live with that. She worked for her uncle, was probably busy during weekdays. He didn't want to take her out at night. No point in adding that kind of risk factor to riding with a passenger.

Her expression of pleasure faded. "There's church tomorrow. I can't miss it."

Yeah, her dad was the pastor or priest or whatever.

"Afternoon?"

That would give him time to track down a helmet for her and maybe a jacket. She needed to wear protective gear, and he doubted she owned a lot of leather.

She nodded, expression happy again.

"I could do that. Maybe, one o'clock?"

"That should work." He'd talk to Benny, see where he might be able to find a helmet. He stared at her head, guessing her size.

"What should I wear? Can I meet you at Benny's?"

He frowned. Did she not want him to pick her up because she didn't want anyone to know she was spending time with him? Would it cause too much talk? Would it upset her dad?

For some reason that bothered him, but it only made sense. It would be easier to outfit her with the gear at Benny's, rather than try to bring it over here on the bike.

"Wear jeans, and boots that cover your ankles. Leather gloves. I'll get a helmet."

Rachel nodded and took a bite of the pineapple-tarnished pizza. She looked a little tired, but her face was still lit up from the idea of riding on his bike.

He could do this for her.

Ryker shrugged, and decided he could manage to eat pineapple on pizza.

He hoped he could manage the rest of this, as well.

BENNY GAVE RYKER a strange look when he asked where he could get another motorcycle helmet.

"Dude, I don't have one. I don't ride."

Ryker had been careful in what he said for the first couple of days, unsure how Benny felt about being in his chair. Ryker was impressed by how well Benny had adapted. He made jokes at his own expense and appeared comfortable receiving them. Ryker had relaxed around him.

Ryker didn't apologize for his question.

"Who around here does?"

Benny gave him a considering look. "I'm not sure if you want to talk to the guys who ride around here."

Ryker nodded. He'd had to change some of his behaviors and the people he spent time with to gain and keep his sobriety. He understood Benny was giving him a heads-up.

"Any secondhand stores? Places like that?"

"There's a pawnshop in Oak Hill."

That was a possibility.

"Thanks, I'll try that."

"Who are you taking out on your bike?"

Ryker shook his head. "You wouldn't believe me if I told you."

HE WAS UP EARLY on Sunday and drove over to Oak Hill. He was lucky enough at the pawnshop to find a helmet. It looked like it should fit Rachel.

He checked that it hadn't been in an accident

or showed any signs of weakness. Half of him hoped one ride would be enough for Rachel, so that after today she wouldn't want anything more to do with the bike.

Half of him wanted her to like it, and he was worried about that half. That half was imagining spending time with Rachel and seeing what else she came up with for her project to change the town's perception of him. That half was going to get him in trouble.

In any case, the helmet needed to protect her. If, God forbid, the bike went down, she had to be as safe as he could keep her.

He didn't need this kind of confusion. There was no good reason for him to stay in Carter's or Cupid's, whatever they wanted to call it. Not once the house was sold.

No need to get more involved with Rachel than necessary. It would be safer for her and him both.

Still, when he saw a bright red-and-white women's jacket at the shop, one that looked to be her size, he added it to his purchases.

The first step in staying safe on a bike was to be seen. Might as well do his best to keep Rachel safe. If he didn't, he could leave town now.

CHAPTER SEVEN

CHURCH RAN FOREVER. At least, it felt like it did. Rachel hadn't been this impatient for the service to be finished since she was a little kid.

It had been a long time since she had something she looked forward to this much.

More fodder for the "I have to get out of here" grist.

She took the direct way out the back door of the church, missing most of the people wanting to chat, and slipped into the parsonage to put lunch together. She ate in the kitchen and left a portion for her father on the table. He had lingered at church, happy to talk to anyone wanting conversation.

She normally hung around, as well, but not today.

She went upstairs and changed quickly. Her dad had come home while she was doing so.

He blinked at the single serving set out in front of him.

"You're going out?"

He preferred to eat with someone. Some

weeks he had lunches set up with friends after church, but not this week.

"Yep. I should be back for dinner. If not, there's leftovers in the fridge."

Rachel rarely left him on his own.

"Leftovers?" he echoed, sounding aggrieved. Rachel ignored it. This afternoon she had something she was looking forward to, and for once, she wasn't going to let her father's expectations limit her.

She left him, a puzzled frown on his face, and got in her car and drove to Benny's repair shop. The place was closed on Sundays, so there weren't any other cars in the lot. She saw Ryker's motorcycle sitting out front, and a pleasant shiver shot down her body.

She'd never been on a motorcycle. It seemed tremendously daring.

Then again, almost anything was daring for her.

She wasn't sure what to do. Stay in the car? Get out and wait here? Go upstairs and knock on the door?

She saw Ryker's boots first, coming down the stairs. Decision made. She got out, hoping she'd dressed well enough.

She was wearing the new jeans again. Her sweater, under her jacket, was a plain navy, but it was warm. She'd put on her hiking boots and carried the leather gloves she normally wore when she dressed up in winter. Her hair was tied back, and she'd chosen a purse that crossed over her body, leaving her hands free.

She didn't know if this was motorcycle-ready, but it was the best she had.

Ryker had a helmet in his hands, but Rachel could see the one he'd been wearing hanging on the bike.

The one he was carrying must be for her.

Then she noticed a bright, red-and-white leather jacket tucked under his arm. He was wearing his own black jacket and had black chaps over his jeans. She sighed.

Ryker wearing leather chaps was almost too much for her.

But the red-and-white jacket looked too small for him.

He crossed toward her, holding out the jacket and helmet.

"Is that for me?" Her voice squeaked. Literally. She felt her cheeks warm.

Ryker nodded. "I didn't have a spare helmet, so I picked one up for you to wear. They had this jacket there—it's nice and bright. You need that so drivers see you."

He passed the helmet and jacket to her. She accepted them with shaking hands. She'd never, ever in her life had anything anywhere near this cool in her hands.

Sad that this was a truth when she was almost thirty years old. And sad that she was this excited about it when she was almost thirty years old.

Rachel set the helmet on the car roof, and pulled off her own jacket, dropping it in the passenger seat of her car. She held the cuffs of her sweater, carefully pulling on the leather jacket.

It fit. It was snug, not loose. She zipped it up and was sure she was grinning ear to ear. She was wearing a motorcycle jacket!

She reached for the helmet, but Ryker put up a hand.

"Wait a sec. We have to talk about some stuff, and you won't hear properly once that's on."

It was actually an effort to set the helmet back down. She wanted it. No, she coveted it. She was ready to break a commandment for it. She wanted to feel cool, daring for once. But Ryker had a serious look on his face.

"Okay." She rubbed her hands on her jeans.

"You've never been on a bike?"

She shook her head.

"Okay. Do you know what we call a passenger on the back of a bike?"

She shook her head. Was it a cool name? She bet it was a cool name. And now she'd know it. She had the inside edge.

"Luggage."

The happy dance in her head stopped. Luggage?

He was watching her closely. Again, the corner of his mouth pulled up. Despite her disappointment at being luggage, she felt a little thrill at that quirk. She was pretty sure Ryker didn't smile much. She wanted to make him smile, upset his composure the way he did hers.

"Luggage," he repeated. "Your only job is to sit there. You do what I do, and nothing else. Don't try to drive or help drive the bike."

She was a little confused. How could she help or not help?

"You'll be hanging on to me." For a moment her brain fried. Hanging on to him? She glanced over at the bike. There weren't any handles, anything for a second person to grip.

She was going to be hanging on to Ryker. That made her belly shimmy. And almost throw up her lunch.

"When I sit upright, you do the same. When I lean over, you follow. Just keep your arms around me and do what I do. When we corner, we're going to lean in. You might want to stay upright, think you're balancing so we don't fall. Don't do that."

She pictured the bike leaning low around a corner. Well, that was definitely something new. That shimmy she was feeling was a different shimmy from the hanging-on-to-Ryker one.

"When we stop, I'll put down my foot. You don't. You stay sitting, same as always. There are footrests for your feet. You keep your feet there until we're getting off the bike."

He put his hands on his hips. With the leather, the chaps, the scruff, since he hadn't shaved—he looked anything but nice. She swallowed.

"Do you understand?"

She nodded. "Luggage. Lean when you lean, straight up when you're straight up, don't put my feet down."

He spent a long minute watching her, as if making sure she truly understood what she'd just parroted back to him. That she wasn't mocking him.

Then he nodded.

"Those boots cover your ankles?"

She pulled up the leg of her jeans, showing that the boots went up over her ankles.

His gaze traced up her legs, over her jacket, checked on the purse, examined her gloves.

She felt that gaze, through the denim and leather.

More shimmies.

He jerked his head toward the bike. "If you're sure you want to do this, then let's go."

Rachel nodded, grabbed the new helmet and followed him over. He stopped at the bike.

"Should I put the helmet on now?" She wasn't sure what the protocol was. Was she supposed to throw it on as they pulled out? No, that didn't match with Ryker's safety talk. Did you only put on a helmet once you were on the bike? Maybe it was bad luck to put it on first.

Ryker nodded, but when she reached for the straps, he took the helmet from her, and she let her hands drop. He raised it over her head and lowered it, moving with slow care. It settled over her head, briefly tugged on her ears, then the inside cushion landed firmly on the top of her head.

Sounds became remote.

He jiggled the helmet. She stood, waiting.

"Fits pretty good. We need the straps tight enough to keep it in place."

She could hear him, but not clearly. His hands brushed her chin as he wove the strap through the buckle, firming it on her head. Noises were muted, echoing slightly in the helmet. He dropped the clear plastic face guard down over her face and stepped back.

Rachel felt like a robot, head encased in plastic.

Ryker pulled on his helmet and gloves. With languid grace, he slid his leg over the seat, and then tugged it forward off the kickstand. He turned back to her and nodded at the seat behind him.

Rachel was awkward, trying to stretch her leg up and over the seat. She had her supporting leg on the ground, the other mostly draped over the seat.

Ryker flipped up his face guard.

"All the way on. Don't worry about the bike. It's my job to keep it upright. You're the luggage."

She wiggled till her butt was centered on the seat. She picked up her feet, shoved them onto the footrests Ryker had flipped down.

She was on a motorcycle. She grinned.

"Slide forward and wrap your arms around me."

There went the shimmy in her belly again.

Rachel did her best, but she wasn't used to this. She never had her body pressed up against a man. She put her arms around his waist gingerly.

He gave her arms a tug and wrapped them

tighter around his torso. The pull brought her closer to him, so that her chest was pressed against his back. Her helmet conked against the back of his.

"Sorry!" The word echoed in her helmet. She wasn't sure he heard her.

He pushed the bike until it was straight upright and then pressed something. The engine roared to life, vibrating the seat between her legs. He checked again that her arms were wrapped tightly, then put both of his hands on the handlebars and they were moving.

Rachel gripped even tighter, her belly clenching for new reasons. The bike pulled onto the road and picked up speed. The air moved past her in a rush, cooling her arms and legs where it whipped by.

They passed the town limits, and the bike picked up more speed. There was nothing between Rachel and the world zooming past her, nothing but the helmet, the jacket and her jeans. She was exposed, vulnerable...and free.

She felt a smile grow, and she laughed out loud.

This? Was fantastic.

RYKER HADN'T DRIVEN with a passenger for a while, so he took extra care. He felt Rachel's grip tighten around his waist as they moved onto the paved road. He maintained the speed limit, watching for other vehicles. As they left the town limits behind, he increased speed, still paying close attention to the woman wrapped snugly around his back.

He waited for her grip to tighten to a stranglehold, for a sign that she was not enjoying the ride and wanted to stop.

It didn't happen.

They came to the first corner, and he leaned in, preparing to counterbalance her body if she fought to stay upright. There was a moment, a short one, of resistance, and then she leaned with him, the bike gripping the corner and moving forward, smoothly, swiftly. After a couple more corners, some acceleration, and Rachel still wrapped around him with every indication she was enjoying herself, he let his worry blow away and gave in to the pleasure of the ride.

Half an hour later he turned into a roadside waypoint empty this early in the year. He came to a halt, dropped his feet to the ground and turned the bike off. He flipped up his visor and told Rachel she could get off.

She released her grip around his waist, then slid sideways, landing on one foot and awkwardly pulling the other one over the seat. Ryker shifted the bike onto its stand and followed her off the bike, pulling off his helmet, waiting to see how she'd felt about the ride.

She tugged the helmet over her head, and her flushed face was glowing.

"That was awesome!"

For a moment he let himself enjoy the expression on her face. Huge grin, sparkling eyes, messy hair and *happiness*. If he had a photo of this moment, that was what he'd call it.

He felt his own expression relax, a smile crossing his face. He didn't smile much these days, but it was impossible to resist the joy emanating from Rachel.

"You weren't afraid?"

Rachel glanced over at the bike. "I was, for a minute. When we first took off, and I realized there was nothing around me. But then it was like flying. Oh, sorry I hit your helmet."

He shook his head. That was nothing.

"So will you teach me to ride the motorcycle? And can I buy this helmet and jacket from you, or should I find my own?"

He took a moment. Taking Rachel for a ride was one thing. Teaching her to ride herself? That was different.

The smile faded from her face. Her jaw tightened. He could see her bracing herself. She expected a refusal.

He wanted to refuse her. Riding a bike could be dangerous. It would attract attention, and Rachel was not ready for some of the attention she'd attract on a bike.

Plus, teaching her would involve a lot of time spent together, and despite her intention to walk a little closer to the wild side, that might be more than she was ready to handle. And what about him, and the way spending time with Rachel made him dream of things he couldn't have? Those were all good reasons. But watching that light die from her face— that was something he didn't feel right about.

"You have to do exactly what I tell you."

The words escaped his mouth before he realized they were coming out.

Her eyes widened.

"Safety is a big issue. If I tell you to stop, or slow down, or that you're not ready for something, you do exactly what I say. For now, you can keep using the helmet and jacket as long as you need to. Take them with you if you want."

As if they were anything but a gift.

She was nodding before he'd even finished his sentence.

"Anything you say, I promise." The excitement was back on her face.

He drew in a breath. He'd committed himself now. He considered how this would work.

"We need to start somewhere off-road. A parking lot would be good. Maybe the church lot?"

That would get people talking, for sure. Was that what she wanted?

Rachel chewed on her lip and looked down.

"Um, maybe not the church."

He considered that. He hadn't been in the lot. Maybe it was full of potholes?

Or maybe she wanted to hide this. Why did that thought bother him? It was the smart call.

"The lot at Gifford's is too small. We need space."

She needed to get used to the bike, how to turn and start and stop somewhere off-road.

She fidgeted with the straps on the helmet.

"I don't think I want anyone to see us."

Disappointment stabbed at him. She didn't want to be seen with him. Maybe at the church bazaar, with other people around, but not just the two of them. He was still a Slade.

"Maybe this isn't a good idea." He made sure his voice was level.

Her eyes flew up.

"No, I want—I need to do this. But…" Her voice trailed away.

"But what, Rachel?" She might be trying to be kind, not wanting to say the words out loud, but he needed to hear them. He needed the truth. He needed a reality check.

She drew a breath. "This is going to sound... weak. I know, I am weak. That's why I get talked into doing all this stuff for other people. I don't say no, that I don't want to do something. People think I'm nice, but I'm just weak.

"I need to change that. And this, riding the bike? It makes me feel strong, and free."

She finally met his eyes. She had such hope on her face.

"I don't want the town knowing about this, talking about it, telling me all the reasons I shouldn't do this. I should just tell them all to take a hike, but—"

She looked away again.

Ryker could picture it, all too easily. All those old ladies, and the old geezers from the bazaar yesterday, sharing hair-raising stories of some horrendous accident that had happened to a friend of a friend...

"Everyone means well. And I don't want to hurt them. But it's time I do some things just for me.

"When I move away, no one is going to think, 'Oh no, Rachel can't do that. That's not like her.'"

Ryker had grown up with the burden of the Slade reputation, and it followed him still, here in Carter's Crossing. He didn't realize that Rachel had her own burden.

He'd been expected to do stupid, reckless, selfish things. He hadn't been trusted, and he hadn't been relied on, either.

Rachel might say she was weak, not nice, but that wasn't accurate. She was nice. Kind, considerate, grateful. Her weakness was not wanting to hurt people.

If only more people had that weakness.

Giving her a small chance to be selfish, to do something of no value beyond making her happy? He could do that. And he would. But they had to find a place that worked.

"Nelson Carter's farm? It has a long driveway."

She considered; brows creased.

"I'd have to tell him about it. And Mariah. And the noise might disturb the horses."

He didn't know horses, but that sounded like a possibility.

"My place?"

He mentally smacked himself. Why had he offered that? The house was the place he was avoiding.

"I thought you said Gifford's lot was too small."

"No, where I grew up."

Rachel stared at him. It was difficult to meet her gaze.

"Are you ready for that?"

She was perceptive.

He turned, looking over the view that this waypoint served to highlight. There was beauty in these hills, even during this early spring season before the deciduous trees had returned to life. He'd grown up with this, hadn't realized he'd missed it.

He imagined going back to the house with Rachel. Taking the bike, teaching her to balance and ride up and down the drive. They had a loop, back behind the house, back to the old shed.

For this? The lessons? It would work well.

They didn't need to go inside. They could drive up; he could give her lessons on handling the bike and then leave. He could deal with the memories and mess from the outside. It might be an easier transition, to go there with Rachel, before he approached the inside again.

It would be easier to teach her in a parking lot, but the old place would do. It would do for both of them.

He turned back to Rachel, who had stepped away and was now gazing at the ravine falling below them. Giving him time, giving him space, giving him *nice*.

Nice might be confining Rachel, smothering her, but *nice* was certainly something he valued. There hadn't been enough *nice* in his life.

"When do you want to do this? It has to be daytime. I'm not going to try to teach you to handle the bike when it's dark. Otherwise, I can be flexible about hours."

Rachel didn't ask him again if he was prepared to do this at the house.

"We close up the office Wednesday afternoons. And I can make sure I'm free on Saturdays. Sundays, well…"

They could work with that.

"There's gonna be homework. I'm going to give you a book to read, about motorcycles, safety, the issues with other drivers, and you need to read that first. Then let me know when you're free, and if the weather permits, we'll get started."

The smile was back on her face, and he had put it there. There was an answering smile inside him, but he kept his expression neutral.

She needed to take this seriously.

"That is awesome, Ryker! Thank you so much. I'll read every word, promise."

With Rachel, you knew that promise would be kept. He wasn't used to that, either.

He nodded at the bike. "Do you want to go back now, or ride some more?"

He needn't have asked, not after seeing how her face had lit up. He knew what her answer would be. They were riding.

He got back on his bike, and Rachel climbed on behind him. She wrapped herself around him, and he felt an inner warmth that he hadn't felt in a long time. So long, he couldn't remember.

He had a feeling he was heading into a different kind of danger, but he didn't back down.

CHAPTER EIGHT

RACHEL WASN'T THE first one to the diner this Tuesday night.

Ryker had found her the book online, and it arrived that morning. It was about motorcycle riding, and she'd been reading it every chance she had. She'd been distracted enough that she'd almost missed the meeting.

The book went into a lot of detail about the dangers of riding a motorcycle. Rachel wondered if Ryker had hoped to scare her off. Not a chance. She'd enjoyed the ride too much.

Still, she was reading it carefully, ready if he wanted to test her on it. She didn't want to be reckless, at least not more reckless than getting on a motorcycle in the first place.

That, she was eager to do.

Jaycee and Mariah were already there. This time she'd arrived to find her drink waiting on the table, while the others were already focused on the plans for Jaycee's wedding.

She slipped into the side of the booth. The other two were poring over a calendar.

"What's up?"

The two jerked upright.

"Rachel! Hey. What kept you?"

Without waiting for a response, Mariah answered Rachel's question.

"Abigail has suggested a July Fourth wedding date. She thinks we can make it a whole town event, with lots of video and photos, something that will look great on the website. Maybe you can do a Cupid to go with it? With fireworks?

"And since the monster-in-laws are heading south the middle of July, it's a way to force them to attend."

Jaycee winced. Rachel covered her hand.

"Are you okay with that, Jaycee?"

Jaycee sighed. "My first choice would be spending a year picking out every detail and making everyone sick of hearing me talk about my wedding. You know, like I dreamed. But that would include having Dave's parents on board, and that's not going to happen.

"Dave is really upset with his parents, and I don't want to make a permanent rift. So yeah, let's go big. Let's make this wedding such a huge success that it will be the one everyone compares others to for years to come."

"Exactly," Rachel encouraged. "Around here people will use it as a landmark. 'Where were you when Jaycee and Dave got married?' Or, 'I remember that happened the same year as *the* wedding. You know, that amazing wedding when Jaycee finally married Dave.'"

Jaycee's expression lit up. "Exactly, Rachel. And Dave talked to his sister, and they're coming up for it. So there, Monster-in-Law!"

Mariah nodded, but she was in planning mode.

"We have to go with red, white and blue, then, for colors. Adding in anything else would get too busy. Can you live with that, Jaycee? Pink or green will clash with the town decorations that Abigail says will be up everywhere. I want this to be a wedding that will involve the whole town. The bunting we'll put up everywhere will be part of it. The fireworks display will send you two off on your honeymoon."

Jaycee frowned. She nodded, slowly.

Mariah pulled out her tablet and started a presentation of the ideas she'd come up with.

"We're going to cross our fingers for a clear day. The Farmers' Almanac says it will be, and apparently, that's considered golden here.

"I want to use the park. We'll do something different than the usual bunting around the gazebo."

That was where Mariah and Nelson got engaged on Valentine's Day.

"Red and white flowers. There are few blue flowers that look good, so I thought we could use blue in the bridesmaids' dresses and the guys' ties. Here are the colors I'm thinking of."

Jaycee and Rachel almost bumped heads.

"How many bridesmaids are you thinking?"

Jaycee held up a hand. "You two, of course. Dave's sister. She's going to be big as a house, she said, but I still want her there. She's super supportive of us, so it's important that she's part of it."

Mariah made a note. "We'll get to the details of the dresses soon. What about the guys?"

"Nelson, and Micah and Jonas from Oak Hill. He considered his brother-in-law, but then I'd have to find someone else, as well. Jonas has a girlfriend, but I don't know her that well, and I don't know if they'll still be together then."

Mariah stared toward the counter, apparently focused on the breakfast menu posted above. That menu hadn't changed in ten years, so Rachel knew her friend was lost in her planning somewhere, rather than considering ordering pancakes. They waited for her to come back to them.

"I think the three attendants on each side is the right size for the gazebo. Let me see if I can come up with some way to include the brother-in-law. Is there anything I need to keep him away from?"

Conversation continued as Mariah ran over the details for a July Fourth wedding.

Rachel's attention drifted. She'd made up her own ideal wedding plans when she was a kid, and had updated them, through college.

Then, when she began to worry that she'd never have a real wedding, she'd stopped, afraid to jinx herself. Her priorities had changed. She didn't worry about colors and themes. She asked only that she find a good man. Someone who loved her. Then she didn't care whether the wedding was big or small, fancy or plain.

Apparently, she was too desperate now to be fussy.

"Rachel!"

She brought herself back to the here and now. "Sorry, thoughts were wandering."

"Did Ryker Slade really help you at the bazaar this weekend?" Jaycee asked.

Rachel willed her cheeks not to turn red. "Yes. I asked if he'd help out with some of the heavy stuff."

Jaycee's eyes widened. "Really? Ryker Slade? Why did you ask him? Why not Nelson or Dave?"

Because they were always busy when she asked them?

Mariah spoke up. "Ryker's working on the website, and Rachel is helping him. So that's my fault. It's not a problem, is it?"

Jaycee was frowning. "How did you even know Ryker would do something like that? Are you sure you want him involved?"

Rachel frowned. If Ryker was good enough to design a website for the town, why couldn't he help out at the bazaar? It wasn't like he was going to steal doilies from the craft table or poison the plants.

Mariah shook her head. "Wow, I didn't understand just how much this town hated the Slades."

Jaycee looked abashed.

"Sorry. It was a long time ago. I don't know what Ryker is like now. But his brothers are in jail, and his dad…well, I know everyone is relieved he's in a home now and not causing more trouble."

Rachel held herself back from attacking Jaycee. "Ryker helped set up for the bazaar and came back to pack up, as well. He's here to take care of his dad's place and sell it, since no one else is willing to do it. So maybe we can cut him some slack and not expect him to steal the Sunday School offering."

Okay, not quite as controlled as she'd hoped.

Jaycee held up her hand. "Okay, okay, I retract what I said. But you have to admit the Slades were always trouble. Even Ryker, back in high school."

"Tell me again about the story with the Slades," Mariah requested. "Slade senior was a piece of work What did the kids do?"

Jaycee pointedly looked at Rachel.

Rachel shook her head. "Mrs. Slade died when the kids were really young. Mr. Slade is an alcoholic. He lost his job at the mill because he was drunk and he wrecked a machine, but Mr. Slade always blamed the mill. The kids regularly didn't show up at school, and they sometimes had bruises. Like Jaycee said, the two oldest, the twins, are in prison. Grand theft auto. They suspected Ethan was part of it, but he vanished." She swallowed, feeling guilty, but this was the story everyone in town knew. "Ryker crashed a stolen car into a tree while he was drunk and joined the air force so that he wouldn't be prosecuted. The girls left, one after the other. I'm not sure what happened to them."

She wondered if Ryker knew, if he kept in touch with his siblings.

"When you tell it like that, well…" Jaycee trailed off. "I guess the Slade kids had a tough time. If Ryker has cleaned up his act, then that's great. I hope things work out for him, especially since he did serve."

Mariah was focused on her job. "Rachel, if there's any reason I should worry let me know, but otherwise I'm going to assume that Ryker has made a success of himself. You're doing okay with him, right?"

Rachel nodded, and let the conversation proceed. She continued to think about Ryker, as she did much too often.

People had heard that he helped at the bazaar, and the people working there had been impressed by him. But there was still a lot of bad history to overcome before people would see the man Ryker was today.

It wasn't really her problem. She was leaving. Ryker might stay or he might not.

But he'd helped her at the church, and he was teaching her to ride a motorcycle. She wanted to do something of equal value for him. She just had to figure out what she could do.

She wasn't giving up, though. He deserved better.

RYKER CAME INTO the shop, ready to pick up a couple more computers that Benny had let him know needed work. Benny was on the phone, so Ryker headed to the table where Benny left the computers for him.

There was a note. Moonstone's reservation system wasn't working properly, and they would like him to stop by to check it out.

Ryker paused.

Moonstone's was what passed for fine dining in Cart—Cupid's Crossing. Not a place he would be welcomed.

This kind of work wasn't his specialty, but he'd done it before. He'd never expected to be asked by Moonstone's to access their computer system. Fourteen years ago he'd been banned from the place. He and some of his "friends" had thought it would be hilarious to put a dead opossum they'd found in Moonstone's kitchen one night.

Maybe Rachel knew more about what she was doing than he'd given her credit for. He'd happily move tables every weekend if it meant people would give him a chance.

He paused. Did he really want that?

He could bail on the town as soon as he sold the house. He didn't have to worry about his reputation in this town after. Anywhere else, he could start with a fresh slate.

But maybe he did want that. Maybe he did want the people in this town to know he'd changed. That he'd overcome a crappy start and made something worthwhile of himself.

Maybe Rachel was right. He shouldn't be willing to let people think of him as one of those Slade kids. He was a better man now. Maybe he deserved the same things everyone else had.

He called the number Benny had posted on the bottom of the note.

"Moonstone's. Jaycee speaking. How may I help you?"

"Jaycee, it's Ryker. Ryker Slade."

A short hesitation, very short, but he'd been listening for it.

"Benny told you we have a problem?"

Two problems, actually. The computer, and the fact that Ryker was the only IT in town.

"He left a note and your number."

Jaycee sighed. "I'll be honest, Ryker. The guy who left here fourteen years ago? I wouldn't let him anywhere near our systems. But Rachel vouches for you, and Benny swears you're a genius with computers, and there's no one else who can get here right away."

Thanks to Rachel and Benny, he'd gone from "out of the question" to "possible" if there was no one else available.

It was a start.

"I understand, Jaycee. I wouldn't trust that kid, either."

A reluctant laugh.

"Rachel would say I was being mean, but I thought it best to be honest. Despite what I said, would you help us?"

"It depends on what the problem is, but I can look. I might be able to fix it, might not."

She sighed.

"*Might* is better than anything else I've got."

"I don't have anything time-sensitive, so I can come over now if that helps."

Her tone softened. "That would be wonderful." She drew a breath. "But if you mess us up, I'll—well, I won't be nice. At all."

"I can't promise to fix things, but I won't make them worse. If I do, feel free to do your worst."

He was about to hang up when she spoke again.

"Rachel is putting her own reputation on the line for you, Ryker. You mess her up, and you'll really feel my wrath."

She hung up then, while he stared at the phone.

Crap. He hadn't asked Rachel to do that.

He needed to tell Benny he was leaving, but Benny was staring at his cell phone with a glare that wanted to burn holes through it.

"You okay?"

"Define *okay*," Benny countered.

"Safe to be left alone. Do you need help? And if so, is it something I can do?"

Benny looked at him, and then back at the phone. "Maybe you can."

"Why do I feel that I'm going to regret offering?"

Benny managed a smile. "My dad wants me to talk to the high school. They're doing an assembly and want me to talk about being a cripple. Sorry, physically challenged."

Ryker would rather ride through town on his bike naked.

"Sorry, Ben. Can't do that for you."

Benny got a glint in his eye.

"But you could talk about being in the air force. That's gotta be more interesting than talking about a wheelchair."

Ryker shook his head.

"I signed up so that I didn't go to prison for drunk driving and grand theft auto. That's not the story they want those kids to hear. You're on your own for that one."

Benny grimaced. "I can't do it. Not the way they want."

Ryker heard a dark tone in Benny's voice, one Benny normally didn't indulge. He cocked his head.

"What's the way they want?"

"They want the Benny who doesn't whine. The one who doesn't make them feel bad about being disabled. I can do that here, and I can be happy with the life I have. Really. But to go back, to that time when I first figured out I was spending the rest of my life in a chair? That's not a pretty story."

"Your call, Ben. But that's the story I'd like to hear."

Benny shot him a look.

Ryker shrugged. "I'm in AA, man. Those are my kind of stories."

RYKER PUSHED HIMSELF away from the desk in the back office of Moonstone's. Jaycee was hovering over his shoulder, but to be fair, her anxiety appeared focused on the computer and not on him.

"Try that."

He stood up, and Jaycee dropped into the chair, fingers moving on the keyboard. The tension lifted from her shoulders in a rush, leaving her relaxed against the back of the chair.

"That's wonderful, Ryker. Thank you so much."

He had his phone out. "Check to see if my

reservation showed up. I placed one from the phone app."

Jaycee hit some keys, and they both saw his name show up on the screen.

"Ryker, I could kiss you right now, but Dave would be a little upset with me."

Ryker held back a grin.

"Dave used to play hockey, as I recall. Probably better not to make him mad."

Jaycee turned and raised her eyebrows. "You were in the air force, Ryker. I doubt you have to worry about my Dave. They probably taught you about a million ways to hurt people."

Ryker no longer felt like grinning. She was right. He'd learned a lot about hurting people, and he didn't want to be like that anymore.

Jaycee sat back, eyes wide. "Oh, sorry. That was a rotten thing to say. Um, can we just go back to you being wonderful again?"

Ryker nodded, then shrugged into his jacket.

"I'm sorry, Ryker. Really. I have foot-in-mouth disease, and I've not found a treatment yet."

"It's okay, Jaycee. I need to get back now."

"Right. Of course. You know, if you want to keep that reservation…"

"I appreciate the offer, but no. Let me know if that problem pops up again."

It was a nice offer. But he didn't need to

come and eat here alone. It would only emphasize the other problem he'd experienced.

My Dave. Twice Ryker had been *my Ryker*, but it hadn't lasted. This was the kind of nice thing he didn't have, because he couldn't care for it.

It would be nice to have someone to dine out with. But romance didn't take with Ryker.

Ironic, when he was working on a website for a town named Cupid's Crossing. But to work on the website, all he had to do was have some skills with software. Romantic connections were not required, fortunately. As Diane and Erica could attest. Because he had two divorce decrees to show that Cupid didn't work with him.

RACHEL FROWNED AT her uncle.

"The Exeters want that divorce settlement soon."

Her uncle waved away her concerns. "I'll get to it. Just want to take the afternoon off."

She knew what that meant. A liquid lunch. She took a long breath.

Her uncle was the reason she wanted to sit in on those Al-Anon meetings. His drinking was getting out of hand. No, his drinking already was out of hand.

She'd talked to her father, but he thought

she was overreacting. In theory, her dad knew drunks could be high functioning, but he couldn't see it in his brother.

If Rachel went to one of those meetings, too many people would suspect her father of being the alcoholic she was concerned about. Because anonymous didn't work in a town this small when everyone knew her. She didn't want to just attend; she wanted to ask questions.

She didn't want to enable her uncle because he needed to hit rock bottom. That was what her research said. But if she didn't cover up for her uncle, if she didn't make sure the essentials of this office kept going, a lot of people would be hurt.

People like the Exeters, who needed the divorce filed and the chance to get on with their lives. They had kids who were suffering through the divorce, and moving out of limbo would help them. If Rachel didn't do most of the paperwork and push her uncle, who knew when it would finally be completed?

And the Romeros, who were buying their first house. The Olsens, who wanted their will finished before they left on a world cruise.

She knew these people and cared about them. If she let her uncle's business fall apart, they'd all be hurt.

What about when you leave? The voice in her head. The voice that said yes to all the things people asked her to do. The voice that was so nice.

The voice that was going to lead her to become the town's cat lady.

She'd listened to that voice for years. But there was a second voice, now getting louder.

She wasn't the town lawyer. She didn't get paid the money her uncle did. Why did she have to do most of his work?

The Romeros wanted a house for their growing family. When did she get to find a partner and start her own family?

Why didn't other people worry about things like the church bazaar and setting up for AA meetings and all those other things she did? If they were so important, why didn't other people step up?

But what if no one does step up?

While she'd been listening to the dueling voices in her head, her uncle had slipped away. Rachel sighed.

Tough love wasn't happening today. But she looked through her to-do list, and decided she wasn't going to work on the business license requests that came in. She was going to wait for her uncle to take care of those.

Those people would pressure him and hopefully make him take fewer afternoons off. On his own, he left the personal legal matters to fall by the wayside. Rachel was the one who kept those from getting delayed indefinitely.

She shook her head. She'd made her decision. She was leaving. She'd have to find someone to take her place, someone able to handle this.

She'd do her best to get everything under control before she left. She'd talk to her dad, again, so that he'd be prepared when her uncle came apart.

People were going to have to figure out how to manage without Rachel taking care of them.

After all, she could be hit by a bus any day. Or fall and break most of her limbs. She couldn't take care of everyone and everything all the time.

It was time she took care of Rachel.

CHAPTER NINE

RYKER STOPPED THE bike just off the highway on the driveway that led to his house. His former home.

The bike was balanced between his thighs, his feet keeping it upright. His hands were still on the handlebars, the engine thrumming.

He was ready to escape.

He sighed and stretched his neck. It was ridiculous. He didn't need to escape this place; he already had, fourteen years ago.

There was nothing, nothing physical to fear here. His father was in a home, lost mentally in places no one could follow. Not that Ryker had tried. He hadn't been to see his father. Hadn't seen the man in fourteen years. When he'd left, he'd never intended to return.

He drew in a long breath. Someone had to deal with this place, and Gabe and Rafe couldn't. Ethan wouldn't. Some sense of responsibility had made him agree, instead of leaving it to Ana or Kate. Or Jess, if they'd been able to find her.

He'd left them fourteen years ago. He expected they were angry about that. He would be if the case was reversed. He needed to be the one to step up now.

The things that remained here, the things that made him want to flee, were all memories. Hauntings from the past. The kind of stuff you couldn't hurt with your fists or escape on a fast motorcycle.

The things he'd always escaped with alcohol.

He heard a car slowing down on the highway. A quick glance showed him Rachel's car, and with relief, he kicked the bike in gear and drove up to the house.

He wouldn't give in in front of Rachel.

Rachel pulled off to the side of the house, where cars in the past had created a parking strip not far from the porch. Her door swung open, and he saw she was wearing the jacket. She had the helmet in her hand, and jeans, boots and gloves on. Everything he'd told her to wear. Not as sweet as she usually looked, but appealing all the same.

There was a sparkle in her gaze, and he knew she was excited about this. But her forehead was creased, and her voice concerned as she asked how he was.

He shrugged and dismounted, kicking the bike onto its stand.

"We don't have to do this here."

Part of him wanted to snarl at the niceness, the consideration in her voice. She knew, no, she guessed, how difficult this was. He wasn't used to kindness and consideration, and it corroded his defenses, the behaviors that kept him strong.

Another part of him wanted to soften, to let someone else in. Someone to feel his pain, comfort him, numb the edges the way alcohol had. He knew Rachel would do it. Those kind eyes, the soft voice—she'd take anything he wanted to share with her and try to make it better.

He straightened. He wasn't going to take advantage of her niceness, not like everyone else in this town did. She was helping him already, and he wasn't going to abuse her generosity.

If he softened, he wasn't sure what would happen. He hadn't been able to be soft for a long time.

He shook his head.

"Let's make some better memories here." He paused, suddenly aware of how much of a come-on that could sound like.

But not to Rachel. Rachel, who had an innocence to her, one he didn't plan to mar.

She laughed. "Will memories of me falling down make it better?"

"You're not going to fall down." He smiled, still, at the image of her wobbling down the driveway like a five-year-old making a first attempt without training wheels.

A fall with his bike would be more serious, but there was no reason she should fall. They'd be going slow. She could balance a bicycle, so she could do this. And he'd stay close. Not only to protect his bike.

"Can you promise that?" She sparkled, happy to be doing something she wanted. She'd accepted his refusal to revisit the past and had focused on her lesson.

He appreciated that she was giving him space.

"I'm not letting my bike get damaged."

Her eyes shot open. "Oh no. I don't want to do that. I didn't think—"

He touched her arm, slid his glove down her leather sleeve to where her hand gripped the helmet.

"That was a joke, Rachel." Either a bad one, or he wasn't good at joking. "The bike isn't that fragile, and the ground here is soft. But most important, you're not going to fall."

Rachel stared at him, eyes searching his.

"Don't count on it," she muttered, almost to herself.

Rachel thought she knew what learning to ride a motorcycle would be like. She'd sit on the bike, turn a key, then push off like she did on a bicycle.

She was wrong.

"Have you driven a car with a choke? Or a stick shift?" Ryker asked.

She shook her head.

His motorcycle wasn't an automatic. And it had a choke. Rachel had to listen to Ryker explain what the choke did, and when she should use it. Then she had to learn about a clutch and shifting gears.

This was going to be a lot different from driving her car. A lot more complicated.

He crouched beside the bike, showing her where the choke, the clutch and the gear shifter were. He made her repeat everything back to him. It took a few tries. Her brain didn't really run in mechanical circles. And Ryker in his black leather was a little…distracting. He was close enough that she could see he'd shaved recently, and the freshly cut hair looked soft and touchable.

And she was going to fail at this if she didn't concentrate. She blinked and paid attention to the choke again.

She finally got to sit on the bike. It was bigger and taller than it felt when Ryker was in front of her, taking all the responsibility.

"We'll go slow, and I'll be with you. You remember where the brakes are? Just start it, in Neutral, let it roll down the hill, then brake."

Rachel drew in a breath. She firmed her jaw, took a grip on the handlebars and then started the bike. She released the brake, lifted her feet and rolled.

She was a little wobbly. She hadn't been on a bicycle for a while. But she kept the motorcycle upright, and even that slow lumber was fun, enough that Ryker had to remind her about braking.

He was right there, beside her. He wasn't going to let her fall.

She braked and let her feet hit the ground, keeping her upright.

She'd kept her visor up, since she wasn't generating enough speed to need to protect her face. She heard Ryker, panting slightly from keeping up with her, tell her to turn the bike around.

It wasn't pretty, but she managed to roll/tilt/shuffle the bike till it was facing back the way it came from.

"We'll try first gear now. You're going to hit the clutch, use your foot to get it in first, let out the gas, then slowly release the clutch.

As soon as you're back where we started from, pull the clutch and the brakes together and put your feet back down."

Rachel stared at the machine. She mentally replayed the steps she'd have to do to make this happen. Then she nodded.

This was it. This was going to be actually driving the bike.

First gear. Clutch and gas. And then, the bike lurched forward.

She gripped the brakes hard, and it stalled.

Her feet were on the ground, and Ryker was behind her, holding the seat, making sure she was upright.

"I'm sorry!" She felt the heat rising in her cheeks. "I forgot the clutch. Did I hurt it?"

Ryker moved beside her. He touched her arm, gently squeezed it.

"It's okay, Rachel. No harm, no foul."

"Are you sure?"

"You're not the first person to do that. I promise. You'll probably do it again. Are you okay? Do you want to keep going, or do you want to break for today?"

Rachel moved her gaze from the hand on her arm, to the bike and back to Ryker's face.

"Do you mind if we keep going?"

He shook his head, lips tilted upward. "Not

at all. How about you turn, glide back down and try coming up in first again?"

Rachel nodded, and worked the awkward turn. Then glided down the hill again to work another turn.

At least the glide was a little smoother this time.

Ryker was beside her, every time. She figured he was getting a full cardio workout with this.

He didn't remind her of all she needed to do. He waited, let her think it through and then followed her up the hill as she found first gear, accelerated, and at the top, managed to hit the clutch with the brakes, bringing the bike to a halt, engine still rumbling.

She knew she was grinning ear to ear.

"I did it."

He nodded.

"I want to do it again. Make sure I can. But maybe…" Her voice trailed off as she realized she was asking him to run up and down the hill with her.

"Do you want to try without training wheels?"

"You're the training wheels, right?"

He nodded.

"I'm going to need to do it eventually, unless you plan to run down the road behind me all the time?"

She loved the way his mouth hitched up.

"Not gonna do that."

"Okay, so I'll do it on my own. Can I put it in gear to go down?"

"If you feel ready to do that, give it a try."

SHE DID IT five more times, up and down, never out of first gear, but becoming comfortable with the steps, starting to follow them without looking like she was listing them in her head each time.

"That's probably a good start."

Rachel bit her lip, a guilty look on her face.

"This must be so boring for you."

"It's fine." He was sincere. He hadn't had as uneventful and easy a time on this property that he could remember.

It was nice to have a good memory of the place.

Rachel got off the bike with visible reluctance. It was obvious she'd enjoyed riding the bike, even just up and down the driveway.

There wasn't too much more he could teach her before she got her permit and could ride on the road.

He jerked his chin at the bike. "Want to go for a ride?"

He knew she didn't want to give up riding yet.

She tried to play it cool, but he could see how her eyes lit up.

"Well, if it's not a bother."

"Maybe we could stop somewhere, discuss what you have to do to get a permit before you can ride on the road."

She grinned and headed to the bike. "I'm ready if you are."

He got on and waited while she climbed on behind him. She was getting better at it, more comfortable with the bike and knowing how to balance on it. She wrapped her arms around his waist and clung tightly to him.

He enjoyed that more than he should have.

He drove for half an hour before he felt her shivering behind him. Not that she'd complained. She tucked herself in behind him, plastered herself against his back and hung on, gripping him like a shadow.

He saw a service station ahead with a small restaurant attached. He slowed, signaled, checked and rechecked before turning in to the parking lot.

She slid off the bike and pulled off her helmet. Her lips were turning blue, but she questioned why he'd stopped.

"You're freezing. And we were going to talk about getting your permit."

"Okay, but I pay." Her chin jutted out.

She was clearly ready for battle, but he wasn't going to fight over a cup of coffee. This wasn't a fancy place, and the cost would be low.

"If that's what you want."

She nodded again and headed to the door.

"Have you been here before?"

Rachel shook her head. "No, have you?"

"Nope. I'm not sure exactly where we are, but if we head south, we should find our way back."

She was unfazed by not knowing her location.

There were only a few customers scattered around the small restaurant, but they all looked suspiciously at Rachel and Ryker with their helmets and leather jackets. Ryker led the way to a table at the back.

He was aware of the gazes burning into their backs. He was used to it, but Rachel was not.

As they slid into opposite sides of the booth, she leaned forward.

"They think I'm a biker." She looked thrilled by the idea.

He held back a grin. "Probably wouldn't call you nice at all."

She was glowing. It was fun when strangers looked at you with respect and fear for an hour or a day, but not when everyone did, all the time, even those who knew you. When you were the first person they thought of when trouble happened. Ryker would never wish that for Rachel.

"This has been so incredible. I know you must have been bored but thank you."

The waitress stepped up, a mature woman with suspicious eyes.

"Just coffee for me. Rachel?"

She looked at the board over the counter. "Can I have hot chocolate? With whipped cream?"

The woman waited, as if sure this was a joke, then nodded and turned away.

Rachel, unaware of exposing her nice card, asked about the motorcycle permit.

Ryker had looked this up for her since he'd gotten his license elsewhere.

"You have to take a test at the DMV office, and it costs $10. They have a booklet you can study for the test, the New York State Motorcycle Operators' Manual. If you take your license with you, you shouldn't need other ID. I found a couple of places where you can take practice tests online."

Rachel pulled out her phone and made a couple of notes. Ryker suspected she'd be taking practice tests before the day was over.

"Then you can go driving on the road."

She looked up again, still beaming with happiness. He couldn't remember the last time he'd made someone feel like this.

Not that it was anything someone else couldn't have done. He was just teaching her to ride. There were programs for that everywhere.

Rachel didn't appear to understand that.

"I'll let you know as soon as I get my permit. If you're really okay with it."

He was. This had been more fun than he'd had in a long time. He didn't normally like passengers on the bike, but with Rachel, she wasn't just there because she was going somewhere, and he was her ride. She enjoyed it, and he enjoyed having her tucked up behind him, little squeals of excitement occasionally sneaking into his helmet.

Their coffee and hot chocolate arrived. Rachel blew on the whipped cream before testing it. It must have been hot since she set the cup back in its saucer.

She turned a suddenly serious gaze on him.

"Can I ask you something?" She shook her head. "It's not really a question. I want to tell you something and ask your advice. I think you're the only one I can talk to about this."

Ryker nodded but sat back, concerned about

what Rachel would need to discuss with him that she couldn't with her friends in Carter's.

She pushed at the handle of her cup before shooting a look around the restaurant, as if expecting eavesdroppers, and then returning her eyes to him.

"My uncle is an alcoholic."

And he understood why she wanted to talk to him.

Having broken the ice, she started to fidget with her napkin.

"I know I'm enabling him, but I don't know what else to do."

Ryker didn't know the right thing to do. He was still pretty new in the sobriety business, still needing so much help himself. But he could at least listen, and offer assistance, if he could, for Rachel's sake. Rachel, who had to be so circumspect. He reached out and laid his hand over her restless one.

"Why don't you tell me about it?"

She puffed out a breath.

"I don't know what else to say. My uncle is an alcoholic. I don't know how long it's been, not really, but the past couple of years…well, it's getting bad.

"He's making mistakes at work. I usually catch them, and I point them out. He would just tell me to fix them, so I do that now, without telling him, for anything I can handle.

"He goes home for lunch, and when he does, he doesn't always come back to the office. Things were stacking up, so I started doing some of the work. I make sure he checks it over and signs off on it, but it's not really stuff I should be doing."

She began to clench her hand, so he wrapped it in his.

"I've done a lot of reading and I understand about rock bottom and how alcoholics have to hit that. It sounds awful. But if I don't stand in and fix things, it's going to hurt his clients.

"People buying houses and making wills and trying to get their divorces finalized. I've started to let some of the business stuff go, to let it wait for him because I figure those clients know enough to push him on it, but even some of that, well, people could end up in trouble.

"That's why I want to go to Al-Anon and ask questions, but people know me. Some might think it's my dad having problems, and that's not fair. Everyone trusts him, and I can't damage that trust when it's not easily earned, and I can't really stand up and say it's my uncle."

Ryker had no answers for her.

"Have you talked to your dad about this?" He didn't know anything about churches, other than the smell of their basements and the quality of their coffee after attending AA meetings there, but surely this was what priests or pastors dealt with a lot?

Rachel nodded. "He thinks I'm exaggerating. Since we never drink in our house, he just assumes I'm overreacting to Uncle Stanley's drinking at all. But I'm not. I may not know a lot, but I know when he's not doing his job properly. And I know he drinks at the office."

She sighed. "I don't know what to do. And what's going to happen when I go."

Ryker didn't blame her for wanting to leave Carter's Crossing. Both her father and uncle would quickly learn how much they'd undervalued her.

She'd made the decision to leave. Being the considerate person she was, she didn't only take into account her own feelings and concerns. She was worried about what would happen to those still in Cupid's Crossing when she was gone.

And it appeared there were things to worry about.

"I don't have an answer for you." He couldn't tell her what would happen with her uncle. There were as many ways to be a drunk and hit bottom as there were drunks.

"I just wondered if it was possible for something to happen, to make my uncle and dad see there's a problem without the law practice blowing up. I wondered if, maybe you knew, I guess, how hard someone had to hit to know they needed help."

Ryker sat back. The easy, and probably most honest, answer would be to say no, he didn't have that answer. He didn't know her uncle, didn't know what it would take for him to reach out for help.

For some people, there was no answer.

But he wanted to help Rachel. Wanted to take some of her burden, so that she could leave and enjoy her new life without worrying about what was going on back here.

"I can't tell you what it's going to take for your uncle to acknowledge and deal with his problem, but I can tell you what it was like for me."

Rachel's eyes widened, and her lips fell open.

"It was after I'd been discharged. I still had a lot of issues from growing up, thanks to my dad, and now I also had things I'd seen while serving—I wasn't in a good place. I dealt with it by drinking.

"It was my second marriage."

He felt Rachel's hand jerk, and her gaze was on the table. He wondered if it was part of her upbringing. Maybe her dad's church didn't believe in divorce and remarriage.

"Diane and I both drank. We got married in Vegas, drunk during the service. My first marriage was not long after I enlisted. Erica and I were both lonely and scared and tried being lonely and scared together. It didn't work.

"This time with Diane, we were lonely and drunk. It didn't work any better, but when you weren't sober, you didn't realize that. We fought. A lot. Loudly and…it wasn't good.

"But one night I was angry, and I punched the wall, just inches from her head."

Ryker realized he was now clutching Rachel's hand, squeezing it as he revisited that bad time. He carefully loosened each finger before he hurt her.

"It should have scared her, but instead, she swung at me. She forgot all about it. But it reminded me of growing up.

"My dad would hit us when he was drunk. And when I hit that wall, I saw I was just like him.

"That was it. I didn't sober up right away, but I knew I had to make changes. That scared me—being like Dad.

"It was the end of the marriage—Diane wasn't interested in me if I wasn't drinking. But I couldn't live like that anymore. And it's not easy being sober, but it's better. I hope your uncle finds the same."

Ryker realized that Rachel was now gripping his hand tightly—or maybe he was gripping hers again.

"I'm sorry you had to go through that, but I'm glad it's better now."

He nodded. "I had to get some counseling once I didn't have alcohol to deal with things. If your uncle does sober up, he'll have to deal with whatever his problems are. There's some pain that's causing him to drink. He may never be willing to make that trade."

Rachel's drink was getting cold, but she could hardly pick up the cup with his hand clutching hers. Ryker released his grip and drew back his hand, wrapping it around his cooling coffee.

Rachel picked up her hot chocolate and swallowed. When she set the cup back down, there was foam on her top lip.

So help him, he had to restrain himself from leaning over and wiping it off with his thumb.

"I don't know what it is for my uncle. I'm pretty sure he wouldn't tell me if I asked."

"If it was that simple, he wouldn't need to drink."

Rachel looked up at him. "Thanks for telling me that. I didn't mean to pry, but it did help me understand."

Ryker didn't know if it was going to help her with her uncle. He didn't know if she wanted to understand him any better, but he'd told her more than he told most people. He had no fear Rachel would gossip about him.

He trusted her. And he didn't trust many people. He had three now, here in Cupid's Crossing: Rachel, Benny and Mr. G. He had more roots now than he'd had for a long time. Maybe ever.

CHAPTER TEN

RACHEL SPENT THE rest of her weekend studying up on motorcycle rules. She went over the practice tests online until she aced them. She found the nearest DMV office and put it in her phone's GPS. She made plans to go Wednesday afternoon.

She didn't tell anyone. This was her own secret, one she only shared with Ryker.

Tuesday she met up with Jaycee and Mariah, as usual. Mariah spread out her wedding planner, but Rachel put a hand over it and stopped her from starting her weekly update.

"I've got something to tell you guys."

Mariah and Jaycee looked up with identical surprised expressions.

Rachel didn't push, and she didn't have news. Not usually. She didn't put her hand over anyone's planner for anything and interrupt what they wanted to say. This was the evolving Rachel. And she was making changes.

It wasn't just the new jeans, but they helped. She'd ordered another pair and more tops.

She'd also ordered some motorcycle chaps but wasn't sure if she'd ever have enough nerve to wear them.

"I'm leaving." She threw it out there; no easing into it, just *bam!* There it was.

"What? You just got here."

Rachel shook her head at Jaycee. "No, not here, and not now. Carter's. Cupid's. At the end of the summer."

There was silence. Well, she'd made some kind of impression.

"What do you mean *leaving*? Like a vacation?"

"No. I'm moving."

Again, silence.

"Is your dad being transferred or something?"

This was what people, even her friends, thought of her. She was so boring, so unexciting, that she wouldn't even move on her own.

"No, this is nothing to do with Dad. I want a change. I haven't looked for a job yet because it's too early, but I wanted to let you know I'm staying for the wedding, and then I'll be packing."

"Really?"

Did they think she was going to say, "Just joking!"? That she couldn't possibly be serious about this? The thought hurt.

"Don't say anything to my dad. I don't plan to tell him until I have a job and a place rented. Paralegals are needed everywhere, so I should be able to get a job, right?"

Rachel wished she hadn't made that into a question, but baby steps. She was announcing her plans, to someone other than Ryker, who wasn't really a part of Carter's so it probably didn't count.

Jaycee was looking at her with worried eyes. "But why do you want a change? I mean, this town is changing already. There's going to be a lot of new things, new people...why not stay and be part of that?"

Rachel was tempted to say that yes, she'd think about it some more, even though she wouldn't. Just to smooth things over, make Jaycee stop worrying, and not scare her with doubts about whether she could really do this.

But that was what she always did. That was how she was going to end up a cat lady. She didn't want to be a cat lady.

"Huh? You don't even like cats." Jaycee was looking even more worried. Rachel realized she'd said that last sentence out loud.

Mariah made a movement, as if to cut Jaycee off.

"Let her talk."

"I'm going to be thirty on my next birthday." That was the biggest trigger for her to change.

Jaycee opened her mouth to comment and Mariah poked her in the ribs.

"You two are engaged and getting married. You have families to plan for. I want that."

Mariah poked Jaycee again.

"There's no one for me here. And the people who are going to come here for the Cupid thing are going to be coming as couples. People already paired up." Rachel repeated the point to make sure Jaycee understood.

"There are single guys here." Jaycee wasn't giving up. "Kevin's single again—"

"I already went out with Kevin."

"Oh. Right."

Rachel shook her head. "Jayce, I can count up the single guys around here as easily as you. Some I've gone out with, some not, but even if some interesting, attractive single guy moved into Carter's, he wouldn't be interested in me."

Ryker's face popped into her head and she forcefully shoved it aside.

"Come on, Rachel..."

"Jaycee! Listen! I'm boring, okay? I know this. I'm boring, and I spend all my time roped into doing things for other people and I'm going to end up a cat person unless I change myself and get away from here."

Rachel noticed heads turning their way, so she dropped her voice, which had risen as she finally let her frustration spill out.

Jaycee looked shocked. Mariah was watching Rachel as if she was a problem to be solved.

"I didn't know you felt like that, Rach," Jaycee said.

A stab of guilt hit Rachel. She almost apologized. Almost.

Because Rachel had a pretty good handle on how Jaycee was feeling, about her engagement, her wedding, her future mother-in-law and Dave. She didn't know Mariah as well, but she'd been around Mariah and Nelson, and had observed how they interacted. She'd listened when Mariah talked and asked questions.

She hadn't withheld information from these women. They hadn't asked. They'd assumed. And they'd assumed wrong.

So she shrugged.

Jaycee swallowed. "Did I rope you into helping with the wedding? Do you not want to be a bridesmaid?"

Rachel's indignation died. "No, Jayce. No. I'm looking forward to being in your wedding. I want to help."

"But I'm doing something wrong. I didn't know how you felt."

Rachel drew a breath. "You didn't ask me

much about me, but that's not all on you. I just… It's like my value comes from helping people, but I want to be more. And to be more, I think I have to change. So that's on me."

Mariah took over. "Your father said you'd be happy to help on the town committee. Was he wrong? Did he pressure you into it?"

"He didn't pressure me because he didn't ask. He just told me I was doing it."

Mariah's eyes widened.

"Do you want to be removed?"

Rachel opened her mouth, and then closed it. She shook her head. "I'll help, through the summer. But someone will need to take over then, because I'm leaving."

She'd said it, to Ryker, to Jaycee and Mariah. With a twist in her guts, it was sinking in and becoming real to her. She, Rachel, was going to leave Carter's Crossing, for the first time in her life, going out on her own.

"I'd like it if you could still work on those Cupids after you leave." Mariah held up a hand. "But not if it's a problem for you."

Rachel smiled at her. "No, that's okay. I like doodling, so those Cupids are fun. And, Jaycee, I love you and I'm proud to be part of your wedding. But at some point I need to make me a priority, as well.

"I'm working on what I need to do to be the

person I want to be. There are things I want that I'm not going to find here in Carter's, so I'm going to be selfish and leave to get them."

Jaycee rolled her eyes. "If that's what you consider being selfish, then you really don't understand Dave's mother."

Rachel snorted. "I promise. I don't want to go that far. So now that I've made my big announcement, let's get back to the important stuff about this wedding."

Mariah opened her book again, but Jaycee leaned over to whisper in Rachel's ear. "You're just as important, Rach, and I'm going to do better."

Rachel had to blink back tears. She'd scared herself, blurting this out, but Jaycee wasn't Rachel's friend just because Rachel helped her out. And one thing she was not looking forward to leaving behind was her friendships.

She hoped she'd find friends just as good when she left.

RACHEL CLOSED UP the office at noon Wednesday. She knew her uncle was going home to drink, but she couldn't stop him. He'd had a call from Abigail Carter about contracts for the mill, but he'd brushed it aside, promising he'd deal with it tomorrow.

She hadn't done anything to those contracts herself. Abigail Carter did not suffer fools gladly, so she'd be calling back. If Rachel's uncle didn't do his job, Abigail would find someone else.

It was a relief, knowing that she was going to leave. She didn't have to worry about her job security, and what she'd do if her uncle lost his practice. She had a horrible feeling that it would happen once she left. But if it did, he might finally seek the help he needed.

She grabbed the lunch she'd packed and got into her car, heading to the closest DMV center. She often worked on Wednesday afternoons, so her father wouldn't wonder where she was. And her uncle wouldn't care.

She sighed as she thought of her father and telling him about her plans. It was going to be a lot harder than telling Jaycee and Mariah. He'd be hurt, she'd feel guilty and he might use that guilt to make her stay.

She wanted to be more confident before she talked to him. And it was still a few months away. She decided to give herself another month before she worried about that and focused on the rules for motorcycles instead.

She needed to ace this exam.

Okay, technically she didn't have to get every question right to pass the test and get her learner's permit. But she wanted to. She wanted to tell Ryker she was taking this seriously and got every question right.

She did. She walked in, and no one paid her any attention. She followed the signage, paid her fee and took her test. She waited for the results and was given a learner's permit.

With a perfect score.

Not a single person recognized her. Not a single person cared who she was or why she wanted to ride a motorcycle.

She walked out of the DMV office, feeling for once like an interesting person, and passed a hair salon on the way to her car.

She stopped. Bit her lip. Fidgeted with the strap of her purse.

Then her chin went up. She pushed open the door to the salon. It was time for another change.

A few hours later she was driving back to Carter's, feeling like she'd slain a small, but still fiery dragon. Her long, boring hair was now cut, highlighted and with every swing of her head, assuring her that she could change. Nothing was keeping her back except her.

She realized something else, as well.

Outside Carter's Crossing, she was anonymous. She could cut her hair, get her motorcycle licence, ride a bike, and no one would know or care.

They also wouldn't know her at an Al-Anon meeting. Maybe that was an avenue she could explore while she tried to deal with her uncle.

She had some more research to do.

RYKER WASN'T SURPRISED to get a message that Rachel had her learner's permit. He congratulated her and agreed to meet her again this Saturday at his old house, where he'd give her a chance to try out second gear before they found a road for her to expand her skills on.

He missed seeing her at the church on Thursday night, where she usually set up for AA and Al-Anon. He got there late and was pleased that someone else had stepped up. It was great that someone was taking on one of her jobs, even though he'd have liked to see her.

Unless she was missing because she was sick—he hoped that wasn't it.

If it was, she didn't tell him, and didn't cancel their plans for another lesson.

On Saturday morning he stopped in to see how Benny was doing. Benny was sitting in front of a pad of paper, scribbling words and scratching them out, muttering under his breath.

"You okay?" Ryker wondered if there was a problem.

"Stupid speech for the high school."

Ryker felt some sympathy for Benny but was also relieved that it wasn't him.

Then the bell jingled when the front door opened, and Rachel walked in.

She was wearing the motorcycle jacket, helmet in hand. She also had had her hair cut.

Ryker stood and stared. Benny looked up. "Hey, Rachel. Looking good. Is that a new cut?"

Rachel grinned and swiveled, giving them a full 360 view.

"Nice."

Rachel shot Benny a pleased smile.

Ryker stared at Benny. Maybe Rachel had more admirers here in Carter's than she'd realized. Maybe she had gone out with Benny. Maybe…maybe he shouldn't be worried about this.

"Thanks, Benny. I wanted a change."

Ryker turned his gaze back to Rachel. He knew what the change was about. Benny didn't. That made him feel good.

He tried to view Rachel as if she was a stranger. Not the memory he had of a sweet girl from high school, too nice for her own good. Nice enough to let someone like him take advantage of her.

Rachel looked very appealing. It wasn't just the haircut, though it did make her look…

prettier. Her eyes were brighter, unless that was just the excitement of anticipating her motorcycle lesson.

She was…more noticeable. She didn't blend into the background. It wasn't just her haircut, or the motorcycle jacket.

She stood taller. She was looking directly at Benny, not at the ground. She was changing, like she wanted.

For some reason he didn't much care for that.

"We should go." Ryker didn't want Benny to spend more time looking at Rachel.

"What's up with the helmet, Rachel? You becoming a biker?"

Benny's voice was teasing. When Rachel nodded, proudly, Benny's eyes popped.

"Really?"

Ryker shot a glance her way. She was keeping it on the down low. Didn't want people commenting on what she was doing.

She'd changed her hair. Maybe she'd changed her mind, as well.

"Ryker's teaching me. But don't tell anyone, okay? I don't want a bunch of safety lectures."

Benny's mouth had opened, and he quickly shut it. Ryker knew Benny had been about to give one himself.

Benny swallowed. "Ryker's teaching you?"

He sounded...disapproving. Ryker felt himself tense.

"I talked him into it."

Ryker didn't want Benny to try to talk her out of it. Benny had his own things to deal with.

"You're busy, right, Ben?" He nodded at the desk in front of Benny.

Benny frowned down at the pad of paper, no longer worrying about motorcycle lessons.

"Stupid speech for the high school."

"What speech is that?" Rachel asked. Of course she wanted to help.

"Overcoming adversity. I don't want to do it, but my dad talked me into it."

An odd look passed over Rachel's face.

"When is that?"

"A couple of weeks. I'm supposed to say it's no big deal that I'm in a chair."

Rachel stepped forward to the counter.

"But it is, right?"

Benny's lips tightened in a grimace that was very un-Benny-like.

"Then tell them that."

He shook his head. "I'm not looking for pity."

"Then tell them that, too. It's good to be honest. I'm trying to be more honest, too."

Benny looked up at her. "Is this connected to your haircut?"

Rachel tilted her head.

"You know, it is. I'm being more honest about what I want. And what I don't want."

Benny looked at Rachel as if she was someone he'd never met who'd just walked into the store.

"How are people taking this new honesty?"

Rachel sighed. "I haven't been honest with that many people yet. I think some people aren't going to like it at all."

Ryker thought she was right.

"What made you decide to be honest now?" Benny was curious, and Ryker was, as well.

Rachel shrugged. "There are things I want. And I realized I'm not going to get them unless I make an effort."

Benny smiled. "I guess riding a motorcycle is one of those things?"

Rachel grinned. "It is!"

"Then just let me say, be safe, and I'll let you two have your fun."

Ryker put his hand on Rachel's back, guiding her toward the door. He was anxious to get going, to get away from Benny.

For some reason he didn't want Benny to be

one of the things Rachel wanted. And since he didn't want to think about that too much, he needed to get them moving so he didn't have to.

CHAPTER ELEVEN

IT WAS A bright spring day. Buds were appearing on the branches, crystallized remnants of snow hiding in the shaded areas between the trees. The air carried the aroma of dark earth and decaying vegetation, overlaid by the promises of warmth in the sunlight. It was a great day for a bike ride, but he pulled into the familiar driveway for Rachel's lesson instead of losing himself in the drone of the highway.

Rachel, on the back, swung off the bike easily now, ready for the next lesson. Ryker followed her off, holding the bike upright on the drive.

They reviewed the process she'd learned in her first lesson to start the bike and put it in gear. She had everything letter perfect. Not a surprise: she'd been a straight-A student back in school.

She was applying herself the same way to riding his bike.

He stood aside and kept quiet as she put the

bike in first gear and drove down the slope of the driveway, and then turned and came back.

No stalling, no questions, no problems at all.

She was ready for more.

"Go right to the road in first. Then turn to come back up and see if you can shift into second before you run out of drive behind the house here."

She nodded, eager to try. He no longer had to run behind her. She had her balance. He watched from the parking area next to the side entrance to the house.

He concentrated on Rachel, doing his best to ignore the house behind him. The house full of bad memories and alcohol. He shook himself.

Rachel had a rocky stop by the road, but she got her foot down before the bike was in danger of falling. She managed the turn, then pointed the bike toward the house.

He could picture the look of determination on her face. He smiled to himself.

She pushed off, left toe tapping the bike into gear. He watched her feet, saw her tap up into second, the bike pausing momentarily as the clutch released and gripped again. Then she was beside him, squeezing the clutch and brake, coming to a halt.

She flipped up the visor.

"I did it!"

"I could see. Want to do it again?"

She nodded vigorously.

"One minute." He flipped open a storage area on the seat behind her and pulled out a bunch of garbage bags and some work gloves.

He'd told himself that he'd put this off long enough.

He didn't need to watch Rachel every minute. She could maneuver up and down the driveway on her own, becoming more comfortable with the bike. He needed to make a start on the house. With Rachel right here, needing him to drive her back to the shop, he should be able to gather up some garbage without risking his sobriety.

Baby steps.

Rachel turned her head over her shoulder. Her visor was still up, and once he'd snapped the seat closed, he saw her watching him, a question on her face.

"You go ahead, up and down the driveway, till you've got this. You can try to hit second on the way down, as well. You don't need me to watch you, and probably should know you can do it on your own."

She nodded. "If you need anything, let me know."

He didn't pretend he didn't understand what she was offering.

He stepped back and waited while she flipped down the visor and kicked off with the bike.

He would rather have watched her. He would have rather watched the buds on the trees, waiting for the leaves to burst out, but he made himself climb the steps. He pulled out the keys and opened the door.

The smell hit him hard. It hadn't gotten better.

He closed his eyes, breathed through his mouth. Then, with the determination he'd learned in uniform, he forced himself to snap open the bag and start with the rubbish closest to him.

There'd always been a garbage can near the door. Now it was a garbage area, with rubbish spilling out of the container and piling up on the floor for several feet around the can.

His father had been on his own for years, as far as Ryker knew. He and his sisters had escaped as soon as they could. His twin brothers had stayed till they were incarcerated. That was three years ago, though he'd been drunk at that time and could have the timing off.

He wasn't sure when Ethan had left, just that he was gone.

His father had let things go with no one else around.

There was mail thrown on the table. He left that to deal with later. He focused on the things that didn't need thinking, didn't need decisions. The pile of pizza boxes, take-out bags and bottles.

Whiskey bottles. Cheap stuff, since his dad was only interested in getting drunk, not savoring the flavor.

Under the smell of must and sweat, he could taste the whiskey, lining his nasal passages, layering on his tongue.

The craving punched hard. It was seductive, warm and inviting. In this room, where dents in the walls marked memories of anger, pain and fear, the alcohol promised oblivion, peace and rest.

He knew all the reasons it was a bad idea, but like a siren call, it beckoned him.

No, he wasn't giving in.

He stood, shook his head, leaned down to grab a handful of debris.

There it was. A bottle, still half-full, the tawny liquid rocking where his hand had knocked against it.

He picked it up. Clenched his hand.

It would be so easy… The tension in his body made his hands shake. There was enough left in this bottle to take away the pain and the memories. The times when there wasn't enough food. When their clothing was too dirty for them to go to school. When Ryker had stood between his dad and his sisters so the girls could get away.

There was just enough left there, swirling in the bottle, that he could get through this job, forgetting most of the bad times that lingered in the very air he was breathing.

It was getting harder to remember why he shouldn't.

He didn't know how long he stood there, battling. The door whined as it opened.

Rachel.

He drew in a long breath and threw the bottle in the bag of garbage with trembling hands.

Rachel moved forward. She grabbed another of the bags he'd brought, opened it and began to shove the garbage near her into the bag. Ryker knew he should be doing the same, but for moments he stood paralyzed. Breathing in. Breathing out. Not drinking.

Rachel twisted the bag closed and knotted it. Then she grabbed another.

Ryker finally moved. He picked up more of the foul debris, shoved it in the bag, anger making him forceful, shaky.

No. *No!* He wasn't losing everything he'd fought for. He'd pay someone to clean this place up if he needed to. If Rachel hadn't been here…

He turned to her, but she wasn't looking at him. She was picking up the garbage, his garbage, filling the bag, making the place marginally better.

He knew she undervalued her contribution to things. She thought she was a drudge, someone who got coerced into helping people because she was too nice.

She had no idea how much she made things better, just by being there, by lending a hand, by helping.

He wanted her to get everything she hoped for. An exciting life, a partner, a family, a home. She deserved it.

If learning to ride a motorcycle made her happy, he'd make sure she learned to do it. Whatever she wanted, if he could help, he would.

That was a promise.

RYKER HADN'T BROUGHT that many bags with him, so they were soon filled. They tied them closed, then took them outside.

"I could come back in my car and take these to the dump," Rachel offered. It would take a couple of trips, but there was no way to take them away on a motorcycle.

Ryker shook his head. "Benny already offered his van. But thank you."

Rachel drew in a breath. "I wondered if I was ready to try some turns. On the bike."

She hadn't gone into the house to check on Ryker. She felt confident in her up-and-down-the-driveway spurts, but wanted to try turning the bike, rather than the awkward shuffles she'd been doing to change direction. Then, when she'd opened the door, she'd seen him standing there, holding the whiskey bottle.

Her stomach had dropped. Literally, it felt like a lead weight had landed about six inches from somewhere around her navel and a hole was left behind.

She'd wanted to tell him to stop, to think, to not open that bottle, but what good would that have done? Ryker was a fully grown adult. She wasn't his sobriety companion, or his family. She was—a friend. If that.

She hadn't known what to do, so she'd done what she knew how: she helped. She picked up a bag and started to fill it with garbage.

She didn't know if it was the right thing to do, but he'd dropped the bottle into a bag, and they'd continued to clean up the rubbish until they'd run out of bags.

Ryker turned and met her gaze. "I need to

ride." The tension in his body vibrated the air between them.

She nodded. What else could she do?

"If you want to drop me at Benny's…" She'd left her car there.

His gaze moved past her, looking through the trees around the house.

"If you want to ride along, that's fine. But I need to ride. Now."

He was giving her the option of joining him. "I'm in."

She didn't ponder whether it was the right thing to do; it was the thing she wanted to do. She pulled her helmet back on, and once he'd mounted the bike, she swung her leg over and tucked herself in behind him. Her feet found the pegs, and she wrapped her arms around his waist.

He didn't say a thing. He started the bike and they were off.

For the next hour they wound up and down the hills, curving into corners, slowing for little towns and then racing through the straights.

This must be how Ryker dealt with his ghosts. At least now, when he didn't drink. Rachel could feel the tension slowly leaching out of his body as they rode along. He finally pulled in at a gas station. It was another small town, with a small store and restaurant tucked in behind the parking lot.

He stopped the bike by the gas pumps. Rachel didn't know where the opening was to fill the tank, so she slid off, legs a little shaky.

Ryker braced himself on the ground and pulled the bike back on its stand. He dismounted and took off his helmet.

"Are you okay?" His eyes were intent, checking her carefully.

Rachel nodded.

He frowned and looked behind her.

"Why don't you go get a table and some hot drinks. I'll be in once I've gassed up."

She nodded again, head bulky in the helmet. Ryker leaned over and unsnapped the strap under her chin, carefully pulling the helmet off. He passed it to her.

Rachel gave him a wobbly smile and turned to the small building. Before she ordered any drinks, she had to find the ladies' room, though she didn't think she needed to share that.

She got to the counter in time to ask for coffee before he came in the door, eyes sweeping the space till they found her.

They sat on the stools, hot coffee in front of them. Rachel stirred milk into hers.

"Thank you."

Rachel shot a glance at Ryker. She wasn't

sure if he was bringing up what had happened back at the house. "What for?"

"For being there."

She understood. She hadn't done anything special, but she'd been an outside presence, someone to see what he was doing, and that had been enough.

"Well, thank you for letting me learn on your bike. And taking all that time with me."

He watched her for a moment, then turned to his coffee without responding.

Rachel mangled her lip for a moment, wondering if she should do this.

"I'm happy to help you clean up the house, if you want."

Those eyes were on her again. "I don't want to take advantage of you."

"You're not." She felt like she was taking advantage of him. So far, she hadn't done anything to rehab his reputation beyond having him help at the bazaar. She'd definitely benefited from that.

And defending him to Jaycee and Mariah.

He frowned. "Rachel, isn't part of the reason you want to leave Carter's that everyone asks you to help them, or do something for them?"

She bit her lip again and looked down at her own cup.

He was right. She was always helping, and these past months, resenting it. More and more.

But this was different. Why?

She turned back to Ryker. "You're not asking me, and you're not assuming I should, or acting like I don't have my own priorities. I offered, you didn't ask and you pushed back to make sure I didn't feel pressured."

She remembered his face as he stared at that bottle. She remembered that none of his siblings were dealing with this. Ryker was the only one taking on the burden, and that on top of the fact that he was struggling to maintain his own sobriety.

It mattered to her that he not lose that battle. It mattered that he got past this. He mattered to her.

Her idea of getting over her crush by getting to know him better wasn't working. But she was leaving, and he would be, too. Maybe a little heartbreak before she left would make her a more interesting person.

If these months before she was free to move on could be used to help Ryker, then they wouldn't be wasted. And if that made her an idiot, well, it wasn't the most shocking news out there.

"When my dad said he'd volunteered me to

be on the romance committee, I was resentful. When I offered to help you, I felt good."

She shrugged, then took a sip of her drink so that he couldn't read too much in her eyes.

He picked up his coffee and swallowed the last of it before putting the cup back in the saucer.

She heard him draw in a long breath.

"I don't like asking for help."

No kidding.

"One of the things I most hate about being an alcoholic is that I have to accept help."

And help was about all Rachel had to offer anyone.

"But better to get help than drink again."

He tensed but looked at her. "Thank you." He reached out a hand, brushed her cheek, then stood.

Rachel ignored what was left in her cup and got up to follow him back to the bike.

The sky was overcast, and the wind was getting cold. They were going to have a long, uncomfortable ride to get back, and she'd be freezing by the time they did.

Despite that, there was a little bubble of happiness inside her, and she was grinning inside her visor when she climbed on the bike and gripped Ryker's waist.

She was being admitted into the exclusive

club of those Rykcr accepted help from, and she'd have bet her savings that there were very few people in that organization.

"RYKER, YOU'VE DONE an incredible job."

Mariah was sitting in a booth beside him at the diner, looking over the website. It was almost ready to go live, so they were checking the final details.

There would still be lots to do once it went up. At the moment only three bed-and-breakfasts linked on the page, since the others either weren't operational or didn't yet have websites to link to.

There were links to a few local operations: the diner, the Moonstone, a place to rent kayaks. Mariah was pushing other places to get websites, or at least phone numbers that could be listed on the town website.

He was glad she liked what he'd done. He took pride in his work. Doing well here in Carter's was all the sweeter.

No, Cupid's. He was still glad he didn't have to tell anyone he was from Cupid's Crossing.

"You're ready to go live?"

Mariah nodded, but she still had a crease in her forehead.

"Is there another problem?"

Mariah crinkled her nose. "Something I've been thinking about. This is connected to the

Romance initiative, but nothing to do with the website. Can I ask you something?"

Ryker nodded. He wasn't sure what she was going to ask, but he could always say no.

"I know you haven't been back here for years, so you don't know the place that well, but I'm wondering if we're missing an opportunity."

Ryker felt his own brows rising. Mariah had been extremely thorough. He found it difficult to imagine she'd forgotten anything.

"Our focus has been on couples coming here. Romantic getaways, proposals, weddings, things like that."

Ryker nodded.

What would be the point in changing the name to include Cupid if they weren't?

"But what about people who aren't part of a couple? Should we try to look at that potential market?"

Ryker's specialty was programming and software. Not marketing, not research.

"I don't have any insight into that for you, Mariah."

"I'm not asking you as a business agent. But you're a single guy. Would you consider Cupid's Crossing a place to find a potential partner?"

Not what Ryker expected to be asked. And

there was no good reason why Rachel should pop into his mind.

"I didn't come here to date anyone."

"No, but if you decided you'd like to date someone, is there any place here that would facilitate that? I can only think of the Goat and Barley."

The Goat and Barley was on Ryker's no-fly zone, but Mariah didn't know that. Ryker came to a decision. He'd worked with Mariah for more than a month now. He trusted her.

"I don't go to bars, Mariah. I won't be looking for a date here, unless I find someone hanging out in an AA meeting."

That made him think of Rachel, as well.

"Ah." Mariah quirked up a corner of her mouth. "I assume dating isn't a priority there."

He shook his head.

"But that's an excellent point. If we want to reach out to singles, we need to look beyond the Goat and Barley. I think we need to keep the attention on our current couples focus, but it wouldn't hurt to think of some single events we could have for weekends that are a little lighter on couple activities.

"Just imagine the appeal if people came here and found love they didn't bring with them."

Mariah's eyes were sparkling but Ryker just shrugged. She sighed.

Ryker hoped that was the end of this particular avenue of discussion. Romance was obviously not something he had any mastery over. He'd decided that with his upbringing, the effects of his service and his alcoholism that he was better off single.

And with Rachel *again* intruding into his thoughts, making him think of possibilities that weren't for him, he should finish up these bike lessons or encourage her to take a course.

But she didn't have a bike. He should keep teaching her until she decided if she wanted to invest in one of her own. If she did, he could help her find one…

He had to stop thinking about Rachel because he thought he'd heard Mariah say her name. He caught up with her conversation.

"What she said made me consider it. I hoped that you and she might be able to scout a few possibilities for me. I know she's leaving town this summer, and you probably are, too, but you're the only single people on my committee. Except for Mavis, and I'm not sure I'd want her on a task like this."

He had spaced out at the worst time. What did she want and how was Mavis involved?

"I'm sorry, Mariah, what was that?"

"I was hoping you and Rachel would check

out a few places for me and give me some feedback."

"Places?"

She nodded. "Singles places. Events where people look for dates."

He and Rachel? Together? That sounded like a very bad idea.

"Why don't you and your fiancé do that?"

That sounded like a task better suited to golden boy Nelson and Mariah.

"First of all, if Nelson went out looking for a date, he'd be in all kinds of trouble. This isn't a job for people who are in a relationship. I'd actually like your perspective, as someone who hasn't been part of this town for a while. It would be as close to an outsider as I can get.

"And Rachel is someone who I know is looking to find a partner. And, as I said, there are only so many single people around here. I wish there were more. I'd love it if Rachel could find someone and stay in town, but that's selfish of me."

Finding someone wasn't Rachel's only issue. She wanted to leave for other reasons. He should say no to this, just to make sure this town didn't take more advantage of Rachel and her good nature. For his own well-being, he should spend less time with Rachel. Let alone at some kind of singles thing. That would be dangerously close to dating.

"I don't believe that's something I'm equipped for."

Mariah looked disappointed, but not surprised. "Sure? I can ask Kevin or Jordan to do it with her, but Jordan is a little reluctant to get more involved in anything connected to the Carters, and Rachel used to go out with Kevin."

She did? Had she broken up with him, or had he been stupid enough to let her go? If he had been that stupid, was he smarter now? Would he convince Rachel he was worth a second chance, and then she'd give up her dream? Was Ryker teaching her to drive a bike for nothing?

Was Rachel being pressured again?

"Are you sure Rachel wants to do this?"

"I was going to ask her if she'd like to spend some time with this instead of doing some of the things we have on the list for Jaycee's wedding. Since Rachel's leaving, it's a chance for her to see the area before she's gone and, I may be overstepping, but if she's feeling like a third wheel, she might like to spend less time working on wedding activities."

Rachel hadn't shared all this with him, but it sounded like seeing her friends get married could be one of the issues that had pushed her to leave.

"You might have a point. I would bring a different perspective, having spent time in places other than Carter's—I mean, Cupid's Crossing."

He wanted to punch his own face. What was he doing? But it was too late. Mariah grinned at him and started another list.

Just then Jean stopped by, sniffing as she poured more coffee for Ryker.

Mariah frowned at her as she left.

"People can carry grudges around here."

Ryker didn't pretend to not understand.

"I did things I'm not proud of."

"But have you done anything since you came back? People change."

They did. Ryker just wasn't sure that always meant changes for the better.

CHAPTER TWELVE

RACHEL INSISTED ON meeting Ryker at his dad's place for her next motorcycle lesson. Ryker told her there wasn't much more to teach her there: they'd need to find a large parking lot or something similar to give her a chance to practice the moves she'd need before getting on the road. Things like turning, which both excited and terrified her,

Yes, she needed to get the hang of more advanced moves on the motorcycle, but she had another motive for insisting on another lesson here.

Ryker didn't like to ask for help, and he didn't want people to know how bad things had been growing up, that was obvious. But she couldn't let him struggle through it alone again. Not when she'd seen how difficult it was for him.

How close he'd come to drinking.

She knew her own bad habits. This was how she ended up helping too many people; she *knew* that. This was what she wanted to resist.

But Ryker didn't guilt her into helping him or assume she would. She wasn't going to be admired for doing this. He was more likely to be upset with her.

Maybe it was reinforcing her own bad behavior, but surely, she was allowed to choose what she wanted to do? And she wanted to help Ryker—take this particular problem off his back. He carried enough.

And maybe if he felt obligated to her, he'd be more willing to consider what else she was going to ask him to do.

She wasn't being totally charitable. And that should make her feel bad, but it didn't.

She pulled into the driveway that was becoming awfully familiar, after driving up and down on the motorcycle so many times. Ryker was there, waiting for her. It was impossible to hide the mop and broom filling her backseat. She stopped the car and stepped outside, hoping he wouldn't be too upset.

"I'm pushing, I know." That was almost an apology.

"I didn't ask you to do this." Ryker didn't look exactly angry. Maybe frustrated?

"No, you didn't. And you wouldn't. I'm offering. If you tell me no, I'll let it go."

She sketched a cross over her chest.

Ryker had his hands on his hips and was staring at her under lowered brows.

"Why? This kind of thing is what you're supposed to stop doing, isn't it?"

She wasn't sure if he didn't want the help, or if he didn't want to take advantage of her.

"Not exactly. I have to learn to say no to people. But I'm the one asking to help you, and *you* can say no. And also—" she didn't want him to interrupt with a no already "—you're spending a lot of time and effort, and gas and money—" Rachel waved at her jacket "—teaching me to ride your motorcycle. I understand why you might not want me to help you in the house, and maybe don't want anyone to. But it was obvious that you were having some problems when I was here last time.

"If I'm overstepping, I apologize, and will make sure not to do it again. But I would like to offset some of the obligation I feel to you by helping this way."

Ryker kept staring at her. He finally shook his head.

"You're right. I have to accept help. I want to be able to do this myself, but..."

He wiped a hand over his face.

Rachel didn't let the pleasure she felt show on her face. She was sure he wouldn't like that. But he was going to let her do what she wanted.

"Do you want to do the fun stuff first? Or the bike lesson?"

A snort of laughter escaped him, and it was difficult to keep a beaming smile off her own face.

"Let's try some of your fun stuff first, and then we'll add in a lesson when we want a break."

Rachel spun around and opened the door to the backseat, which was filled with cleaning supplies. She hadn't seen a lot of the house, but it had obviously been long neglected. She was fastidious enough to not want to use any cleaning materials that had been left in the place.

Ryker was right there, taking items from her as she pulled them out.

"You came prepared."

She checked his expression. "It's not my first time doing this kind of thing."

He nodded and headed to the door of the house. Rachel filled her arms with paper towels and a bucket full of soaps and cloths.

The place still smelled terrible. The garbage bags from the last lesson were gone. But this was going to be a huge task.

She started by opening windows. Some of them were jammed shut, so those Ryker worked on to force open. The spring air was cool, but not unbearably so, and anything to help with the smell was good. Since alcohol was a major element of that lingering smell, letting it out of the house could only help.

The memories? Nothing she could do there. Except maybe distract him.

The first hour they filled bags of trash. Rachel had bought the largest box of garbage bags she could find, and they used most of them. Again, Ryker refused to let her put them in her car, promising he'd borrow Benny's van again.

"Kitchen or bathroom next?"

Ryker opted for the bathroom. Since it was small, Rachel passed him some cleaner and rags and decided to make a start on the kitchen. She wondered how the seven kids had survived with only one bathroom. There were two in the parsonage, and she'd been an only child.

She didn't know if there were any triggers from the bathroom that might upset Ryker, but she decided to go ahead with her distraction plan.

"Hey, Ryker. I had a thought."

Ryker stepped out of the bathroom to talk to her. He'd pulled off his bike leathers when they started working on the house. Now that he was in the small bathroom, he'd also pulled off his long-sleeved shirt, and was wearing only jeans and a white T-shirt.

Rachel's mind skittered for a minute. Tattoos and muscles. On the guy she had a crush on. Oh my.

"You had a thought?"

He had a cloth in his hand, spray bottle in the other. Rachel mentally gave herself a slap and remembered why she was there.

"I think you should talk to the high school at that assembly Benny's doing."

She quickly turned around and knelt in front of the open refrigerator. It was honestly disgusting but prevented Ryker from seeing her face.

"What?" He sounded perplexed.

"Mr. G wanted Benny to talk to the kids at the high school because he used to get in trouble in school. He wants the kids to hear from others who had a hard time in high school, give them an idea of how things can get better afterward."

Ryker had turned his life around. He'd had a horrible start, here in this house, but he'd made something of himself. He'd be a great example, if she could convince him to do it.

"You want me to talk at a high school assembly?"

He didn't sound perplexed now. He sounded horrified.

Rachel just replied with a mmm-hmm as she pulled on one of the crisper drawers. What had possibly been in there before it fossilized? She tugged out the drawer and stood to shove it into the sink full of hot, soapy water she'd prepared.

"No." Ryker almost growled the word.

She'd expected a refusal.

"Why not?" She made sure not to turn around and focused on the crud in the crisper. She was glad she'd worn gloves but wasn't sure she had tools that could scrape this thing clean. She might need explosives.

"I don't want to." He sounded final, but he hadn't returned to the bathroom. Maybe he was willing to be coaxed into it. Maybe he was just glad of a break.

From her glimpse of the condition of the bathroom, she couldn't blame him for that. But if he wanted coaxing, she could provide it.

"Benny doesn't want to, either."

"Yeah, well, it's not my dad who's asking." There was tension in the air. Ryker's dad was a whole different animal from Mr. G.

"Benny's not doing it for his dad." Rachel had talked to Benny, when Ryker wasn't around, trying to learn more about the assembly and what it was about. It was something she thought might be good for Ryker and good for his reputation here in town. All part of what she'd said she'd do for him.

Beyond that, if he saw that people had changed their minds about him, maybe he'd stop seeing himself through that lens, as well.

"Then why is he doing it? He's complaining about it nonstop."

Rachel decided the only hope she had of getting anywhere with the crisper was to let it soak, so she turned to look at Ryker.

He still looked endearingly confused, standing with the cleaner in one hand and his strong arms, swirling with ink, holding a cloth over his shoulder.

"He knows that this town has had problems. With the mill shutting down, times have been hard for people. And that means, sometimes, that kids do stupid stuff."

"Like me."

Rachel nodded. "Benny hopes that telling what he did, and what he regrets and why, might help some other kid. And he's even going to talk a bit about his life in the wheelchair. Generally, he doesn't like to talk about that, but there are a couple of disabled kids in the school. Benny promised to offer to talk afterward to anyone who has more questions."

"So I should represent the future alcoholics?" There was anger running underneath the question, and his arms were now crossed. The cloth had fallen to the floor, and Rachel had questions as to the continued survival of that cleaning product with his knuckles now showing white around it.

Rachel wasn't saying this right, or maybe this wasn't the right thing for Ryker. But he had a lot more to offer than he saw in himself.

"I think you're not the only kid who grew up in a home that had an alcoholic parent or an abusive one. I think there might be kids out there considering enlisting when they're done with school, and you could let them know what it's like, at least in some ways. And yeah, there may be some who are alcoholics, as well. You don't have to tell them everything about yourself and your life, but I think you have a lot in common with things they're working through.

"The last time many of the people in this town knew you, you were in a bad place, and a lot of them still see you as that same guy. As soon as you have this house ready, you can leave, and maybe you don't care. But I get the idea that you still see yourself like that. If you talk to these kids, you won't just be telling them about you and what you went through.

You'll show them who you are now. You might even show yourself."

Rachel put a hand over her mouth, shocked by her own outburst. She was pretty sure she'd crossed a line there. More like decimated it, so she swung back to pull out the next crisper.

Ryker didn't respond to her speech. She heard him return to the bathroom and turn on the water. The conversation was definitely over on his end.

She drew in a breath and then choked on the smell of rotting food. She put the second crisper in the sink and started to scrub.

Stupid! She had already pushed him, insisting on helping with the house. Then she tried to push him into speaking at the high school.

Her motives were good. He did have things to share, things that might make a difference for a kid there. And yes, people hearing him talk about being in the air force would certainly make them look at him as an adult, not the troubled teen he'd been.

But telling him it would help fix him? Too much. Too presumptuous. None of her business. And for all she knew, he was afraid of public speaking. Lots of people were.

She had no business trying to fix him.

She dropped the scrubber in the sink.

It wasn't that she wanted to fix him. She

wanted him to see he was already fixed. He wasn't perfect, heaven knows. She'd heard him describe his life. Two tours, two divorces, two years sober.

But he was strong. He'd survived all that and succeeded. He wasn't trouble; he was an inspiration to get out of trouble. She didn't think he saw himself as strong, other than physically, and people in this town looking down on him would encourage that idea.

Her problem? Her crush had made her way too invested in Ryker. It wasn't supposed to be like that. She was supposed to be less attracted to him when she got to know the real person.

After all, she was leaving, and so was he. Letting herself get emotionally involved with the man was setting herself up for heartbreak.

She thought she'd understood that, but now…now it was hitting home. Hard.

The smart play would be to pull back. She'd done research. She could take courses to get her motorcycle license. Some of them provided bikes for people to learn on. She'd already helped with the house, and with the garbage and alcohol gone, the worst was done; she didn't need to do more. In fact, she had a solid idea that Ryker wouldn't want her help anymore.

She could do that. Stop investing in Ryker.

Spend more time helping Jaycee. Maybe figure out what to do about her uncle.

Maybe that was smart, but her whole life she'd always been sensible. And she'd always done what was good for other people.

And the result of that was a desperate longing to get out of this town and do something for herself. A belief that she was wasting her life.

Spending time with Ryker was selfish, and was probably a stupid thing to do, and for once she didn't want to be smart and selfless. She'd probably get hurt, but it was better than not feeling anything at all.

She'd had too much of that in her life.

She'd never been as interested in, or as attracted to, someone as she was Ryker. It was reassuring to know she had that kind of depth. Her nonexistent dating life? Wasn't because she couldn't feel. She could feel so much. And risky as it was, she wanted more.

Of course, it depended on whether she'd gone too far just now.

Ryker wouldn't want her to go any further; that was obvious.

She finished scrubbing out the gross section of the fridge beneath the crispers and decided that she could leave the crispers themselves to soak. She'd done enough for today—she should leave.

She closed the fridge and let the water out of the sink. Time to find out how much damage she'd done.

"Ryker, are you okay if I head out now?"

He stepped out of the bathroom. His T-shirt was wet and showing signs of dirt from his cleaning. It clung to his chest, and more tattoos were visible under the wet fabric.

Heaven give her strength.

"Of course. Let me gather—"

Rachel shook her head. "No, keep the stuff for now. If you want me to come back again, I'm happy to. If not, I'll pick it up later, or you can bring it by when you have Benny's van."

Ryker frowned.

"You didn't get a chance to ride the bike."

"No, I didn't. I think I've pushed you enough for today, and I understand if you'd like a break from me. I'll wait to hear from you, okay?"

He sighed, rubbing a hand over his face.

"Rachel, I'm not angry. I just…have to think about some stuff."

Rachel felt tears at the backs of her eyes. She willed them away.

"You take the time you need. Just let me know."

She was aware of his gaze running over her face, his creased brow.

"Are you upset? I know I'm moody, and not the most considerate person."

Not considerate? She'd almost had to twist his arm to get to help him today. He'd bought her a motorcycle jacket. Even back when she first saw him again, at the church after the committee meeting, when Mariah wanted Rachel to do the Cupids—he'd tried to step back from involving her because he thought she didn't want to spend time with him.

He had his problems, but lack of consideration was not one of them.

Rachel shook her head. "No, I'm upset with me, not you. We should both do some thinking."

The last thing she wanted was for him to feel bad about his response to her pushiness. He was entitled to be upset.

"I'm happy to come back and help some more, but for now I'll give you some space."

She pulled on the sash of the kitchen window, wanting to close it.

She heard Ryker come closer and pulled harder.

His hand rested on her shoulder. The touch increased the confusion swirling inside her, adding shimmies to her conflicting desires to get the heck out of here or to refuse to leave. She was a mess.

"Rachel, it's okay. I'll get the windows. You get to where you need to go."

Yeah, where she needed to go was back home. Where she wanted to go was about a 180-degree turn, so she'd be tucked into his chest.

Instead, she pulled away, grabbed her jacket and her purse and left with a wave in his direction, not meeting his eyes.

These feelings she was having? They were uncomfortable, and embarrassing, but they weren't nice or boring.

Was that a win?

RYKER WAS ANGRY with himself. Rachel had scurried off as if she'd expected him to blow up at her.

He wasn't angry. Not precisely. He was confused, a little embarrassed, grateful and frustrated. But he couldn't be angry with someone who just wanted to help. And who understood when they'd pushed too hard and stepped back.

Especially when she saw him as a much better man than he knew himself to be.

She was a giving person. And people took advantage. He didn't want to do that. But turning down her help upset her.

He might judge himself based on his past, but Rachel judged herself by the help she gave others.

He needed to work on his own self-image, he could see now. There were people in this town who still saw him as a troublemaking kid. But he'd met enough others who were willing to look at the person he had become.

It was critical that he do the same. He might be an alcoholic, but he was sober now, and with help and determination, was going to remain that way.

A hell-raiser in the past, he was a veteran now. He'd gone through some nasty stuff, helping to keep his country safe. He might not have joined up to save the world, but he'd reenlisted, and he'd been a good soldier.

Despite his failed marriages, he wasn't hurting his exes now. His first wife had remarried, and best he knew, was still happily with her husband. His second was still drinking, but he wasn't enabling her. She had his number, if she ever wanted to get sober.

He'd learned he wasn't built for romantic relationships, but he could be a good friend.

And being a good friend to Rachel meant helping her understand that she was more than just the assistance she provided. He needed to be careful that she knew she was appreciated, even without helping.

He paused from the sweeping he'd been doing. While he'd been thinking, he'd channeled his frustration outward. The whole house was now swept clean. The open windows and garbage removal had taken care of most of the smell. The place still looked grubby, but it was no longer a pigsty.

He'd been working here all afternoon, and he hadn't come close to needing a drink. At first, Rachel's presence had helped. Then she'd come up with this crazy idea of him speaking to the school, and he hadn't had time to think about the house.

There were still memories here, but he had more confidence that he could deal with them.

Rachel didn't need to clean up more of his dirt, either in the house or his life. But he'd used her supplies and wanted to thank her for them.

He'd call her about giving her more lessons on the bike, making her accept help instead of giving it.

That meant spending more time with her, and that reminded him of another Rachel issue buzzing around in his brain. Mariah's request. Going to singles events with Rachel.

Mariah was trying to help Rachel. As much

as going to a singles mixer made his skin crawl, he could go with Rachel, support her and try to boost her confidence. She wanted the traditional husband/home/family. She deserved it. She would be an incredible wife and mother.

He'd push her to interact with people who weren't looking for her help, just her friendship. He could do that for her.

He wouldn't talk to the school, though. It was one thing to stand up in an AA meeting and bare your worst self to people who'd been there and wanted to support you. To do the same for a bunch of high school kids who didn't care about him and would be happy to make fun of him? Or the adults, teachers, some of whom had taught him? Who'd think he was just fooling himself with talk of change?

He'd rather run the bazaar single-handed.

RYKER STOPPED BY the shop when he got home, since he needed to borrow Benny's van again. Having all that trash gone from the house would be a load off his shoulders.

"Sure. No problem. Getting the place cleaned out?"

Ryker nodded. He felt lighter, knowing part of that job was done.

"All the garbage is bagged, and we've got

most of the kitchen done, as well as the bathroom."

Benny's eyebrows rose. "We?"

There was no reason for Ryker to feel defensive.

"Rachel helped me."

"Another motorcycle lesson?"

Ryker shrugged. It was supposed to have been.

"You two are spending a lot of time together." Benny had a big grin on his face.

Oh no. He didn't need to let stories get out there about Rachel.

"Rachel likes to help people." Which was true, but he didn't like feeling that he was just one of her charities.

"Yeah, she's pretty nice. But if word gets out, people are going to talk."

Small towns could be gossipy.

"There's nothing to talk about. I'm teaching her to ride a bike, and she wanted to help me clean the house."

"Okay, just making sure you understand."

"Understand what?"

Ryker was sure he knew, but he wanted to make Benny say it. As if that would give him justification to be angry.

Benny raised his hands. "I have no problem.

But some people in this town have long memories, and they don't like you much."

"Something happen?"

Benny nodded at the table where he put work for Ryker. "There's that laptop back for you to clean up. But another customer decided she'd rather go to Oak Hill than let you touch her machine."

A slow burn built up in Ryker's chest.

He shouldn't worry about what people thought. But this time he wasn't going to say it was okay.

He was done apologizing for his youth. He'd been a kid, and it had been a rotten situation. Thank goodness his time here in Carter's Crossing was limited.

He didn't want those same small-minded people hurting Rachel, if they found out she'd been helping him or taking lessons from him. He could stop both. But then, they'd win.

"I've seen the work that guy does on computers. Whoever she was, she deserves it."

Benny offered him a high five.

"Exactly. I think the only reason some of these people aren't all over my case is because of the chair. I guess they figure I've been punished."

"That's a horrible way to think."

Benny shrugged. "Yep. But that's the way

some folks are. I usually charge them an extra service fee, so I feel better about working for them."

Ryker felt a smile curling his mouth.

"Oh, and Nelson and Mariah were by to pick up something. Mariah said to ask you about the mixers?"

There was a question in Benny's voice.

Right.

If he agreed to help Mariah, and people found out, they'd talk. They'd talk about Rachel because she was going to a singles mixer, and they'd talk more if she went with him.

He was angry with those small-minded people. He could take it, but he knew Rachel would be hurt. She didn't have the scar tissue he did.

Even with it, this was bothering him.

He could step aside and let her go with Kevin, whoever he was. There'd be talk about that, as well, and it didn't sit right with him, that she'd go with an ex.

People would talk less if he wasn't Ryker, the hellion from fourteen years ago. If he was just some regular guy, maybe someone who had cleaned up his act, then they might not talk so much, or judge Rachel.

Oh no. If he did the talk at the school, and people knew what he'd done…

Maybe he'd help some kids at the same time.

He glowered at Benny.

"This is all your fault."

CHAPTER THIRTEEN

"You're late."

Mariah had given Rachel a look as she slid into the diner seat, but it was Jaycee who spoke.

"I wasn't aware we were on a time clock." Rachel was as surprised at her response as the other two.

"Sorry," she muttered. "Not a great day."

It hadn't been, but that wasn't the only problem.

Her uncle was getting worse. Today he'd yelled at her about an incomplete file. She'd had to remind him that she was only a paralegal. He hadn't apologized, just blustered. Knowing that she was leaving was the only thing that had kept her from snapping at him.

She normally didn't snap, but she was on edge. After all, what would happen when she was gone?

After the aborted bike lesson/cleaning/high school speech disaster, Ryker had sent her a thank-you email. That's all. She had no idea what that meant. The sinking feeling she had when she read it made her suspect it wasn't anything good. Before coming to the diner to meet her friends she'd been looking up motorcycle classes to join, in case Ryker wasn't willing to help her anymore.

She was not in her happy place.

Mariah reached over to squeeze her arm. "Are you good? Is there anything we can do?"

Rachel felt tears threaten. Again. It was just that normally she was the one offering. She wasn't sure how long it had been since anyone had checked if she needed help.

She took a long breath and gave a shaky smile.

"Thank you. I'm not good, but most of it is work stuff, and I can't tell you about that. Legal issues."

Jaycee leaned forward. "Is this wedding too much? I know, I need to make sure I don't get carried away again like I did for the engagement party. If you want to bow out, then that's okay." Jaycee made a face. "Well, not super okay, but my wedding is not the most important thing in the world. I know, shocking, but…"

Rachel leaned over to give her friend a hug. This support was exactly what she needed.

And maybe something she should have been asking for. Food for later thought.

"No, you're not getting rid of me as a bridesmaid that easily. But I appreciate the offer, so much."

Mariah gave her a long look.

"I do have something to ask you, but you have to be honest with me and tell me if you don't want to do it."

Rachel leaned back. "That sounds a little scary."

"It's not. It's really not. But I want to be sure you're not going to agree just to be nice."

Rachel nodded. "My new goal is not to be nice, so bring it."

"I heard what you said before, that this town isn't a place to *find* someone to love. It's a place for people who are already in love. We've concentrated on making it a destination to celebrate those occasions. That was why I was brought here, and that's my focus.

"But maybe we can do both. I can't distract from my main job here, not right now, but I'm going to consider it as a future project.

"I wanted you to do some research for me before you go. Instead of doing some of these wedding projects that I can cover, if you'd do this instead."

Rachel blinked. This was not what she expected.

"What kind of research are you talking about?" She couldn't imagine finding anything online that Mariah couldn't or hadn't.

Mariah opened a page in her notebook. Rachel thought she was organized, but Mariah left her in the dust.

"I found a few singles events in the area. I was hoping you and Ryker would go, check them out, see if they were lame or useful, and…"

Mariah looked up with a hopeful expression.

"Maybe you might even meet someone interesting."

Rachel was still stuck on the Ryker part.

"Ryker?"

Rachel wasn't sure Ryker even wanted to talk to her again, let alone go to a singles event. A singles event, with Ryker. Where Mariah hoped Rachel might meet someone. When she was there with Ryker. As if.

As if Ryker would do that.

"I appreciate that the two of you want to help me find someone, but is this the best you could come up with?"

Mariah crossed her arms and frowned at her.

"Honestly, Rachel, I think this could be an

untapped potential market. A big one. And I would trust your input on this."

Rachel glared at her. She smelled shenanigans.

"Why not go yourself?"

Mariah gave her a look. "Yeah, Nelson isn't going to go for that. And no, I'm not going to go with him and pretend we're not together. If you go, you'll be someone participating, hoping it works the way it's intended. It'll be a real test. And there's a chance you'll have some fun, too."

Rachel's first response? No way. She didn't want to announce that she was looking for someone and was too much of a loser to find anyone in her regular life.

But that wasn't productive thinking. Would she call the people she met at something like that losers? No, so why say that about herself? She hadn't found anyone. And she wanted to. If people didn't know you were looking, they couldn't help you.

It wasn't the worst idea ever. Maybe, in the new life she was looking for after the summer, this might be the kind of event she'd attend. Maybe getting her feet wet now was good practice.

Her second response was the one she shared.

"I could do that. But I don't think Ryker will be interested. I'll go on my own."

Mariah shook her head. "I'd feel better if you had someone there with you. And I'd like to get a male perspective, as well."

Rachel wouldn't mind going with someone. But Ryker?

"I don't think it's really what Ryker would do."

Mariah looked down and ticked off something on her list. "He already agreed. The first event is next Wednesday night. Since we don't have a committee meeting that week, I thought you'd be free. You in?"

Rachel opened her mouth, ready to say something else to give Ryker an out, but instead nodded. Ryker was a big boy. He could figure this out for himself.

Now she just had to attend a singles event with Ryker and try to notice anyone else.

Mariah sent them the information for a singles meetup in Malton, a larger town about an hour away. The program was a game night. That didn't sound too scary. Rachel had done some online research about events like this, just to see what she was getting into. Naked dating was something she would definitely refuse. Not even to be less *nice* and meet someone was she going to an event naked.

Though for a moment she grinned at the thought of what people would say.

Ryker had brought back her cleaning supplies. He'd driven them to the parsonage in Benny's van, and her dad had answered the door first. Ryker had thanked her for her help, and her dad had commended her for helping out.

Rachel had quietly seethed. She didn't need her father to reassure her that she was making good decisions. She was an adult. She could make good *and* bad decisions for herself.

Fortunately, she hadn't expressed those thoughts. Neither her dad nor Ryker would have appreciated them, she was sure.

Instead, she'd shoved the mop and bucket into her dad's hands and suggested he put them away. He'd blinked in surprise but taken them and left. He hadn't returned, which was what she'd expected.

Ryker could have said or done something then, but he hadn't. She'd been disappointed that he hadn't asked for more help, but she had to respect his limits.

The only information he'd offered was that he was going to find a parking lot for them to practice turns on the bike, so she didn't know if he was upset with her or not. She suspected he felt obligated, and that didn't warm her up at all.

She really wished she'd had an answer to how he felt before they went on this…not-date together. She was parsing through what he said or didn't say to try to work it out. She'd suggested they ride over together. He said that wasn't a good idea, not if they were supposed to be singles.

True, but she would have liked the confidence of arriving with someone she knew.

She'd given herself a pep talk on the drive over. And she'd made a promise to herself that she was going to approach this as if she was on her own. She was not going to cling to Ryker or be disappointed if he didn't show up.

Okay, she would be, but no one would know.

She pulled into the community center. There were a lot of cars in the lot, so the fear of being the only person to show up was removed from her list of concerns. There were still a lot of things on the list.

She'd worn another new outfit. She was gaining confidence in her shopping now. At least she was trying out colors, and even her father had noticed she looked "different." The frown on his brow indicated that *different* wasn't necessarily good, but she wasn't trying to please him with her appearance. Not now.

Mariah and Jaycee had been complimentary, and they were a better judge of the look she was going for.

Not a game-changing act of rebellion, but baby steps.

Still, she sat in the car, hands on the steering wheel, screwing up her courage to go in there. Alone.

She wasn't sure what to expect. Maybe game night was code for something, and she was going to be the same awkward, outside-looking-in person she'd always been.

Could she ask if she could just watch? Or was that strange and creepy?

Her stomach was twisting up, and her palms were sweaty. She was going to have to run to the bathroom. If anyone shook her hand, they'd have to wipe their own hands after. This wasn't going to work.

Maybe she should wait to do a singles event after she'd moved. After all, what if she found someone she liked tonight? Then she was in trouble. She was planning to move away. She was dooming things from the start.

But this town *was* away. If she found someone, maybe she could find a job near here.

No, that was probably too pushy. It would

scare the guy away. He'd feel crowded, and either want to talk limits, or just start ghosting her.

Then she'd be stuck in a new town, with a bad ex already. He might bad-mouth her to all the other single guys and—

Before she went any further into her hypothetical failed relationship, there was a knock on her car window.

She jumped, but then, through the dusk, recognized Ryker.

Great. He'd seen her sit in her car dithering. Maybe it would be easier to learn to like cats.

She'd been sitting with the engine off too long for the power window to lower, so she opened the door a nudge.

"Want to head in?" he asked.

She'd prepared herself for the idea that he wouldn't want to be with her, not if they were supposed to be "singles." But she stopped herself from asking.

She wouldn't have asked in a nice tone of voice.

Her stomach was no longer roiling. She felt more comfortable going in with someone, and she didn't want to have to tell Mariah and Jaycee that she'd chickened out. She'd accept his escort and be grateful. She wouldn't assume anything more.

She wiped her palms on her pants, reached for her purse on the seat beside her and opened the door to get out as Ryker stepped back.

He was wearing his leather jacket, a T-shirt and jeans. With his dark hair, messed by the helmet he'd probably just removed, and the boots, he looked like a poster for the kind of guy nice girls should avoid.

She obviously was not a truly nice girl, not anymore, because she didn't want to avoid him. At. All.

Feeling more confident, she smoothed down her pants and walked with him to the doors. She saw two women about her age pause to check Ryker out. And fought an urge to put her arm in his, claiming him.

He wasn't hers. And she really didn't want him to find someone tonight, which was selfish and mean of her.

She was becoming less nice every day now. Apparently, it wasn't as hard to do that as she'd feared.

THE WHOLE THING turned out to be so much less scary than it had been in her head. There was a check-in table, with a short questionnaire. Based on the answers to the questions, she had her name printed on a colored name tag and was sent to a particular game room.

Ryker had shown skepticism in every gesture but filled out the form and got his own name tag. He was not sent to the same room as Rachel.

Apparently, Ryker liked different games than she did. Now there was a surprise.

Rachel found herself in the board game room. There was a fairly even split between men and women, and a few different games set up on tables. No long games, like Monopoly or Risk, but Scrabble and Pictionary.

Rachel had fun.

None of the guys made it to her romantic possibility list, but she got along really well with one of the other women, and they exchanged numbers to meet up. Rachel was calling the night a success, even if she was just as single as when she'd arrived. She could make friends. She'd already recognized that she was going to need friends in her new location, wherever that might be.

Okay, so she'd almost weaseled out of this, and might have if Ryker hadn't been there, but she'd be ready for the next one. She was confident now.

After the games' time limit was called, everyone gathered in the main room to mingle and hear announcements and have some drinks and snacks.

There was another event in two weeks—a musical one. Surveys were being distributed online and they were asked to fill them out so that the organization could better serve their needs. Rachel dutifully accepted the invitation to join the group online.

People tended to clump together in the same groups as the game rooms. Rachel was beside her new friend, with others from their board game group. They'd found drinks and were re-hashing some of the more interesting pictures that had been drawn in Pictionary.

Rachel finally spotted Ryker across the room. From the looks of it, his game room had been the cool one. The guys near him all carried themselves in that too-cool-for-school posture, and the women…well, that was where the hot women had been.

It wasn't surprising that a couple of those women were standing near Ryker. Rachel felt a spasm of jealousy that was all too inappropriate.

Ryker and she were friends at best. He'd never kissed her, or put his hands on her, except for bike lessons. Or that time with his hand… Most of the time she'd been the one pushing for them to do things together. He hadn't taken that initiative, except for meetings related to the town website.

She'd known she had a crush on him in high school. She'd also been smart enough to know that it was superficial. She hadn't known the real Ryker. She hadn't known how bad things had been in his home. She hadn't known the trouble he got into, or why he did. She hadn't seen him for fourteen years, so the man he was now was a stranger to her.

Her hope that getting to know him better would end the crush had backfired. She liked this man. She'd seen beneath the stoic, strong surface. He'd shared things with her, things she didn't expect he shared with many people. She'd talked to him, and even told him about her plans to leave before she'd told her friends.

She knew he didn't have any kind of a crush on her. She wasn't his type. She was nice and boring. Less nice and boring than she'd been, and he'd helped with that, but Rachel needed to be realistic.

She'd gained something from this time they'd been together, but she needed to put a pin in it. She couldn't imagine it to be more than it was, as much as she wanted it to be.

When one of the guys from her game group offered to get her a drink, she gave him her best smile.

The guy was…nice. She was nice. She needed to manage her expectations. Someone like this nice guy could give her a nice life. And it would be her life: she could have her own home, her own person, a family of her own. It might not be chills and excitement and mountaintops, but it wasn't cats alone.

She shouldn't find that…depressing.

When she'd put in enough time that it didn't look like an escape, she said goodbye to her group. She got away before her nice guy could get her number; she wasn't ready to try dating someone like him just yet. Not till she was able to stop comparing him to Ryker. She promised the people at the check-in desk she would fill out the questionnaire and made her way out to her car.

RYKER WAS NOT a fan of game night.

The only thing he'd ever done that came close to game night was going to a bar to have beer and play pool or poker with friends.

He didn't have those friends anymore. They'd gone with the alcohol.

He should have filled out the questionnaire differently, because he ended up spending the evening with the kind of people he'd cut out of his life when he'd chosen sobriety. He'd been invited to a bar after this event was over and had to refuse, more than once. He didn't want to tell them he didn't drink anymore. He just wanted them to go away.

Finally, the end was in sight, and they'd all gone to the main room. He'd been counting down the time till they could leave. He spotted Rachel with a group of people she seemed to like. One man was claiming as much of her attention as he could.

He was a good match for her. Ryker imagined the guy was an accountant or insurance adjuster. Maybe a dentist. Someone with a stable, safe job. Ryker hoped he wasn't someone who'd take advantage of Rachel's self-sacrificing tendency. She deserved to have someone sacrifice for her.

He turned down another invitation to go to the bar. When the two women didn't want to take no for an answer, he told them he was on his bike and couldn't drink.

They wanted a ride.

Mentally, he rolled his eyes.

He didn't want passengers and told them that he had no spare helmets. Then, when he looked again, Rachel was gone.

The guy who'd been hovering near her was still around, so she hadn't left with him. Ryker was more relieved by that than he had any right to be. He made his way through the room and headed out, barely acknowledging the guy behind the check-in table reminding him to fill in his questionnaire.

He didn't care about the questionnaire.

Rachel was unlocking the door to her car.

"Rachel!"

They were supposed to be doing this together, weren't they? That was why he was so disappointed that she'd left without talking to him.

She turned around, surprise on her face in the parking lot lights.

"You don't have to leave on my account."

He tried to examine her face, read her mood.

"I just needed an excuse."

She fiddled with her keys.

"You didn't enjoy yourself?" She sounded surprised.

He shook his head. "Our friend at the desk there really doesn't want me to fill in that questionnaire."

He heard a gurgle of laughter escape her.

"Did you have fun?"

She cocked her head. "I did, actually. More than I expected."

That shouldn't have made him feel...sad.

"I made a friend."

She certainly had. "Did you give him your number?" That was the point of this, right?

She blinked at him. "I gave *her* my number. I didn't find any guy I wanted to go out with."

That shouldn't have made him feel better. Because Rachel not dating someone else had nothing to do with him. He wasn't someone she should date. And that wasn't even a thought he should have.

"You didn't find anyone?" Her voice was a little high, nervous.

He shook his head.

"Really?"

"Those people were like the friends I had before. They asked me to go to a bar after."

"Oh. Maybe you could have gone somewhere else?"

"No. I know what it's like with people like that. I can't do that anymore."

"I'm sorry." Her voice was soft, kind.

"It's okay. That's not fun now. Should we compare notes, something for Mariah?"

"I guess."

She didn't sound very enthusiastic. Maybe she was upset with him that he hadn't asked her for more help with the house. He should explain that to her, if he could find the right words.

"I found a place we could have the next bike lessons, but it's only empty on Sundays. We could do both things then—lessons and notes for Mariah. Does that work for you?"

"Are you sure you still want to?"

Definitely. He didn't like the hesitation in her voice. But he knew why she was asking.

"Rachel, I appreciate that you helped me start on the house. I really do. I hate asking for help, and instead, you almost forced it on me so I didn't have to. It got me over the worst, and I appreciate that more than you know. But I don't need you to help me all the time. I don't want to be a project for you."

He was tired of being the person always taking.

"I didn't ask you to help me clean the rest of the house, but I'm happy to spend some time with you, teaching you to do something you want to do. That's assuming you do still want to learn to ride?"

She smiled. "Yeah, I do. I can make Sunday afternoon again."

The relief was too large for what his expectations should be. He had to remember who he was and what was within his grasp.

"We could go to dinner after, make the notes for Mariah."

She nodded, her cheeks creasing from carefully holding back a smile. "But only after we fill out the questionnaire."

CHAPTER FOURTEEN

RYKER STOPPED AT the town gas station to get some fuel in the bike. It didn't use a lot, but he wanted a full tank for the lesson with Rachel tomorrow.

A white van had been parked on the opposite side of the gas pumps. As Ryker opened his tank and reached for the pump handle, he read Carter's Crossing Veterinary Clinic on the van. Then he noticed a man who could only be Nelson Carter coming out of the little convenience store at the back of the lot, headed toward the same van.

Ryker shoved his credit card in the appropriate slot. He'd never been a friend of Nelson Carter's. They moved in very different groups back in school.

"Ryker? Ryker Slade?"

Ryker lifted his gaze to the man now facing him across the fuel pump.

Life had been good to Nelson Carter. He was tall, his scrubs showing a fit physique. He looked younger than Ryker, well cared for.

Someone who'd never gone hungry or feared for his life.

The Carters lived a completely different life than the Slades.

"Nelson." He nodded and turned to put the nozzle in his tank.

"I heard you were back."

He didn't sound thrilled by the prospect, but then again, who was? Even Ryker hadn't wanted to return.

But Ryker wasn't that kid anymore. He knew how people were supposed to behave. He turned back to Nelson.

"Congratulations."

Nelson's brow creased. Ryker continued.

"On your engagement. Mariah is good people."

Nelson's face lit up. "She is. I'm lucky."

Ryker didn't respond because he couldn't imagine anything else they had to talk about.

"Mariah told me you and Rachel are doing some things for her. Going to singles events."

Well, they'd gone to one.

Nelson jiggled the key fob in his hand.

"I probably shouldn't say this."

Ryker's tank was full. He removed the nozzle, returned it to the pump and braced himself.

"Mariah trusts you, and she's a good judge

of character. But she doesn't know you, not like I do."

Ryker shook his head. "You don't know me, either, Nelson. It's been fourteen years."

Nelson gripped his keys.

"You're right. I don't know you now, but the guy you were, well, that guy wasn't someone I'd trust. And Rachel is…naive. She wants to help everyone. I just—"

Ryker's chin came up, and he met Nelson's gaze. "You think I'll take advantage of her? Maybe guilt her into helping me, along with everyone else in this town?

"I haven't asked her to do a single thing, and I've refused some of the help she's offered. I'm not the one who's taking advantage of her."

Ryker's words were more heated than he'd intended. He grabbed his receipt and credit card and shoved them in his pocket.

Nelson was watching him intently, and he felt uncomfortable under that stare. He didn't need to prove himself to anyone.

But he had a reputation, and now Rachel's friends were worried about her. He understood a lot about her now, knew she'd defend him to them, but he didn't want to add to her troubles.

Nelson quirked up a corner of his mouth.

"That's fair. And I guess, when I think about

it, the only person you hurt back then was yourself. I apologize for making assumptions.

"But if you do hurt her—"

The suggestion made him angry.

"Yeah, I know. Still, maybe I'm not the one you should be talking to."

It was none of Ryker's business. But he wasn't the one making Rachel want to leave Carter's Crossing. That had happened before he showed up. And it seemed he wasn't as jaded about being labeled the town villain as he'd thought.

It would be nice if people would give him a chance. Realize he'd changed. That he'd done something of value, at least for part of his life. That he could be an asset to a community.

Like if he gave that high school talk Rachel mentioned.

Ryker got back on his bike. Nelson hadn't moved; instead, he was watching him, brows lowered.

Then Nelson sighed and turned to his van.

"Guess you've got a point. Have a good day, Ryker."

RACHEL WAS FIZZING as she parked at Gifford's Repairs. She was looking forward to improving her riding. Not that it was much riding yet. But being on the back of the bike with Ryker had given her a sense of freedom. And driving it herself gave her a feeling of power. She wanted more of it. She wanted to drive the bike herself, feeling both strong and free.

And, there was no sense fooling herself, she was looking forward to spending time with Ryker.

She liked him more than she should. But she was leaving and so was he, so if she kept that in mind, she should be okay. She was learning how to be around a guy she found attractive and be comfortable with who she was. She was learning a lot of things she'd use in her new life.

Yes, it would hurt when he left, but she was gaining more from knowing him than she'd ever regret.

She got out of her car and locked it. Ryker's bike was there, but there was no sign of him. She double-checked the time.

She was on time, and he was here, so she waited.

After ten minutes she was getting impatient. They didn't have that long to practice, and she wanted to get a lot better on the bike.

Gifford's was closed; it was Sunday, so she couldn't wait there. She sent a text.

Nothing.

Finally, she was done waiting. She knew

Ryker lived on the second floor. She'd see if he was there. Maybe he'd hurt himself and couldn't answer the phone...

That thought sent her up the stairs at a run. She knocked at the door, waited and knocked louder.

"Ryker? Are you there? Are you okay?" She bent over to look in the keyhole. Except it wasn't that kind of lock.

Suddenly, the door was pulled open, and she straightened, flushing.

Ryker was there, and he was fine. She'd been silly. He'd forgotten.

Her excitement fizzled away.

He ran a hand through his hair. She couldn't help tracking his arm, the colorful tattoos running down it and the white T-shirt tight around his chest. Her cheeks flushed.

"I'm sorry, Rachel—"

She didn't wait for more.

"It's okay, we can do this another time—"

She turned to go, but he reached out a hand to grasp her arm. He didn't grip tightly, and she could have pulled away, but that touch brought back the fizzing, and her body didn't hear her brain telling her to go.

"No, Rachel. I didn't forget. Not exactly. I was distracted by something."

Something or someone? If he had a girlfriend here, she was going to die of embarrassment. The problems she was having breathing in air, the hole she felt where her internal organs used to be—she was literally going to die, she feared.

"Come in for a moment—I'll get my stuff."

That didn't sound like there was a girlfriend with him.

She pulled in a long, shuddering breath and followed him in, looking around with curiosity. When she didn't find another person, the queer feeling inside settled, and blood returned to her brain.

The place was plain and sparse. There were some laptops on a table, with one opened in front of a chair. Ryker reached over to save something, then closed the lid. He passed a kitchenette on his way to a back room: bedroom or bathroom, probably.

There were no photos on the walls or side table. Ryker's jacket and helmet hung on wall hooks beside her, his bike boots and some running shoes below them on a mat. There were no dishes in the kitchen, no mess anywhere, beyond the laptops, and some notepaper and pens beside them.

She found it all way too interesting.

Ryker returned, wearing a sweater. She was

both disappointed and relieved that there was less of him on view.

He looked at her and made a face.

"I was working on a speech for the high school."

He was grumbling, as if confessing a weakness.

Rachel felt the smile creasing her face.

"That's awesome!"

She could hear the words climbing up her throat. *Do you want me to help?* But she held them back, almost by physical force.

Ryker could ask if he needed help. And was she the person to advise him? She'd never been through what he had, knew nothing of what he was comfortable sharing. She wasn't a great public speaker.

She remembered his words, that he was happy to spend time with her without her needing to help him. Had anyone ever said that to her before?

Maybe she was more at fault in becoming everyone's little helper than she'd realized. She didn't just say yes to everything; she offered help to everyone, every time.

Not that that was a bad thing, but was she doing it because it made her feel important? Valued? Did it make her feel superior because she was helping, not being helped?

Maybe she should think things through before offering help. Like now.

She let her comment stand and waited for Ryker to respond.

"That's what Mr. G said. Ready?"

Rachel nodded. "Let's go."

RACHEL LOVED MOTORCYCLE RIDING.

She was also exhausted.

She was so impressed with Ryker's patience, because almost three hours of talking to her, watching her, demonstrating to her, encouraging her and probably grinding his teeth when she got things wrong was pretty impressive. But at the end of it, since she had her learner's permit, she'd driven out of the parking lot they'd been practicing in and circled the block. On the road, on her own.

She'd been nervous. But Ryker had been calm and totally confident for her, and she'd done it.

She hadn't been able to resist a dorky little happy dance when she got back and off the bike. Ryker had been kind enough not to laugh.

Now they'd stopped at a diner and were having dinner together.

Rachel would have loved to call it a date, but she knew it wasn't. She'd decided that her time spent with Ryker was a teaching moment for more than riding a motorcycle. She could use the experience for other dates. Because now she was confident she'd get some.

The singles group had sent her an email. She hadn't understood exactly how the group worked, but they'd informed her that two men were interested in getting to know her better. If she wished, they'd give them her contact information, and they could set up time to spend together outside the singles events.

That had been an incredible ego boost. She'd agreed to attend their next event, a musical evening. Karaoke and dancing. Not that she planned to sing, but it should be fun, and Mariah wanted them to go.

She was going to go even if Ryker didn't. Still, it would be nice if he did.

"Did Mariah talk to you about the next singles night?"

He had his hands wrapped around a mug of coffee and lifted his gaze to her.

"Karaoke? Not my thing."

Rachel tried to picture Ryker on a stage, singing to a pop song. No, that took more imagination than she had. He wasn't a guy for being in the spotlight.

"It's not mine, either, at least as far as singing myself. But it could be fun watching other braver people."

He snorted.

"It's not always bravery, but a matter of discretion." A rare smile crossed his face. "I do everyone a favor by not singing."

Rachel had to smile in response. "For me it's both. I told Mariah I'd go, so I can give her feedback. You don't have to."

"You want to go?"

She nodded.

"Okay, then. We'll go."

She cocked her head.

"Are you sure?"

"I may ask a favor in return."

Rachel's eyes widened. Ryker, asking her for help? She nodded.

"Maybe you should hear what it is before you agree."

Maybe it was something he didn't think she'd want to do.

"You want me to go with you to see your dad?"

He froze. Rachel was 1,000 percent confident that not only was that not the favor he wanted to ask, it was also stepping way out of line.

"Sorry, I shouldn't have said that."

Ryker took a swallow of coffee, and Rachel wanted to crawl under the table.

"I was going to ask you to check over this

speech for the high school. I wouldn't ask anyone to go see my father."

Rachel knew it was important to walk a fine line between being a friend and intruding. It wasn't a line she normally crossed. But then, it wasn't normally Ryker.

"I don't want to push into someplace I'm not wanted, Ryker. That just came out because you made this favor sound like a big ask. Your relationship with your father is none of my business."

She still longed to help him, so she needed to restrain herself. But then her stupid mouth just kept moving.

"If you ever did want a buffer on a visit, I'd be happy to help. I haven't seen him very often, only when we were dropping off care packages, but I have heard the talk and I know he's pretty bad."

Ryker's knuckles were showing around his cup. Oh well, in for a penny…

"But all that aside, I would be happy to check over your speech, if you want. Maybe email it to me?"

She would be lucky if he didn't walk out the door right now.

"Do you know what you want to order?" She tried a wobbly grin to go with her question.

Ryker drew in a long breath, then let the volatile subject pass.

RYKER GRIPPED THE sides of the podium in front of him.

His pulse was rapid and shallow. His palms were sweating, and if he wasn't wearing this button-up shirt over his T-shirt, his armpits would be showing damp stains.

He forced himself to take a breath. He looked ahead of him.

He'd never seen the high school auditorium from this side. He'd sat in the seats, usually at the back, though he'd often skipped the assemblies. A sea of faces was staring back at him, and he cursed himself for agreeing to this.

Benny had just left the stage, after talking about his own time in high school and the accident. Benny had practiced the speech with him, so Ryker knew it was good. He hadn't heard a word Benny had said just now, nerves hitting him hard, but the kids had responded well.

The silence stretched out. Kids were getting restless and moving in their seats. Ryker wasn't going to be able to do this.

He caught Rachel's eye. She'd insisted on taking time off work to come support him and was now standing at the back of the auditorium. He swallowed. She gave him a thumbs-up, a silly, dorky gesture that reminded him of her dance after taking the bike on the road.

She thought he could do this. She thought he needed to.

He looked at the back row and saw his guys.

Their clothes were worn, not as well cared for as the other kids'. They were slouched in their seats, too cool for this, carefully hiding the hurtful things inside.

He'd been there. So had his brothers and sisters. He didn't want any of these kids to make his mistakes.

His talking to them might not change anything. But maybe it would.

He took a long breath.

"I used to sit in the back row, that is, if I didn't skip these things."

He could feel the attention moving back toward him. He saw Rachel's brows rise. This wasn't the script they'd gone over. But he knew whom he needed to talk to, and he'd do it the way they might listen to him.

"I didn't want to be here, so that was part of the reason. But I also didn't want to sit up front, where people could see that my clothes were old and dirty. Where they might see the bruises my dad had given me.

"Up front was where people who cared, and who had people who cared about them, sat, and that wasn't me."

One of those kids in the back, a girl, had

lifted her gaze to him. Yeah, she knew what he was talking about.

"My name is Ryker Slade. You might even have heard of us. We were the family everyone was told to stay away from. My dad was a mean drunk, and my mom died when we were small. We didn't have a lot at our house, and we got into trouble.

"I'm not here to blame anyone. Growing up was tough, and when I stole a car and drove it into a tree, drunk off my face, I had to choose whether to go to prison or enlist. I joined the air force. I have two brothers in prison, so we didn't all make the same choices.

"It wasn't fair what we grew up with, and I know it's not fair for some of you. A lot of kids here, they're going to go to college. They're going to get educated and have a life full of choices in front of them, and it's not fair that everyone doesn't get that."

Ryker had focused on those kids in the back. They weren't all listening, and he might not get through to anyone. But the kids in the front, they had people who cared about them, and the chances were good that they'd be okay.

"The air force wasn't a great choice. I didn't rise up the ranks and become a major, and I didn't make it a career. But it got me out of this town, away from my father and away from a lot of bad choices I could have made.

"I saw some stuff that messed me up during my two tours, and I used alcohol to deal with that. Not a great choice, but it runs in the family.

"I'm out of the air force, and I'm sober. None of it was easy. But now, now I do have choices. I've got a skill I can use to support myself. I can choose where I want to live. I can choose not to do stupid stuff that gets me in prison."

He swallowed, not exactly sure where to go from here.

"So yeah, some of us have crappy choices to start with. And I know some of you are going to make bad choices, and anything I say isn't going to change that. But if you're like I was, it may not seem like your choices matter much, but they do. And if you wanted to talk to someone about what to do, there's probably someone here at the school. But if you can't talk to them—and I never did, I get it—stop me if you see me around town I'll talk to you."

He grabbed the papers on the podium in front of him and turned, getting himself out of there as quickly as he could. He'd messed that up. But as the kids in the front, the ones he hadn't been talking to, politely applauded, he knew he'd told his truth.

Maybe it had helped someone. Maybe not.

He felt a load had lifted from his shoulders. He'd finally told the secrets his family had kept all those years ago. And it had been bad. The seven of them had been through a lot.

The twins hadn't done well, but he had. He wasn't that reckless, hurting kid anymore. And no one had stood up and told him he was.

He'd done better than he'd expected. On the other hand, he had every confidence he'd never be asked back.

CHAPTER FIFTEEN

RACHEL TOOK MORE CARE with her appearance for the musical night. She'd decided she'd gone as far as she could on her own, and asked Mariah and Jaycee for help.

They'd been thrilled to go shopping with her, and Rachel realized she'd been so focused on making herself needed by helping everyone else that she'd neglected to let other people feel necessary by asking for help.

At first, she'd wanted to leave Carter's to escape the confined life she felt trapped in. She hadn't been focused on where she was going, just on what she was leaving.

Now she was excited by the thought of a new beginning. She'd recognized some of her own flaws, and those she could work on. She was learning new skills: improving her looks, meeting new people, taking risks.

Saying no.

New Rachel was going to enjoy herself. She wasn't going to be the cat lady with no life of her own.

She'd started to look for a job, checking out sites online. She didn't want to go to New York or Boston. That was too big for her courage right now. But towns within a one- or two-hour drive. Those she was interested in.

She wasn't quite New Rachel yet, but she had left Old Rachel behind. People had noticed the change in her appearance, but now they were also noticing a change in her behavior.

When the fall bazaar had come up in a conversation with her father, she'd told him someone else should be in charge.

His eyes had almost bugged out of his head.

She couldn't do it all on her own. The people involved were getting much older, and new blood was needed *if* it was going to continue. Ryker's help had been great, but she didn't know if he'd even be around for another one, let alone want to help.

The very idea of *if* had shocked her father.

He'd promised to get her help. She hadn't quite been brave enough to tell him she was leaving and wouldn't be in charge of this one. The help wasn't for her; it was to replace her. Instead, she'd told him that as long as she was there, people would assume she would take care of everything. She had her notes and could advise, but if the bazaars were going to continue, someone else would need to step up.

Her father acknowledged her concerns, but his eyes were a little twitchy. Rachel escaped to her room, hoping he'd be concerned enough to talk to his management team. Hopefully, they wouldn't decide that pressuring her was the way to deal with this.

If they did, she was going to have to flex her "no" muscle.

She'd worry about that later. Tonight she was going to have fun. She looked good, at least two guys were interested in her and she'd spend some time with Ryker. CVs and bazaars could wait.

This time, when she pulled into the parking lot for the mixer, she wasn't racked by nerves. And this time Ryker was there, waiting for her.

His expression made it obvious he wasn't looking forward to the evening, but he was a grown-up, he'd agreed to come on his own and she wasn't going to worry about it. Much.

This time there weren't separate rooms set up with different kinds of games. Again, there were name tags and colored stickers to fill the space below. The different colors were for different kinds of music. The karaoke and dancing would include most music styles, but by personalizing your name tag, you could signal your own musical tastes.

Rachel put pop, country, rock, gospel and

blues on hers. Ryker left that part of his name tag blank. She had to know.

"You don't have a kind of music you like? Or is it something they don't have here?"

He frowned. "Doesn't seem like a good idea. I don't want someone coming up to tell me why what I like is crap, or to try to dissect the components of it with me. I just like to listen to what I like."

Rachel shrugged. Ryker wasn't here because he wanted to meet anyone, at least as far as she could tell. He was only here to do research, so if he wanted an unmarked name tag, he was entitled to that.

She suspected he might have people coming up to him to ask him why he didn't have a type of music on his tag often enough to make him second-think that decision.

The main room was transformed from last time. A bar stretched along the back wall, and a stage was set up at the front. There was a DJ and a karaoke machine. Along the walls were chairs, for those wanting to sit out. In the middle a large group of people had gathered, some with drinks, some talking, everyone waiting for the music to start.

Ryker offered to get Rachel something to drink. She asked for water. She was driving home, and she wasn't much of a drinker in any case. He nodded and she stood, not far inside the doors, watching everyone with interest.

"Rachel!"

It was her new friend Marcia from the last meetup and one of the guys from their game group. Rachel was happy to see them again.

"You've got almost every type of music covered there," Cliff observed, looking at her name tag.

Rachel shrugged. She liked a lot of music.

"You know, when it comes to gospel music…" he started.

Rachel and her friend were relieved that Ryker showed up with water for Rachel and interrupted what was undoubtedly going to be the kind of explanation Ryker was trying to avoid by not choosing any music genres.

He might have had the right idea after all.

"Thanks, Ryker. Do you know Cliff and Marcia?"

Ryker nodded as they all agreed it was nice to meet each other. Cliff frowned at Ryker.

"You didn't put down any music genres."

Ryker took a swallow of his own water and nodded.

"Were you claiming that you like all music, or were you making a statement about how these separations are artificial constructs imposed by critics and merchandisers—"

"I didn't want to talk about music."

Cliff's mouth was hanging open.

Rachel bit her lip. Perhaps fortunately, the DJ stepped up to start the evening's entertainment.

There was a sign-up sheet for karaoke at the side. They'd alternate between the DJ playing songs and karaoke singing, depending on how the karaoke went. Several people rushed to sign up for karaoke. Rachel did not. Neither did Ryker, but that didn't surprise any of them.

Marcia teased her. "Come on, it's fun. We could sing something together."

Rachel shook her head. "Sorry, not my thing. But I promise to cheer you on if you want to do it."

Marcia wavered until Cliff encouraged her and went with her to sign up.

Rachel rolled her eyes at Ryker. "No one bugged you to sing."

The corner of his mouth tilted. "Told you it was smart not to dress up my name tag."

Rachel grinned back at him.

"Well, thanks for coming with me, even if this isn't your kind of thing."

Ryker turned to watch the crowd of people. The DJ had started with an upbeat number, and people in front of the stage had started dancing.

He reached over and grabbed her empty water. Placing the cups on a nearby tabletop, he pulled her toward the dancing crowd.

"Oh no." Rachel hung back, even though she loved the feel of her hand in his.

He glanced back. "No what?"

She nodded at the dancers, just in front of them.

"I don't dance."

He turned around, still holding her hand, backing toward the dancers.

"You don't like it?"

She opened her mouth, closed it and decided to own up. After all, Ryker was under no illusions that she was or ever had been cool.

"I don't know how. Preacher's kid didn't go to the school dances."

"I'll show you."

He didn't tug her farther, nor did he let go of her hand. He stood, staring at her, a coaxing almost-smile on his face.

This did not compute. Ryker liked to dance? Ryker, the reserved biker who wouldn't even list a music genre on his name tag?

But she was nodding and following him into the crowd before she'd consciously made a decision. She was very much afraid that if Ryker had asked her to karaoke, she'd be up there, making a fool of herself behind a microphone in front of everyone.

And she wouldn't even care.

Once they were in the crowd, he took both her hands and put them on his shoulders. Those shoulders were firm and warm, well muscled, and she felt her belly start to shimmy again. Then he put his hands on her hips, and she almost stopped breathing.

He leaned his head down so she could hear him over the music.

"Relax. Follow me."

As if she would say no to him.

Ryker could dance. He was good at it. Rachel was on the dance floor, and Ryker was dancing with her, and suddenly the world was upside down.

They danced for a couple of songs before the first karaoke singer was ready. Rachel hated to stop. The chance to be this close to Ryker, touching him while he moved her hips, showing her body how to move to the beat of the music, would be a dream come true if she'd ever dreamed anything this amazing.

She needed to dream higher, or nothing was going to top this.

The dancing crowd dispersed as the first karaoke singer stepped forward. Rachel's friends found them and brought a couple more people along with them. They hung around together and applauded the first singer, who was good. The DJ played another song, and Ryker went to find her more water instead of asking her to dance.

Rachel reminded herself to not be stupid. Maybe dreaming higher was not the answer.

The next singer was bad. Truly awful. But he was having fun, and the crowd cheered him on. The next music break Rachel excused herself to go to the restroom, to be sure she didn't allow herself to even think about dancing with Ryker again.

Two hours passed in a lot of fun. Some members of what had become their group would sing karaoke, and they'd cheer them on. When a dance song was played, they started to dance as a group, which helped Rachel control her expectations.

Ryker was asked to dance by a few women, and Rachel refused to be disappointed when he left with them. But he always returned, making sure she had water to drink. Rather like a chaperone, she gloomed.

Rachel had not become any more enamored of Cliff, since he tried to lecture her on music any chance he got. She couldn't understand why he'd want to spend time with her if she was as idiotic as his conversation indicated he thought her to be.

The DJ announced the final song, a slow number. Rachel could see Cliff turning to ask her to dance. She scrambled to find a polite way to say no when a strong hand grabbed hers and tugged her toward the center of the floor.

Ryker pulled her into his arms, and she forgot everything else.

"Thanks." Her voice was breathless. But she was held against the firm body of Ryker Slade and her teenage self was speechless. Her adult self was almost as bad.

"I didn't think you wanted to dance with him, and you'd be too nice to tell him that."

She couldn't be disappointed by that. He was being nice.

But her face must have shown something, because he added, "And I like dancing with you."

Part of her brain wanted to argue about the whole *nice* label, and that she had been planning to find a way to say no, but she was so happy to be dancing with Ryker instead of Cliff that nothing was going to pull her down. She let the comment drift away.

She didn't know how to slow dance any more than she knew how to fast dance, but he was holding her, and she just had to follow his lead. She kept her gaze on his chest, afraid of what her face might reveal if she looked at him. He was wearing a button-up shirt, and she could see the hint of a T-shirt and a tattoo where the buttons opened near his throat. She wondered what the tattoo was. She wondered if she'd ever see it.

She wondered if she should be talking, but she couldn't think of anything to say beyond *Please never stop.*

She wasn't so crazy as to not know that she couldn't say that.

The music came to an end, unfortunately. Ryker released her, and she held back a protest. She followed him to rejoin the group they'd been with most of the night.

Later, she'd be happy that she'd found friends. They'd talked about meeting up again for a Sunday brunch. She wasn't sure if she could manage that, what with church, but she was making a life for New Rachel.

Yes, that was all food for thought…later.

Now, though, she was floating on cloud Ryker. It was a bad place to be, and she'd hit earth soon enough, but she was going to let herself enjoy the ride while it lasted.

They said their goodbyes and talked again

about plans to meet up. Rachel nodded and smiled and hardly heard a thing.

Then Ryker waited for her to precede him out the door, and she found herself heading down the hallway, promising to fill in the questionnaire again, definitely and for sure, and then out the door.

Out where the air was cool and real life came rushing back. Ryker walked her to her car, and she knew he'd make sure she was safely on her way before he headed back on his bike.

The magical night was about to end. She pushed the thought aside, unwilling to taint a single moment.

She just needed to unlock the car, turn and say good-night to Ryker without wrapping herself around him, and then she'd be driving home in the dark, free to relive every moment.

She reached for the car door when a hand came down on top of hers. His hand. It clasped hers, and slowly turned her back to face him.

She blinked and looked up, wondering what was wrong. His free hand gripped her waist and pulled her close.

The shimmies and jitters and goose bumps all broke out as he leaned his head down. She stopped breathing, sure that she'd somehow wandered into one of her dreams.

Then his lips touched hers.

RYKER HAD NO IDEA what he was doing.

Just like back in high school. Fourteen years ago.

Back then some part of his brain, the part that wasn't totally self-destructive, had prodded him to get some tutoring, suggesting that graduating high school would be a smart thing. Fate had given him Rachel as a tutor.

She was sweet. Kind. So earnest. And it wasn't hard for him to recognize that she had a crush on him.

It had amused him, at first. He hadn't shared it with his friends, knowing how they'd make fun of her. He and Rachel were so opposite that he couldn't understand why she'd see anything appealing in him. But he found himself looking forward to the tutoring sessions. He even began to imagine seriously graduating from high school, getting more education. Becoming more like Rachel.

Then one of his teachers had kicked him out of class and promised to fail him. He hadn't been able to complete an assignment. His dad had been on the rampage the previous night. He'd started to rip up the homework Ryker and his sisters were doing at the kitchen table, so he'd shoved his toward his dad and swiped his sisters onto the floor where they could rescue it later.

It wasn't an excuse he could offer his teacher. After all, he was one of the Slades.

Those dreams of his were never going to happen. He wasn't going to get a high school diploma. There was no point in getting tutored in English when the other classes were all going to be failures. There wasn't going to be anything after high school.

He should have told Rachel he was quitting. That had been his plan. He wasn't a complete jerk. But when he'd said he had something to tell her, she'd looked so...hopeful. And for once, he'd wanted something nice for himself. So he'd kissed her.

She responded, enthusiastically and without any skill. She'd had no restraint, no sense of how much trouble she was asking for. Some slice of decency had made him stop and push her away.

He might not be going anywhere, but she was, if he didn't mess it up for her.

Then he'd dropped out of school, and never seen her again until a few weeks ago.

He knew she was interested in him again. He wasn't any better for her than he'd been all those years ago, but he'd assumed that crush would fade over time, since other women found him less interesting as they got to know him better. Example: his two marriages.

In the meantime, he'd enjoyed helping her. It had been nice to spend time with someone who liked him. That was part of Rachel's nature. And paying her back, at least a bit, by teaching her to ride his motorcycle and doing some strong-arm work at the bazaar, that had all been a way to apologize for his teenage behavior.

She was still talking about leaving Carter's, and he had no intention of staying, so he hadn't seen any danger in the two of them spending time together. Danger to his own expectations of what he could have in his future.

Not until these singles events, when he had to face other men being attracted to Rachel.

He understood. She didn't think men noticed her. Her physical appearance wasn't dramatic and eye catching, but she was pretty. In a restrained, quiet, *nice* way that he knew she'd never appreciate. But he did, and so did these guys.

And that was what was right for Rachel. Some nice guy, without an ugly history; someone who wasn't carrying around an addiction and divorces and a family that should scare any sane woman.

He'd known he didn't need to dance with Rachel. And that he shouldn't. But she'd been standing there, enjoying the music, looking wistful…and he wanted to make her happy. He'd actually thought he might be the guy who could…for a few moments.

He'd been smart enough to avoid the next dance, and she'd caught on and avoided the one following that. And then they'd been group dancing, and he'd gone to dance with other women, the ones that were his type. Flashy, troubled and trouble.

When that last dance was announced, Ryker had seen the guy who wanted to ask her to dance. The music snob. She had, too. She'd stilled, bit her lip. Ryker could see the way her shoulders slackened as if she'd made the decision not to say no, even though she wanted to.

The guy had only talked about himself all night. He was a self-absorbed blowhard. But Rachel was too nice to say no.

Ryker had grabbed her hand, pulled her into the dance to give her an out. And he'd enjoyed it too much. He'd imagined doing this again, in the future.

She felt good in his arms. Nice. She hated that word, but to him, it was everything he'd been denied, and he found himself soaking it up whenever he was with her. Having her that close had filled a hole in him he'd never managed to deal with in all his life.

He'd told himself he'd make sure she got to

her car without the blowhard bothering her. He'd be just possessive enough to make the guy back off. So that Rachel wouldn't have to be nice and say yes to the guy when she didn't want to.

He'd liked that slow dance too much. And she had, too. He could see it on her face, in the way she carried herself.

He needed to tell her that he was no good for her and would only get in the way of her getting the life she deserved. The way he should have in high school. He was an adult now. He needed to deal with things. That was part of the purpose of AA. Not avoiding.

But when she looked up at him, expression exposed under the illumination of the parking lot light, he'd felt that same urge he had fourteen years ago. Hope, as if he could deserve these nice things, not destroy them. A chance to touch Rachel, kiss her, a chance to believe that things could be better.

So instead of telling her they shouldn't spend time together, making her face fall with disappointment, he pulled her close and kissed her.

She came willingly, melting into him.

Her lips were soft and welcoming. She was tentative. He liked that she didn't have the experience most of the women he'd known did. She followed his lead, pushing up on tiptoes to grip his shoulders, the way she had when they were dancing.

For a few precious minutes he let himself enjoy it. The way his body warmed from contact with her. The way his heart beat faster as her lips moved on his. The peace that flooded his mind when his thoughts were limited to the softness of her lips, the texture of her hair in his hand, the breathy moan that filled his ears.

And for just a moment he thought…maybe.

But the chatter of people leaving the building, heading to their cars, broke into the bubble.

He pulled himself away from her. His breath was coming hard, and he could see her chest rising. She raised her hand to her lips.

He had to tell her this was a mistake. He had to turn off that light in her face. He knew better. She deserved better. Why had he indulged himself at her expense?

This was not one of the choices he should make.

He was no better than he'd been at seventeen.

He needed a drink.

Just like returning to his home had dug up the old responses to deal with problems, so had this revisit of his past.

He had to get out of here. He had to call his

old sponsor, find a meeting. Because hurting her was inexcusable, and it woke the monster inside.

He opened his mouth, but nothing came out. Hands shaking, he turned for his bike.

He might have set a record for getting his helmet and gloves on. Then the engine throbbed between his legs. He pushed the bike forward, put it in gear.

When he was on his bike, he had to focus on the road and the other drivers who wouldn't see him. He couldn't dwell on her face, on her lips, on the way he thought he could be better when he was around her.

My name is Ryker, and I'm an alcoholic. That was who he was. And he wasn't going to make three years sober if he didn't get help. Now.

CHAPTER SIXTEEN

RACHEL WATCHED RYKER FLEE. There was no other way to describe it. He kissed her and fled like wolves were after him. Or maybe ghosts.

The ghosts of Rachel's bad kisses.

She couldn't believe it had happened *again*. But the look as he'd left? Yeah, that wasn't the look of a guy who wanted to kiss her anymore.

Why had he kissed her? And then why had he left?

Because for her, that kiss had been something.

Prior to this, his high school kiss had always ranked as her best kiss. Best on her side at least. It couldn't have been that great for him.

But she'd kissed guys since. Guys who had kissed her more than once. She'd even done online research on what constituted a bad kiss. She didn't think she was too messy, or spitty, or whatever.

But now was not the time to dwell on it. Before someone recognized her and wanted to talk, she got into her car, slammed the door and drove out of the parking lot.

She bit her lip, blinking back tears. Because this kiss had been even better than the high school one. For a few minutes she'd felt pretty, safe…loved. Again. But it was an illusion.

At least as far as Ryker was concerned. She was afraid that she'd fallen, hard.

HOPE WAGED A WAR with common sense. Maybe she'd just imagined the look on his face. Maybe he'd remembered an appointment he had to go to. Maybe they'd still have motorcycle lessons, and she'd help him with the house and they'd work on the website and…

And nothing. Because common sense was much smarter than hope. And with each day that went by that she didn't hear anything from Ryker, hope lost more ground in the battle against common sense.

Tuesday evening with Jaycee and Mariah, she told them about the musical night, without mentioning the dances with Ryker or the kiss. Hope still held out enough of a possibility that she wasn't heartbroken, not quite. Her eyes were dry, and she spoke normally—enough that no one looked at her sideways.

But Jaycee asked if Ryker had been there.

Mariah answered. "He already sent me his

impressions. He had to go out of town for a few days."

Mariah didn't even look up from her checklist. She assumed Rachel knew this.

Hope gave up the struggle. Ryker was gone. He might come back to Cupid's Crossing, but he wasn't coming back to Rachel.

Why had she ever thought he would? She could change what she wore and ride a motorcycle, but she was still just Rachel.

But no. She'd had interest from a couple of guys at those singles events. She was interesting, at least interesting enough for some people.

Just not for Ryker. At least, not enough to stay. Not enough to work through difficult things. She wasn't an idiot; she knew he came with problems. Problems that would take a lot to resolve.

She could help people in town see how he'd changed, but she couldn't make him see himself. And she could only help as much as he'd allow.

He wasn't allowing anything now.

Mariah had a new project for the town, making a video series about the renovation of the mill, something to keep people interested in what was going on in Carter's Crossing. No, the renovated mill was for Cupid's Crossing. The singles idea would have to wait.

Rachel was relieved.

With a six-week countdown to Jaycee's wedding, the clock was ticking, and Rachel threw herself into helping with plans. She sent out her résumé to several places in towns a few hours' drive away. She started looking at apartment listings. She got together with some of her new friends from singles nights, though she begged off attending another singles event because there was no point.

No point in looking at other men, not right now.

She refused to let herself cry. Crying would mean that she'd felt something real for Ryker and she couldn't allow that. She would cop to being a pushover, to being nice, to trying to earn affection and attention by helping people. She was not stupid, though, and falling in love with a man who'd never even asked her out, and who'd twice fled after she kissed him, was beyond stupid.

She wasn't stupid. She wasn't. And if sometimes, late at night she suspected her intelligence might be overrated, she got up and searched for more jobs and apartments because she was *not* going to cry.

She was doing so well that she almost convinced herself. Then came the news.

Rachel had been out of town for dress fittings. With the last-minute nature of Jaycee's wedding, the bridesmaids had had to scavenge for dresses in the right color. At least style-wise they could do as they wished.

She and Mariah and Jaycee had gone shopping together, and they'd all found dresses. The right shade of blue and cocktail length. Since the wedding was on the Fourth of July, it was going to be hot. Rachel didn't know if it was Mariah's doing, but she was grateful to whoever decided against floor-length gowns.

Rachel's dress had to be taken in a little. She hadn't been eating much lately.

Mariah was checking out the three of them in the mirrors in their tacked-up dresses.

"Have you heard about a job yet?" She turned those searching eyes on Rachel, who promptly pretended to examine her own reflection.

"I have an interview next week."

"That's awesome!" Jaycee swirled on her stand, floating on a wave of bliss and chiffon.

Rachel shrugged. "They might need someone before the wedding, so I wouldn't be able to take it. If they even offer me the job."

"Rachel!" Rachel turned at the note of command in Jaycee's voice. "We can do this without you being on-site. Mariah has everything under control. If this is your dream job, you take it and we'll work it out."

She tilted her head.

"Have you told your father and uncle yet?"

Rachel shook her head. "No one knows but you guys." And Ryker, but that didn't matter because he wasn't around. "I'm going to tell them when it's a done deal. After all, you don't tell your boss you're leaving till you have your new job, right? My boss just happens to be my uncle. I'll make sure he finds some help before I go."

When she left, that help wasn't going to cover for him, and she'd decided that was a good thing. It was.

"And your dad?"

"He's my landlord."

"He's more than that," Jaycee admonished softly.

Rachel deflated. "I know. But he's going to make me feel guilty, even if it's not on purpose. I'm a coward, but..."

"Come here." Jaycee waved her hands at Rachel, until Rachel was right in front of her. Jaycee grabbed Rachel's hands and squeezed them. "You're going to leave this town, where you've lived all your life, to find the life you want. That's brave. If it's better to tell your dad later, then that's fine.

"You always do things for other people. If we can help you with this, just say the word. Well, as long as it's not the week before or after the Fourth of July, but once Dave and I are back, we'll help you pack, move, tell your dad, whatever."

Rachel felt the tears threatening but fought them back. She'd been on the verge of crying for days now, and she was afraid that once she started, she'd never stop. If she was going to break down, it wouldn't be in the dressing room of a bridal salon.

Leaving was necessary, or she'd never find the life she wanted. But it was also hard.

Mariah reached an arm around Rachel's waist and pulled her tight. "Same here. But if either of you mess up your dresses…"

They broke apart with a laugh, and Rachel was in control of herself again. Friends. Friends were awesome. And she was lucky to have them. She was going to miss them when she was gone.

She'd find a boyfriend after she left. After all, it wasn't like there was any future for her with Ryker even if he had liked her. He wasn't staying in Cupid's Crossing. He wasn't staying anywhere. He'd take off on his bike, free to work from anywhere he wanted.

In fact, that was what he'd done. Left her behind.

ON THE WAY HOME she got a call from her dad. The news was bad. He normally was calm and reassuring in those events.

This one he was having trouble handling. Her uncle had been in an automobile accident.

He was in the hospital, and her father wasn't sure what his prognosis was. Her dad sounded dazed, not like the pastor who'd been through many hospital visits over the years. It didn't sound good.

Rachel promised to come immediately. Her hands trembled, and her mind spun between worry and guilt and fear.

There was no black ice, not this time of year. The roads were clear. Had Uncle Stanley been drinking? Could she have prevented this?

Mariah redirected her vehicle and let Rachel out at the front of the hospital. She and Jaycee offered to come in with her, but she sent them on home. She would have her dad with her, and they could support each other. Until she knew more, she didn't want to have them wasting their time.

Rachel promised to let them know what was

going on, and they'd come back with provisions, if it was going to be a long stay. Rachel rushed in the front door.

She'd been here with her dad many times, so she knew where to go. Somehow, though, the corridors were longer, and her feet had difficulty handling the smooth floors. She gave her uncle's name and was directed to the ER. There she found her father.

He looked confused and distraught. She sat down beside him and grabbed his hand.

"What happened, Dad? How is he?"

"He's...well, in one way he's okay. He only had a few cuts, and they gave him stitches."

Rachel's shoulders dropped down a couple of inches as the tension dissipated.

"Okay, that's great. How's his car? What happened? Can we see him?"

Her father shook his head.

"The police took him away, just now."

The tension ratcheted back up. She was afraid to ask, sure of the answer.

"Why?"

"He was drunk. He was driving drunk, and he hit someone."

Rachel closed her eyes. One of her worst fears come true.

"You were right, Rachel." Her dad was now gripping her hand so hard it almost hurt. "You told me about his drinking, and I didn't listen to you. This is my fault."

Rachel was vindicated, but she couldn't enjoy it. And her dad was wrong about one thing. She'd learned a bit from hovering around the AA and Al-Anon meetings. She reminded herself as well as him.

"No, Dad. This is his fault. I talked to him, and he wouldn't listen. I should have maybe done a little less at the office so that other people knew he had a problem, or he hit his rock bottom."

Her father closed his eyes. "I think this is rock bottom. He hit a motorcycle, and I don't know if the young man will survive. We'll get the prayer tree going as soon as we get home—"

Rachel felt ice spearing down her spine, radiating out to her limbs. Her heart beat heavy and slow. There were many people who rode bikes, and most of them were young men, but she knew. Somehow, she knew it was Ryker before she asked.

"Who was it? Who did he hit?"

Her dad turned grief-stricken eyes her way. "Someone from Carter's. It's one of the Slade boys."

RACHEL WASN'T SURE what happened next; it was all a blur. She must have responded to her father, and she must have gone through the motions of getting information at the hospital. The details were lost, until she found herself upstairs in ICU, looking through a glass window at Ryker.

His face had some bruising, but his helmet had done its job. The rest of him was covered in bandages, and his right leg was in a cast. There were machines hooked up to him and there was talk about internal injuries.

She couldn't process it. Just that Ryker was hurt, her uncle had caused it and there was nothing she could do but pray.

She couldn't even go in the room and touch him, to be sure he truly was alive. It was only because it was a small hospital, and who her dad was that she was able to do this.

She wanted to offer bargains to God. She'd stay in Cupid's Crossing and spend her life working on the bazaar. If that wouldn't cover it, she could do something to hurt herself to offset his pain. She wanted to scream or cry, do something to release the agony that was pushing out the previous numbness.

Right now, though, her body refused to listen to any commands. She stood there, staring through the glass, unable to fully grasp that Ryker was hurt.

He'd gone through two tours of duty, and

now he was hurt because her uncle refused to acknowledge he had a drinking problem. Rachel hadn't forced him to face it. And now Ryker was paying.

But Rachel was paying, too. Because she couldn't argue that she hadn't fallen in love with him. Not now. The pain she felt, while it might not have a physical source, was too real, too strong, too debilitating.

She'd trade places with him in a heartbeat. He didn't feel the same about her, and would be embarrassed if she told him, but it didn't change a thing.

She stood and watched.

Her father had been there, had said something to her about leaving or eating, but she'd ignored him. Nurses had finally forced her to go sit in a chair in a waiting room. They promised to let her know if anything changed. There was no one else to tell.

She'd thought this feeling might just be a crush, and if she got to know Ryker better, it would pass. Then, when that didn't happen and her feelings grew, she'd thought she might have a little heartbreak when she left but that she'd get over it, and it would make her a more interesting person.

Hard to believe just how wrong she'd been.

Was this fate? Had there been something

about Ryker, even back in high school, that had been it for her? Or had that just been a crush, and these past few weeks had taken the crush and matured it into love?

Did it much matter? She was still here, gutted over a man who didn't feel the same about her. But she didn't care about that, not now. She had to know he would be okay. She might never see him again, and if that was the cost of her bargain with God, she'd live with it.

He deserved better.

After some time, she wasn't sure how long, they told her he was going to make it. She went to see him through the window one last time. He looked to be the same to her.

Still, there was nothing left for her here. Ryker would recover, and he wouldn't want her to be there. So she wouldn't be.

She called Jaycee, who came and picked her up and drove her home. She told her dad that Ryker should make it. She didn't ask about her uncle. She had no further capacity for compassion. She went to her room and collapsed, fully dressed on her bed.

She finally cried.

RYKER CAME TO, knowing something was very wrong, but not sure what it was.

He hurt. Almost everywhere.

There were strange sounds. The smells were strong and antiseptic, and there was constant noise. He wasn't in his apartment over Gifford's. He wasn't in any place he could remember being before.

He couldn't open his eyes.

Someone came in the room, picked up his hand and took his pulse. That, he could understand.

He was in the hospital.

He didn't remember why. But it explained the pain, the sounds...the smells.

He finally willed his eyelids open.

"Nice to see your eyes open, Mr. Slade. Do you know where you are?"

The woman was wearing scrubs. She had a stethoscope and some kind of name tag. He didn't try to read it, didn't care if she was a doctor or nurse.

Her question. Right. He opened his mouth, had to clear his throat before he could get the word *hospital* out. It came out rough.

"Good. Can you tell me your name and what year it is?"

He gritted out the answers, then asked his own question.

"What happened?"

"You were in an accident."

His brows pressed down. An accident?

"You were on a motorcycle. I'm not a proponent of motorcycle riding, but at least you had a good helmet on. You were hit by a car. His fault, not yours.

"You had some internal bleeding, and we had to remove your spleen. Also, your leg was fractured in several places. You're going to be uncomfortable for a while."

He gave a short nod. He was definitely uncomfortable.

"We're going to move you out of the ICU now. There's a button by your hand you can push if you need anything. You should make a full recovery, so I'm going to get back to the patients who need me more urgently right now."

He looked up. She had circles under her eyes, lines bracketing her mouth. She looked tired.

"Thank you," he rasped.

"You're welcome. I'll see you later."

He closed his eyes for a moment.

He didn't need to push the button, because there was nothing he needed that they could get for him. Nothing that he wanted, either, because what he wanted was something he didn't deserve.

While he'd been away, he accepted how he felt about Rachel. He'd kissed her, not merely because he hadn't wanted to put that disappointed look on her face, but because he wanted to. He wanted kissing, and time together, and a home. And because of that, he needed to let her find it with someone who deserved her.

He shoved the unwelcome thought away and tried not to think. At some point he stopped thinking, sleep taking over.

HE WAS IN AND OUT of consciousness, his memory telling him about people taking his pulse and temperature and blood pressure and asking him questions he often ignored. When he finally came to, fully aware of who and where he was and what had happened to him, it was daylight. His eyes squinted, getting used to the glare coming in through the windows of his room.

There was someone sitting in the chair beside his bed. Not a nurse, or doctor, or anyone in scrubs.

It was Rachel.

Rachel.

His stress dropped, and he felt lighter. He felt...whole.

The pain level didn't change, and the room was still too bright. But seeing her was good. It was right.

His eyes moved over her face, drinking it in. She had those shadows under her eyes, like the doctor had. She was staring at the phone on her lap, complexion pale, hair drawn back.

Her sparkle was gone, but at least she was there.

Did he do that?

His happy left. She wasn't for him. He cared for her too much to take advantage of her generous nature. He'd changed, but he couldn't erase the past. He was still an alcoholic. He was still the guy who'd been married twice. She deserved someone as shiny and bright as she was.

He hadn't thought he'd see her again. He'd planned not to, for her own good. He'd planned to double down on finishing the house and leaving. But this was something he had no control over, so he was going to add it to his memories.

He wasn't sure if he should be upset or relieved if he was the reason she looked so sad. He was still a little confused, memories soft around the edges of his consciousness. He knew Rachel was better off without him, but he was selfish enough to hope she wouldn't get over him too easily.

More evidence that he didn't deserve her.

Suddenly, her eyes were locked on his.

They widened, and then her whole expression shut down.

Yes, he'd done that.

He couldn't really have expected a warm welcome. He'd kissed her, torn away on his bike and never reached out to her.

"You're awake." Starting with the obvious. "Are you in a lot of pain?"

He shook his head. The pain in his body was manageable.

"I need to talk to you."

He wanted to shake his head again, refuse to discuss this with her. There was nothing pleasant they could have to talk about, not after what he'd done.

But he owed her, so he clenched his jaw and waited for whatever she needed to say.

"My uncle is the driver who ran into you on your bike."

He blinked. That wasn't what he'd expected.

"The lawyer?" He wasn't sure if she had other uncles.

She nodded. "He was drunk."

Oh, lovely irony. The sober alcoholic hit by the drunk one. Fourteen years ago he'd been the one driving drunk.

"He's entirely at fault. He failed the Breathalyzer, badly. He's now in a rehab facility."

She wasn't looking directly at him, not anymore. She was staring over his shoulder at one of the machines they kept in the room to monitor his condition.

Was she only here to try to get him to sign something?

His mood nose-dived.

"All your hospital bills and rehab are covered. I know it isn't enough to make up for what he did, but you should know that financial issues will not be a problem for you."

He hadn't thought that far ahead yet. But it would be a relief. As a freelancer, he didn't have an employer's health program to cover him.

He wondered if Rachel had strong-armed her uncle to do this. He didn't know her uncle, but he didn't think philanthropy would have been his thing. Drinking was your thing if you were an alcoholic.

"Do you have any questions about that? Your hospital bill is covered, and there's an amount for loss of income. Your therapy is covered until you're able to resume your normal activities."

He wished she'd look at him. But again, he was relieved she didn't. He didn't want to see pain in her eyes, and he didn't want to see them blank and cold. He didn't think any other expression would be directed his way.

"Did you make him do this?"

Her lips tightened. "My father has his power of attorney. My uncle isn't able to make decisions now. My father is horrified and feeling guilty."

Part of Ryker wanted to refuse the assistance. Part of him knew that was a gesture he couldn't afford.

Rachel might not admit to being behind this, but he was sure she had been an influence. This wasn't costing her, not financially, so it would be cruel to refuse. He'd been cruel enough.

And you need the money.

"Thank you."

She raised her face to him for a moment, eyes wide again.

"Okay." She bit her lip. "There's one more thing."

He could feel his body tensing, adrenaline urging him to fight or flee. He couldn't do either. He was going to lie here and take whatever reprisal she wanted to give him.

Her gaze was focused behind him again.

"I wanted to talk to you about us. That kiss."

Despite the dry throat, he tried to stop her. "You don't—"

"Please, Ryker. I have something to say."

He released his clenched fists and waited.

"You probably knew I had a crush on you back in high school."

Yeah, I knew.

He nodded, but he wasn't sure she saw.

"You were the first guy to kiss me. And I know it didn't mean anything to you, but—"

"No."

That got her glance back his way.

"It did mean something. But I was bad news, Rachel. I was going nowhere. I wasn't going to take you down with me. I knew you had a crush, but you didn't know the real me."

Her lips twisted.

"You're right. I didn't know you, not very well. I made up a character from what I did know. Is the kiss why you stopped coming to tutoring?"

He nodded. She didn't need to know he'd stopped coming to school because of that, as well. She'd take on that burden, like she took on so many.

A small smile quirked up one corner of her mouth. "Good to know I wasn't that bad a kisser."

His breath caught. Had he really done that to her?

What did you expect?

She focused back on her prepared speech.

"Anyway, when you came back, well, that

crush came back. But I knew I didn't know you, so I thought if I spent time with you, I'd get past that."

He should be happy about that. It was exactly what he'd thought, and it was the best thing for her. But *happy* was not the way this was making him feel.

"I want to thank you—you were a lot of help to me. It wasn't just the bike lessons, though I want to keep learning."

A quick glance his way.

"Oh, maybe that wasn't the right thing to say right now."

He shook his head. Anyone who didn't acknowledge the risks of bike riding had no reason to ride. Right now he wasn't sure if he'd be back on his bike—

His bike was probably gone. Destroyed. Good thing he had insurance.

He swallowed.

"It's okay, Rachel. Just be careful."

"Anyway, you opened my eyes to more things than motorcycles. I wasn't happy with my life, and some of that was my own fault. I realize now that I am a valuable person even if I'm not helping someone. They'll still be my friend. If I need help, I should ask for it. And it's okay to say no.

"That's all stuff I should have known but you made it real for me. So thank you for that."

"Rachel—" She was gutting him. Thanking him for doing nothing? She'd helped him, more than anything he could have done for her, and she should know that.

She held up her hand.

"I'm almost done. With all that, I got to know you better. And my crush wasn't any longer on an imaginary character. I got to know you, and I liked you."

She closed her eyes.

"No, it was more than like. I fell in love with you."

Her hand was up again, as if she expected him to interrupt. But he could only think to tell her she was wrong; she couldn't love him.

I'm not worth it.

"I didn't plan on it. If I was listing my perfect guy, I wouldn't have picked an alcoholic with two ex-wives. I mean, I've heard enough setting up those AA meetings, and I've seen too many couples come to my dad for counseling or my uncle for a divorce.

"I'm not stupid. I know those things have messed you up, but they've also made you strong. Kind. More than you know.

"And I know I scared you with how I responded to that kiss. I'm not super experienced, and you could tell how I felt, I'm sure. I understand why you left like that, but it hurt."

He closed his own eyes because he hadn't wanted to hurt her. He'd known he had, though. He had been scared, but not for the reasons she thought.

"But you did the right thing."

He had, but he hated that she knew it.

"Because this thing I feel for you, it's more than I expected. It's big, and it's strong and it kind of scares me. And since you don't feel the same, I needed to know, because this new Rachel isn't settling anymore.

"If you need something, connected to your hospital stay or rehab, let me know, but otherwise, I can't be your friend, Ryker. I'm sorry. You have Benny and Mr. G and I hope you find other people, but I have to take care of me first.

"I still wish all the best for you. I want you to make a full recovery. I hope you get the house sold and find what you want from life. And don't give up on love, either. You have a lot to offer."

He opened his eyes again, but she was already leaving the room. He had an urge to follow her, his hand moving to wrench out his IV, when his brain caught up and made him pause.

What would he say to her? That he was a bad bet, that his sobriety was still a thing he had to fight to maintain every day? That there was something lacking, because women didn't stay with him, and he couldn't bear for her to discover what it was that was wrong with him?

He needed to let her go. It was the right thing to do. If you loved someone, you did what was best for them. And sometimes, even a Slade could do the right thing.

CHAPTER SEVENTEEN

BENNY CAME TO pick up Ryker in his van when Ryker was finally released from the hospital. Ryker was finding life on crutches to be awkward and tiring. He thanked Benny for taking the trouble.

"Of course. I'm glad to have you back. There's work piling up for you."

Benny squinched up his face. "Oh, when you can, obviously, no pressure. I wasn't supposed to mention work. Forget I said anything."

Ryker was still on pain meds, though he was cutting them back as much as possible. He was concerned about the addiction angle, considering his alcoholism, but the meds also blurred his focus. It sounded like someone had told Benny how to treat him. He was pretty sure his doctor wasn't supposed to talk to anyone else about his posthospital care, so he didn't know what was going on.

"Who told you that?"

"Um, Rachel. She was setting everything up for you."

Rachel. He was torn between asking Benny never to mention her name again and asking for every detail about her.

Just because he knew he wasn't good for her didn't mean he didn't appreciate her.

That's what it is? Really?

He hoped his accident hadn't set up that voice in his head permanently.

"What did she do?"

So far, he hadn't had to reach out to her, but other than the hospital bill, which had been taken care of, he hadn't been in a situation to need her help. He'd known it would be a pain to get up the stairs to his place, but once he got up, he could stay there most of the time. He'd planned to borrow Benny's van when he needed to get something or ask Benny to pick up some food for him.

It shouldn't surprise him that Rachel hadn't waited for him to ask.

Benny shot him a glance as Ryker settled himself into the passenger seat and slid the crutches down the middle of the van between the seats.

"Well, there was some little stuff. Groceries. A cart so you can push things around up there—you know, cup of coffee, laptop—anything you can't carry now that you're on crutches."

Okay, that was thoughtful and not too big a deal.

"The handrails in the tub. The stool for the shower."

Right. The hospital had mentioned something like that, but he'd planned to worry about that later. He'd just wanted out.

Rachel had taken care of a lot of things.

Like that was a surprise.

"And, well, there's the chair thing that goes up the stairs to your place."

Ryker turned to Benny, who was now driving out of the hospital parking lot.

"What?"

"It's great—I tried it out. If you move out, I might see if I could live up there. Well, probably not, because if something happened to it, I'd be stuck, but I could come up and visit you. Make sure you're good."

"That's… It's—"

"Awesome? Too much? Ryker, people feel bad that this happened to you."

Ryker shook his head. "Stuff happens."

"Yeah, but right now a lot of people are upset this happened to you."

It was hard to be shocked by the crappy things life could throw at you after you'd drawn the short stick and been born a Slade. It was the good things that surprised him. And people in this town upset that he'd been hurt? By the town lawyer? That was a surprise.

"Well, a lot of stuff has happened to you, and it's time some of it was good. I'm glad, because I'd rather have you working on those computers than wasting all your time pulling yourself up and down the stairs."

Benny winced.

"Don't tell Rachel I mentioned work again. Really, your recovery is more important. Just ignore me."

Ryker didn't think he needed to worry about telling Rachel anything. She'd made it clear she didn't want to see him again.

"It's okay, Benny. I spent too long in the hospital with nothing to do except sleep. I need something to keep me from climbing the walls."

They pulled into the parking lot at Gifford's. Benny came to a stop by the bottom of the stairs to Ryker's place.

There was a metal track going up the side of the stairs, and it supported a moveable seat.

"Seriously?" Ryker asked.

"Yeah. It's supposed to save you from walking up and down the stairs."

Ryker thought it looked incredibly lame. But Rachel had done this. For him. He'd give it a try.

Benny had made his way into the back of

the van and hit the buttons to open the rear door where the lift was for his chair. Normally, Ryker would help with Benny's chair, but he couldn't now. His hands were tied up with his crutches.

This cast could not come off soon enough.

When Benny made his way out, he wheeled over to the staircase, Ryker following behind awkwardly on the crutches.

Fortunately, he didn't have anything to carry. His helmet had done its job to protect his head, but it was now too badly damaged to be worn again. His clothing had been cut off him. He suspected Rachel had either brought the spare clothes to his hospital room or arranged for someone else to do so.

Benny showed him how the stair chair worked. With a sigh, Ryker sat on the seat and endured Benny watching him with a smirk as he pushed the buttons to make it rise.

Once he'd made it to the top, he stood back up on his crutches, and Benny waved before wheeling himself toward his own quarters.

Ryker opened the door and crutched in. He wouldn't admit it, but the ride home had exhausted him. The stair chair might be odd, but right now he was grateful even for that.

His place was clean. Cleaner than he remembered leaving it. He made his way into the kitchenette and found his fridge stocked with ready-to-heat meals. He grabbed a water bottle, about all he could carry while on crutches, and noted the little cart by the table. It had a handle he could push and wheels, to make it easy to move around the place.

He hobbled to the couch and threw himself down. It was a relief not to have the crutches under his armpits. His hands were no longer calloused, and his palms were sore.

These next weeks until the cast came off were going to suck. It was going to be a while.

Which meant he was staying in Cupid's Crossing for the foreseeable future. Even without a cast, he'd lost his transportation. But for the first time, despite what he'd been through, staying here felt okay. It felt good.

And most of that was down to Rachel, whom he'd hurt. Hopefully, by the time he was mobile again, she'd have left town, because he needed to start not missing her.

He raised his legs, including the heavy, awkward cast, onto the couch. He grabbed the remote, and before he'd finished his water, had fallen asleep in front of the TV.

RACHEL'S LIFE WAS flipped upside down.

It wasn't just because of Ryker. No, actually it was. She wasn't the same as she'd been.

She'd planned to change things before he returned, but his return had made those changes happen. She wasn't the same pushover, nice person she'd been.

Now his accident had changed external things, as well.

Since her uncle was in rehab, Cupid's Crossing no longer had a lawyer. There were a lot of legal issues to be dealt with. These issues weren't as simple as transferring a pile of paperwork to someone else.

It meant that Rachel was busy. Very busy. Too busy to think about Ryker…except at night when she was trying to sleep. But she let people think work was the reason for her tired looks.

She'd done more than a paralegal's job would normally entail because of her uncle's drinking anyway. His workload had been increasing with the legal demands of all the new initiatives being set up to transform the town into Cupid's Crossing. With her uncle gone, things were in chaos. Some files just needed a signature, but most of them weren't complete. As her uncle's drinking had gotten worse, so had his work habits. Documents were scattered everywhere, even digital versions were in the wrong folders. There was a lot for Rachel to deal with.

She was the only one with a hope of making heads or tails of it. Which meant plans for leaving were now on the back burner. She'd had to tell the people who'd arranged the interview that she wasn't available.

She called around the listing of local law offices to find what lawyers in the area could take on extra work, and what their rates and specialties were. She made a list of current cases. She created a rough grouping of who could go where, so that when clients called, she had a reference for them.

Her father had received a big shock. He apologized to her, several times, and asked her if he'd overlooked anything else she'd brought up.

She'd told him that she was going to need to find a new job at some point, and that would mean moving. That shocked him, as well. After he'd made a few suggestions, such as commuting from Carter's—to where?—and finding work in another field—what field was she qualified for, and would she earn as much and was there anything in that field required in Cupid's Crossing?—he'd had to face a future without his daughter.

It was making him appreciate what all Rachel did for him. Finally. And it put him on the verge of panic.

She should have been able to appreciate

finally being valued but…she shrugged and kept on.

Her experience with Ryker had even changed her dynamic with her friends.

She'd had to confess to them, since she'd been dragging herself around as if she had her own personal black cloud hovering over her. She told them about the bike lessons, their arrangement to help each other and that she'd fallen in love with him.

"I can't blame you for that." Mariah shrugged. "I mean, he's got the whole bad-boy thing down."

"But he's not!"

"I know—if I thought he really was I wouldn't have worked with him. I'm relieved that he's been getting better and started working again."

"He has?" Rachel squeezed her eyes closed. "No, don't tell me. I don't need to know. I have to move on."

"I just can't picture you and Ryker." Jaycee shook her head.

"I can." That was Mariah.

"Really?" Jaycee and Rachel echoed.

"Ryker brought you out of your regular routine, and you're better for it. You're trying new things, moving to a new place and hey, you were really brave to talk to Ryker like that."

Rachel had repeated her hospital speech the best she could remember. "That's something that's happened these past few months."

Jaycee frowned. "But…he's a Slade."

"That's not fair, Jaycee!" Rachel was angry with her friend. "Dave's mom is horrible, right? But you don't blame Dave for that."

"I know, but remember what Ryker was like? He crashed a stolen car into a tree while he was drunk."

The sound Rachel made was scarily close to a growl. "That was fourteen years ago. He's not the same guy. He served in the air force—two tours. Maybe you should cut him some slack!"

"See?" Mariah said. "Rachel is more fired up than I've ever seen her. And Ryker has changed. I mean, that talk he gave to the high school. I heard from a lot of people about that—they were impressed."

Jaycee shrugged. "Okay, I admit I should give him a chance. He did a good job on Moonstone's computer when I had to call him in."

Rachel glared at her.

Jaycee raised her hands. "I get it! Sorry. It's just those Slade kids were all trouble."

"They had a crappy time in that house, Jaycee. You guys might not have had a lot of money, but you had food, you weren't beaten and you had security that those kids never did."

"Okay, okay, I'm a horrible person, and I'll do better. Cross my heart and pinkie swear. But please, can we just take a bit of time to make sure the wedding is going okay?"

"You mean, since your evil M-I-L insists that your brother-in-law be in the wedding party and now you're short a bridesmaid?"

Jaycee sighed. "I knew she was going to do something. I mean, beyond saying big weddings are tacky and hating the colors and..."

Rachel gave Jaycee's hand a squeeze.

Mariah sat up with a smirk on her face. "I talked to the dress shop where we got our dresses, to see what sizes they had in sample bridesmaid dresses in the same blue as we've got, and using that information, and a list of women you are friends with...what about Andrea?"

Jaycee considered. "I don't know her that well."

"She was a good friend of Dave's sister, so she knows Dave's brother-in-law, if you pair them up for the wedding. I've been working with her on the mill, and I admire her a lot. Heading up a construction company isn't easy for a woman, so I like her moxie."

"You know, Dave's mom couldn't complain since she's a friend of Dave's sister, but she won't like Andie because of her job." Rachel nudged Jaycee.

Jaycee squealed. "Rachel, I like this snarky side you've got coming out. I'll talk to Andrea."

She reached to hug both Rachel and Mariah.

"I promise, once this wedding is over, and we're back from our honeymoon, I'm going to properly thank you two. Dave's mom invited his dad's boss to come to the wedding, so that is the official seal of approval from Mommie Dearest."

"Isn't that going to put out your count?"

"No, Dave had already marked them down as coming. His mother didn't know, though, so while I suspect she liked the thought of causing me trouble, she must think the wedding is going to be good enough to impress them. And it is."

Mariah nodded calmly. "It's going to be incredible. That's what I do."

RYKER HAD FORGOTTEN how much healing took out of a body. And getting older made it worse.

As his body recovered from the trauma, and he had more energy, he slept less. That gave him more time to think and remember. He worked as much as he could, but there was still too much time to think about Rachel.

He knew he'd made the right decision, for her, but it sucked that he'd hurt her. He hadn't expected that she'd feel…that strongly. He'd underestimated her, like everyone else did.

He hadn't understood how much it was going to cost him, as well.

Carter's Crossing was not a place he'd wanted to come to. He'd been fortunate to make some friends here. Benny and Mr. G hadn't just provided him with a place to live and a job, they'd also become friends. Before the accident he had found himself stopping in at the shop every day, to check on work and talk to Benny.

Mr. G was at every AA meeting. And after, it had become a standing date to go out for coffee.

He wasn't best friends with most of the town, but after helping Rachel at the church, and giving his speech to the school, he didn't get those looks anymore. Not from everyone. There were still people who saw him as one of the Slades and always would. But others were pleasant or sometimes smiled with apparent sincerity.

Jean, at the diner, had brought him his coffee without a sniff, sigh or slam. And it had been from the fresh pot. Mr. G explained that her son had enlisted after Ryker's talk. He'd been starting down a path similar to Ryker's and Benny's.

Which meant his speech had reached someone. That felt...good.

Then there were the people in town who needed computer help. Those people waved and greeted him happily.

Most of the people opening up B and Bs in the town were older, and not very tech savvy. Ryker had started with Mavis Grisham. Except for her Great Dane, who had wanted to sniff his crotch all the time, he'd enjoyed taking the photos for her house, advising her how to make the most of what she had to offer and showing her how to run her website.

He made sure Tiny, the Great Dane, wasn't in any of the photos. He didn't agree with her belief that he would be a selling factor.

He'd looked up the organizations for B and Bs for the state and given her that list. She'd sent him home with pie and patted his hand whenever she saw him.

He had a few more to get set up, people who'd been reluctant to work with him because of his last name. Now they needed his help. He didn't blame them, but he was human enough to enjoy that they had to wait to reap the rewards of an online presence until he could get around better.

He'd put down roots here. And now that people didn't look at him like he was…well, a Slade, he was less eager to leave.

He was surprised at how lonely he found the time in his apartment. He had become used to solitude, after he'd stopped drinking and no longer had those superficial friends. For those first weeks in Carter's he'd enjoyed having the place to himself. Now he was getting cabin fever. He actually…wanted to be around people.

Not only was getting around awkward, he didn't have his bike to provide transportation, if he'd been able to ride it. Benny would let him use the van, which he could drive with the handicapped controls, but Ryker wouldn't presume unless he needed to go for food or a doctor's appointment. Something essential.

And he was still weaker than he wanted to be.

The person he missed most was Rachel. He hadn't realized how much she'd become part of his life until he'd excised her. He emailed her his thanks for her and her family's help, but her reply had been brief. She hadn't encouraged a response.

That was what he'd wanted, or at least, what he knew was best. This time alone, with little to do but work and sleep and try to engage with online entertainment, exposed how much he'd grown to care for her.

Care for her? Sure, call it that.

Thanks to that annoying voice in his head, he'd finally admitted to himself that he'd fallen in love with her. It wasn't a surprise. It was more surprising to him that more men hadn't.

But that only reinforced his determination to do what was best for her. Ryker Slade wasn't the best for anyone, let alone Rachel.

One morning, feeling especially morbid, but fortunately less tired, he filled a computer bag with the couple of laptops he'd cleaned up—including his most frequent subject, the laptop again full of viruses—and threw it over his shoulder. He had a pair of shorts on, loose enough to fit over his cast, and a T-shirt. Spring had finally rounded the corner to summer, and jackets were no longer needed.

Just as well, since his was gone.

He crutched out of the door and sat on the stair chair that he was finally getting accustomed to. He let it lower him down the stairs, and then made his way to Gifford's front door. Of course, it had a button he could push, opening the door automatically and allowing him to make his way in.

Ryker had a new appreciation for accessibility these days.

Benny looked up from his workbench.

"Hey, man. Good to see you. How are you doing?" Benny raised a hand. "No, for real, how's it going?"

Ryker hitched his way around the corner and set the bag on the table that Benny had allocated for computer work. He rested against the table, weight on his good foot, crutches set aside.

"I'm surviving."

Benny shrugged. "Some days, that's all you get."

"I was getting tired of my own company, so I came down to see what was going on."

"You're always welcome, and you can drive the van if you need to get out."

"I appreciate the offer. I think I'm good—there's still a lot of food up there."

Benny shook his head. "We're going to miss Rachel when she's gone."

Ryker couldn't move. He hadn't been prepared for talk of Rachel. He swallowed and struggled to sound normal.

"She's leaving?"

Benny shot him a glance. "She worked for her uncle, and, as you know, he's not practicing right now. There's not another lawyer in town for her to work for, and I expect she'll be glad to leave."

She did want to leave, Ryker knew.

"She does a lot for this place."

Benny nodded. "After my accident I ended up one of those sideline people, you know? I couldn't do much, so I watched from the sidelines. Overlooked. Rachel was one of those people, too. Always ready to reach out, the kind of person who noticed when someone needed help. I think it was a result of her mom dying."

Ryker frowned. He'd known her mother had died, but he didn't know the details.

"When did her mother die? What happened?"

Benny's eyebrows shot up. "You don't know? Rachel was twelve, I think. Her mother was a really nice woman, I heard. A lot like Rachel—always helping people. When her mom died, I think Rachel stepped up to take her place, the best she could."

And everyone let her, Ryker thought. Benny continued.

"My mom died when I wasn't much older. I remember Rachel brought us food, offered to talk to us if we wanted. Her mom died of breast cancer, mine of ovarian cancer. So we had that in common.

"I didn't talk to her—too focused on not

letting anyone know I was hurting. My dad started drinking. I started to get in trouble—it wasn't a great time.

"But Rachel would stop by with cake from time to time—and she wasn't that much older than me. After the accident, when Dad got this place set up for me, she stocked up the place with everything I'd need. It was the church, in theory, who set me up, but I know she did most of the work."

Ryker nodded. That was exactly what Rachel would do. And why it was good for her to leave.

"I was glad you were giving her bike lessons," Benny continued. "Well, maybe I should have been more worried about accidents, but it was something she was doing for herself. And you guys seemed… Okay, none of my business, but I thought maybe you guys were a thing."

A thing. Yeah, whatever they'd been was as vague as that description, *a thing*.

"We were friends."

Right.

"Were? I haven't seen Rachel's car out there, and friends would visit, right?"

Ryker started to reach for his crutches but halted. "Yeah, we're not a *thing* anymore."

Benny's eyes expressed sympathy. "Cause of this mess with her uncle?"

"No!" Ryker would never hold her uncle's behavior to her account. "That's nothing to do with her. It…we…before the accident."

"You mean, when you ghosted out of here for a few days?"

Ryker kept his gaze on the ground. "Yeah. I kissed her. So I had to leave."

"I would do some squealing here, because I called it, but obviously, something went wrong."

"Of course it did. This is me, one of the Slades. I'm not exactly Rachel's type."

Benny held up a hand. "Whoa, wait. Are you telling me Rachel thought she was too good for you? Rachel?"

"She is too good for me."

A moment of silence. "Ah. This isn't a Rachel thing. It's a stupid Ryker thing."

"You have a lot of *things* going on in that head of yours."

Benny sighed. "Okay, you have your own issues. I get it. But I'm going to say my piece. I don't think people around here know the real Rachel. Rachel's been put in a box for a long time now, and she didn't even try to get out. But lately, lately she's changed up how she looks, she's learning to drive a motorcycle and some of the old biddies were complaining that she wasn't going to do the fall bazaar. It was like she finally figured out what she wanted and started getting it.

"I thought you were part of that. But I guess you see her in that same box everyone else does, and you don't want to let her get what she wants."

Ryker could do a good "don't mess with me" face, and he employed it now.

"No, that's not right. I'm glad she's not letting people take advantage of her. But I don't want to take advantage of her, either."

"Rachel is a lot stronger than anyone thinks."

The face was not working the way it normally did, because Benny was totally ignoring it. Ryker pushed himself up on his good foot. "I know she is."

"No, you don't," Benny growled at him. "Or you wouldn't be making decisions for her."

Ryker grabbed his crutches and swiveled to the door. He used the end of a crutch to activate the automatic door. Waiting for it to open took a lot of the zest out of the gesture of storming out.

He left all the computer stuff behind. He

wanted to take off on his bike for a ride. Or get a drink. Or go for a run.

All he could do was ride the stupid chair rail up to his own place so he could brood in peace.

CHAPTER EIGHTEEN

RYKER NEEDED A MEETING, and he needed not to run into Rachel. Fortunately, Mr. G was willing to drive him over to Oak Hill. No questions asked.

Ryker was getting better with the crutches, but still found the hassle involved with doing the simplest things frustrating. On the other hand, everything was frustrating him right now.

And why was that?

"Oh, shut up," he grumbled as he pulled himself up on his crutches.

"Sorry, what was that?" Mr. G looked startled.

Ryker took a breath. "No, I'm sorry. Just talking to myself."

"If you're telling yourself to shut up, then maybe you need this meeting more than I realized."

Ryker knew Benny had been talking to his father. Ryker was rethinking the benefit of friends right now. The good kind who hung around when things were messed up—the kind he'd never had before. Now they cared enough to give him a hard time.

This church was fully accessible, and Ryker was able to crutch up a ramp to get inside. There was an elevator to help him to the basement, but he refused to take advantage. The extra effort of working down the stairs both soothed and irritated him.

He needed to get to his meeting and get off the crutches. He'd bypass the coffee, because what he needed most now was to quiet his brain.

He should have known better. Things never worked out.

He hit the last step and turned, following the signs, counting down till he could sit in the room and focus, when he saw her.

He froze, absolutely unable to process at first that she was really there in the hallway in front of him, not some hallucination his twisted mind had dreamed up.

Hey!

Then she turned and saw him.

He was right there, with a front-row seat to watch her response.

First, he noticed the circles under her eyes, the slumped shoulders, the sparkle gone from her face. All the signs that things were not going well with Rachel.

Of course they weren't. Her uncle was in rehab, and her life must be upended.

Then, recognition. And instead of disgust, her face lit up, happy to see him.

Then, when he didn't move, had who knows what expression on his face, the light left. Her expression closed down.

"Hi, Rachel. We didn't expect to see you here." Mr. G at least had enough on the ball to respond to her presence in a socially acceptable way, rather than staring at her like a block.

The corner of her mouth twisted as she moved her gaze to Mr. G, behind him.

"Yes, I can see that. Don't worry. I won't get in your way."

Before Mr. G could respond, she'd turned and slipped into the room beside her, the one with the sign on the door reading Al-Anon. The group she'd found for herself.

Ryker was still unable to move. He heard Mr. G, over his shoulder, let out a long breath.

"I said I wouldn't get involved, but, Ryker, I hope you know what you're doing because that girl is hurting."

As Mr. G passed him, moving toward the AA meeting ahead on the right, Ryker saw the set expression on his face.

He did know what he was doing, didn't he? Rachel deserved someone better.

And you're the one who gets to decide for her? Because you've shown how smart you are to date?

He wanted to tell that voice in his head to shut up again. Anyone would agree that Rachel deserved better.

Anyone but Benny and Mr. G, right?

He was arguing with a voice in his head. If that wasn't an indication he needed to get his butt into this meeting, he didn't know what was.

He moved forward quietly as he passed the Al-Anon doorway. He couldn't resist glancing in, needing to see Rachel, as much as it hurt him to see her sadness.

She was in the back row, and the look on her face broke his heart. Just like he'd break hers someday.

Someday has already happened, idiot.

What he wouldn't give for a drink.

"ONE WEEK. IT'S one week. How are we going to get everything done?"

Rachel tugged Jaycee's hand away from her anxious teeth. "No biting your nails."

Jaycee put her hand down.

"We're fine, Jaycee." Mariah was unbothered, calm and patient. Like she was used to this.

She was. Which was a good thing, because Jaycee had a bad case of bride nerves.

"But there's so much to do!"

Mariah put a hand on her laptop. "Everything is here, everything is assigned a time and person and everything will get done. And all the plans on the computer are backed up in the cloud, so nothing bad is going to happen."

"What if it rains?"

"The forecast is looking good so far, and we have tents."

"What if it's a thunderstorm or a tornado?"

"The church hall is our backup."

Jaycee stuck out her bottom lip. "But it won't be as pretty."

"No. But you'll still be married, Dave's family is all here to see it and then you're off on your honeymoon."

"I'm sorry." Jaycee sat down. "I'm such a mess about this."

Rachel leaned over and put a hand on Jaycee's. "What were you doing this morning?"

Jaycee shot her a look and winced. "I was at Dave's folks' place."

Mariah shook her head. "Do your best to avoid Dave's mother for the next week, okay? If she asks you questions, tell her to come to me. I can handle this. It's going to be a beautiful wedding, and you're getting a fireworks display thrown in for free."

"And then your mother-in-law is moving away, and you'll live happily ever after."

Jaycee turned wide eyes to Rachel. "That's almost mean, Rachel."

"I'll stand up for my friends."

Jaycee leaned over to give Rachel a hug. "Yes, you will, and I love you for it."

"Good." Rachel turned to look her friend in the eye. "I have one favor to ask of you."

Jaycee tilted her head. "What is it?"

"You won't just promise me?"

"I'm a nervous bride. I'm not taking any chances."

"Okay, but this is serious. I really mean this. You cannot throw me your bridal bouquet."

Jaycee paused, a guilty look on her face.

"But, Rach…"

"Jaycee, I'm not kidding. If you throw it at me, I'll walk away. I'll headbutt it to someone else or let it land on the ground. I am not catching that."

"It's not a real thing, Rach. It's just… showing everyone that you're an amazing person and someone should notice it."

"I know you'd be doing it for what you consider to be good reasons, but, Jaycee, I'm not over Ryker yet. That's going to take time."

"Stupid Ryker."

"It's not his fault, Jaycee. He didn't do anything but kiss me, once, and I took too much from that. I told him that if he didn't feel the same way, I didn't want second-best. And I meant it."

"But he made you all sad for my wedding."

"I promise I'll be happy on your wedding day, Jaycee. I'll be so happy that you and Dave are getting married. But if you throw that bouquet my way… You know what this town is like. They will go on and on about it, and I'm not ready to leave just yet. We're still working things out with the practice."

A firm in Oak Hill had worked out an arrangement to take care of the town's legal needs until they were settled or another lawyer was found. Rachel was running the office here, and twice a week a lawyer would come from Oak Hill. Rachel didn't think she could make her own plans to move until a better process was established.

She should be more frustrated by that. But she'd been changing herself, and that had changed how stifled she felt here. And, masochistic as it was, she didn't truly want to leave while Ryker was here.

Yeah, not over him yet.

Mariah put a hand on Jaycee and gave her a little shake. "We know you mean it for the best, Jaycee, but Rachel is having a tough time, so let's make things easier for her."

"Of course, if that's what you really want, Rachel. I'm still used to you not asking for anything, and we had to figure out what you really wanted. I promise, cross my heart, that I will not throw you the bouquet at my wedding."

Rachel thanked her but felt that somehow, she hadn't quite closed up all the possibilities there. Surely, Dave couldn't toss her the garter. That went to the single guys.

She didn't want to burst Jaycee's bubble, but she could not face another round of people promising to find her a nice guy. She'd found a guy. He just wasn't nice enough in his own head or didn't want a nice girl.

RYKER OPENED THE DOOR to Moonstone's and slid through on his crutches. It was the middle of the afternoon, so the place was close to empty. He'd timed it well.

Jaycee came forward from the back when she heard the door. She frowned when she saw who it was.

Despite that, he was glad to see her. He

hadn't been sure, this close to her wedding, that she'd be at the restaurant.

"Ryker."

Her voice was cool.

"Can I talk to you?"

She deliberated. "What about?"

"Rachel."

Her face pinched, but she nodded and led him to a table at the back. He sat down, resting the crutches against another chair. She appeared to wage an internal battle before she asked if he'd like some coffee.

His first instinct was to say no, but he might need the caffeine to get through this.

"I'd appreciate it."

She set a cup in front of him, just this side of a slam. The liquid sloshed to the brim, but not over.

Jaycee was good at her job.

She sat down across from him with her own cup.

"I told you not to hurt her."

He nodded.

"I didn't think it would hurt her, not that much."

Jaycee cocked an eyebrow.

"I know my flaws, Jaycee. And while Rachel sees something in me that I don't, I thought hurting her now would be better than later.

I've been divorced twice. I'm an alcoholic. Not much of a prize."

Jaycee crossed her arms. "I'm not going to argue with you."

The side of his mouth twisted. Jaycee was honest, and that was what he needed.

"I've had a couple of people telling me I shouldn't be making that decision for her."

"They have a point. So why are you here?"

Because Benny and Mr. G had made him hope.

He leaned back and sighed. He didn't want to talk about this, but he wanted to make Rachel happy. He wasn't sure why she'd picked him, but it wasn't fair to decide for her. Maybe. That indecision was why he needed an opinion from someone who knew Rachel.

"I'm asking you. You're her best friend. Should I leave her alone?"

"You need me to make up your mind?"

"I'm asking you if you believe she's better off without me. If I ask *her*…I'm pretty sure she'll say no."

"That sounds like you do think you've got something to offer."

Ryker ran his hands through his hair.

"I have something, but it's not enough. Not for her. But she thinks it is. My family has done enough selfish and destructive stuff that I don't want to add to it."

Jaycee watched him, eyes narrowed.

"You really do care. You're just trying to do what's best for her."

"Of course."

Jaycee didn't look like she thought it was obvious.

"How much do you care for her?"

His fists clenched. "Enough to walk away from the best thing that's ever happened to me."

He hated exposing himself like that. But if there was a chance that he might not have to let Rachel go, he would do it.

"You want *me* to decide if you're not good enough for Rachel?"

"No, not that. We can take that as a given."

Jaycee uncrossed her arms and leaned forward.

"Maybe you're wrong."

This time it was Ryker whose eyebrows shot up.

Jaycee sighed. "Okay, I hate to admit this, but you were good for her. I don't know exactly what you did, but after you came back and she was spending time with you, she changed. For the better. Not a big thing, but she was less… passive? I don't know exactly. But she started to stand up for herself. Like she finally thought she was worthwhile.

"We had been taking advantage of her, without realizing it."

Ryker nodded. "I don't want to do that."

"No?"

He allowed a small smile to escape. "It's not easy—she tries so hard to help everyone."

"But you have—stopped her?"

"Probably not as much as I should have."

"She needs that. She's working to take care of herself now, but I know her. It'll be hard for her to say no. She needs someone to keep an eye on her, make sure she doesn't get taken advantage of."

He nodded. "But she also will always be helping someone."

Jaycee took a long breath.

"Maybe you are good for her. She can help you and you can make sure she takes care of herself. I cannot believe I'm saying this, but you just may be the perfect guy for her. Who'd have guessed?"

He certainly hadn't. It meant he had to do the best he could with the material he had. If she was going to choose a Slade, he would make it as close to a dream come true as he could.

"If I can possibly believe that she might be

willing to settle for me, and that it wouldn't be the worst thing she could do with her life, I'd be a fool not to try. And I would do almost anything to make her happy."

Jaycee let out a long breath.

"You've convinced me, Ryker. What do you want from me?"

"I want Rachel to know I want her. I want her as much as I think she wants me. Maybe more. She needs to know how special she is, as well. She doesn't want to speak to me, I know, so I need help.

"I'm not very good at asking for help, but I'm learning. That's thanks to Rachel."

Jaycee pursed her lips. "You need to make a grand gesture."

"If that's what you want to call it."

"So what exactly do you want this gesture to say? You're sorry? You love her? You want to go out with her?"

"All of that. And more."

Jaycee's eyes lit up. "I have an idea."

JAYCEE'S WEDDING WAS BEAUTIFUL. The weather cooperated fully, providing a sunny day with enough breeze to keep the sweating down to acceptable levels. Dave and Jaycee said their vows in the town gazebo. Rachel wasn't the only one blinking back tears as the two pledged themselves to each other. She kept her thoughts firmly focused on the here and now, doing her part to hold the bouquet, adjust Jaycee's veil and follow her now-married friends over to the gardens for pictures.

At the wedding, since she was maid of honor, she was paired up with Nelson. She didn't begrudge him when his eyes kept wandering to Mariah, his fiancée. Theirs would probably be the next town wedding. She wasn't sure what Mariah had planned for her own nuptials, but she had refused to breathe anything about it until after Jaycee's wedding.

The reception was a town picnic. There were potluck items brought by the locals, along with catering Mariah and the Romance Committee had arranged. Rachel knew Mariah wanted catering facilities locally, but that would have to wait on the mill renovations, currently underway.

Rachel suspected Mariah wasn't going to plan her own wedding until that venue was available.

The whole town appeared to be in attendance. Everyone knew Dave and Jaycee, and free food was a strong lure. Rachel saw Benny in his chair with his dad beside him, but no one else. She tried not to look for Ryker, but whenever she slipped the leash on her attention, her gaze wandered over the crowd, searching for that dark head.

Maybe he'd moved on. She hadn't heard anything, but—

No, she wasn't doing this.

She was able to eat some of the food, speak to most of the crowd, gracefully accepting compliments on her dress while avoiding all the "when is it your turn" questions that people who'd known her all her life felt compelled to ask. Did they really think she had an answer to that one? *Two more weddings, and it's my turn.* Like she'd drawn a number at the butcher shop.

She kept the smile plastered on her face, but it was wearing on her. She'd been sleeping poorly lately, and though her makeup, provided for the wedding party, was stellar, time and warm temperatures were starting to wear through. She'd stay until Jaycee and Dave had their big farewell, then she was leaving. She could watch the fireworks from home.

Since her father officiated at a lot of the marriages in Carter's Crossing, she knew the rhythm of a wedding. The toasts were over, the cake was cut. It was time to toss the bouquet and the garter, then the happy couple would leave, Rachel following as soon after as she could.

All the single women were being gathered

up. This was her least favorite part of the day. She allowed herself to be shepherded in with the others, keeping a wary eye on Jaycee. Jaycee had promised, but she had a look on her face. Rachel knew that look and wondered what her friend was up to.

All the single women were gathered, but Jaycee was delaying. Rachel tried to glare at her, but Jaycee was looking out of the park, not at Rachel. Rachel followed her glance, and her breath caught.

A man on crutches was slowly crossing from the sidewalk to the gathering in the middle of the town park. He was wearing dress pants with a button-down shirt. She'd never seen him in anything but jeans or shorts before. He was moving awkwardly, but deliberately.

Ryker.

Her silly heart did its shimmy again, and Rachel tried to ignore him, she really did. But she couldn't resist looking at him. He was thinner, she thought. She'd left lots of food in his place—wasn't he eating? His hair was a little long, but he was clean-shaven. She could hear murmurs through the crowd, but he was ignoring everyone but Jaycee.

Oh no. What were they up to?

Suddenly, Jaycee turned back to the group of women, all waiting with various degrees of excitement for the flowers to be tossed. Rachel tried to ease her way to the back of the group. Jaycee was staring right at her, and Rachel shook her head, mouthing, *You promised...*

Then Jaycee turned and threw the bouquet directly at Ryker.

The crowd hushed. Ryker managed to catch the flowers, but one of his crutches fell, leaving him standing awkwardly balanced.

Next thing Mariah was pushing Rachel from behind. Rachel hadn't known Mariah was anywhere close. She stumbled forward, the confused crowd allowing her to pass through.

Her face was burning. She didn't know what her friends had done, but she was going to kill them. If she survived the next few minutes, they were dead. So dead.

Finally, she was standing in front of Ryker, red-faced and nervous, looking only at the ground. He was wearing one of a pair of boots, and the crutch was lying beside his cast. She could see his bare toes. She focused on those toes.

How did he even have attractive toes?

"Rachel." She heard him call her name, but she was looking only at those toes until she could escape.

"Rachel, could you look at me?"

She closed her eyes. She shouldn't do this.

It was going to be embarrassing and hurtful. But her head slowly moved up, and she finally opened her eyes, ready to shut them closed again. Ready to flee the park, truth be told.

She met his gaze and felt the shock run through her.

"Rachel, I'm sorry."

Yeah, this wasn't what she wanted to hear. Not now, not ever, not especially in front of the whole stupid town. She braced herself, trying to pretend she was somewhere else.

"I didn't think I deserved you, so I ran, and didn't give you the chance to make that decision, about whether you wanted to give us a try. I know I'm not any of the things you deserve, but what I feel for you is big, and strong and scary, like you said in the hospital. I love you, and if you're willing to take a chance with that…"

He struggled to get down on one knee and Rachel grabbed for him. She lost her balance, and they both landed on the grass, his other crutch slipping away.

"Are you okay?" She checked to see if his cast had cracked.

Ryker reached a hand to her chin. He forced her to look at him again.

"I will be. But I'm hoping you can answer my question."

The flowers, Jaycee's bouquet, were still under his arm, apparently unscathed, and he passed those to her.

She took them, then didn't know what to do with them.

"Thank you." She wasn't sure how else to respond.

Then Ryker reached into his pocket and pulled out a ring.

"It's not much, like me. It was my mother's. If you could find a way to take a chance…"

His voice trailed off. Rachel stared at the ring in his hand.

She couldn't make sense of this. She was trying to get over Ryker. He didn't like her that way. She shook her head to clear it.

She saw his hand drop, his face closing up. It hit her. Ryker had…proposed. He thought she was saying no.

Her whole goal, back when she made her big plan to leave and change, was to find her happy-ever-after. Once Ryker was back in town, she'd seen what that looked like, but she thought she'd lost it.

And now, now he was there, hers for the taking?

She reached forward, grabbing his face. "Yes. Yes. Yes. Three times yes. But you can't run away this time."

His face slowly relaxed, and then a smile, a real, face-creasing smile, appeared.

"Really?"

"I will marry you, if you can kiss me and not run away."

He shoved his crutches away and leaned close enough that their breath mingled.

"Watch me."

EPILOGUE

RYKER STEPPED OUT of Rachel's car, landing carefully on his walking cast. He stared at the house. Rachel slipped her hand into his.

It was empty now of everything but memories. Those had lost their hold on him.

Growing up here had been bad. For all of them. But now he'd truly moved on. It was just a house, one with scars and wounds, but someone else would buy it. They might fix it or tear it down. It wouldn't affect him anymore. He hoped his siblings could also find their peace.

He heard a car approaching, and they turned, waiting for Abigail Carter, who'd requested this meeting.

The limousine that pulled up looked incongruous in their drive. Nothing that luxe had ever been there before.

A rear door opened, and Abigail Carter stepped out.

Ryker's father had cursed her after his accident, called her a bloodsucker, liar and much worse. Blaming Abigail rather than accepting his own guilt.

Ryker saw in front of him a proud, silver-haired woman, growing older, strong, but still human.

The past was gone. He didn't hold any grudges. If she wanted to buy the place, he was happy to let her. He was ready to let go.

"Rachel, Ryker Slade." She walked up to him, immaculate and well-dressed, slightly reserved, yet he saw no expression of judgment on her face.

He nodded.

"Your father was the most contrary man. Anything I suggested, he would do the opposite. I didn't learn that quickly enough. I am sorry."

Ryker turned to watch her, rather than the house. He hadn't known why she wanted to meet him here, but an apology hadn't been expected. Or required.

"I never thought you were responsible for the accident."

"I wasn't. No one at the mill was. Your father was…"

"Drunk."

She nodded. "As your family was more aware of than anyone. I offer an apology for not being able to help you, you and your siblings, more. I couldn't do anything to support your father's claims, or he would have had some basis to sue the mill for money. That money would have had to come from funds going to keep the mill going."

Ryker frowned.

"It's not widely known, but our family has been living on investments, not money taken from the mill since well back into the last century. I haven't taken any salary or bonuses since my husband died. The mill was struggling for years before I finally had to close it."

Ryker felt the surprise in Rachel's tightened grip. He wasn't the only one who didn't know this. He lifted his chin toward the house. "What happened here wasn't your problem."

She ran her gaze over the building, so much smaller and shabbier than her own.

"I was taught, perhaps wrongly, that what happened in the town that bore my name was my responsibility. It took too long to understand how to manage your father. I hope the air force suited you better?"

Ryker tensed, and Rachel rubbed his arm. Had Abigail been behind the choice he'd been offered all those years ago?

"Yes and no."

She examined him. "We hoped it would give you more options. Get you away from bad influences. Yes, I helped come up with that offer. I thought you had potential, and that your brothers would drag you down with them."

Since the twins were in prison, it was probable he'd be there, too, if he hadn't enlisted.

"That's true."

Her lips twisted. "It caused its own problems, didn't it? That's the problem with meddling. Things don't always fall out as you hope."

Ryker gave her a small smile.

"I still appreciate it. It wasn't all good, but I'm here now, and it's a better place than the twins are at."

"Thank you, Ryker. That was generous of you."

"I call it as I see it."

She nodded, as if closing the door on the conversation. "So your family has no interest in this place anymore."

"No, ma'am."

A sharp glance.

"You're planning to sell it."

Ryker nodded. "We need the money to keep Dad in the home."

"The gentleman in the car might be interested."

Ryker shot a glance at the limousine. He couldn't imagine anyone riding in a limousine wanting this place, for any reason. It wasn't a nice summer home for a rich guy from the city.

"However, I should tell you he has no interest in the house, only the property. He'd pull the building down. You've worked hard on cleaning it up, so you should know those are his intentions."

"He's welcome to blow the place up. If I'd known, I'd have left it as it was."

That might not be true. He'd cleaned up a lot of ghosts, as well as garbage, while working here.

With help from Rachel. His fiancée. He turned, checking that this wasn't a dream, and he'd wake up back in the hospital. But no, she was there, eyes smiling at him, letting him decide this. Offering her love and support.

Yeah, he didn't care about this place at all, not anymore.

Abigail waved at the limo, and the other back door opened. Out stepped a tall man, silver haired, looking wealthy enough to drive everywhere in a limousine. And one who'd never step foot in a house like the one before him.

"Ryker Slade, this is Gerald Van Dalton. Gerry, you've met Rachel."

Ryker held out his hand, examining this stranger.

Van Dalton shook his hand and nodded at Rachel. Then he answered Ryker's unspoken question.

"Mariah is my granddaughter. She's spoken of you."

"Nice to meet you."

"I'm interested in your property. Abigail promises you won't change your price based on my plans, but that's not my usual practice."

Ryker examined the man. He looked like he might be willing to cut corners to put through a deal. Ryker would have a lawyer check out any offers the man made.

But he did trust Abigail. Or he trusted Rachel, who trusted Abigail.

"The money isn't coming to me. It's supporting my father in the home he's in. I'm ready to walk away from this."

Van Dalton's face showed surprise. But when it rested on Abigail Carter, it showed something more.

Interesting. But that was not why Ryker was here.

"Mrs. Carter says you're only interested in the land. That's fine by me. You can bulldoze the house or bury it, I don't care. If it's a fair offer, I'll take it."

There wasn't exactly a lineup of buyers wanting the place. Not because of his reputation, not anymore, but because this town still needed business to keep people working. People didn't have money to buy.

"It will be a fair offer. Then the house will be torn down."

Ryker stared at the house, for what might be the last time. If this man wanted to buy it and demolish it, Ryker wouldn't need to come out here again.

He was okay with that.

"Good luck with what you've planned," he told the man. It would be good if something came out of this place, out of its history, that would be a positive.

"I'm so not in New York," the man muttered.

"No, you're not, Gerry," Abigail responded. She turned back to Ryker and Rachel. "Gerry will send his offer to you, Rachel, and you can get one of the lawyers to check it over. It'll make a lovely small inn and spa. Mariah will be pleased."

Van Dalton shook his head at her. "Why don't you just tell everyone all my plans?"

"They already know, or will soon, Gerry. It's a small town. Now, once we get Mariah and Nelson married, I think my work here is done."

Ryker didn't think he was part of this conversation any longer.

"Then what are you planning to do, Abigail?" Van Dalton's voice was amused.

"Oh, I have ideas."

"Would you be willing to discuss them, perhaps see if they line up with ideas I have?"

Abigail shrugged. "I'm willing to listen to offers, once things here are settled."

"Offers, you say."

Abigail shot him a challenging glance. "Only if it's a good one."

Rachel tugged Ryker's hand, pulling him toward the car. She cast an amused glance at Abigail and Gerry.

"I didn't believe in Cupid, but I think I do now." She kept her voice low, for his ears only.

Ryker lifted her hand to his lips, pressing a kiss. He wasn't going to discount Cupid, not after the miracle of this woman tying herself to him.

Cupid was performing miracles.

* * * * *

HARLEQUIN SELECTS COLLECTION

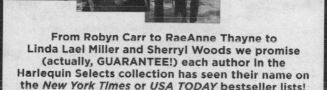

19 FREE BOOKS IN ALL!

From Robyn Carr to RaeAnne Thayne to Linda Lael Miller and Sherryl Woods we promise (actually, GUARANTEE!) each author in the Harlequin Selects collection has seen their name on the *New York Times* or *USA TODAY* bestseller lists!

YES! Please send me the **Harlequin Selects Collection**. This collection begins with 3 FREE books and 2 FREE gifts in the first shipment. Along with my 3 free books, I'll also get 4 more books from the Harlequin Selects Collection, which I may either return and owe nothing or keep for the low price of $24.14 U.S./$28.82 CAN. each plus $2.99 U.S./$7.49 CAN. for shipping and handling per shipment*.If I decide to continue, I will get 6 or 7 more books (about once a month for 7 months) but will only need to pay for 4. That means 2 or 3 books in every shipment will be FREE! If I decide to keep the entire collection, I'll have paid for only 32 books because 19 were FREE! I understand that accepting the 3 free books and gifts places me under no obligation to buy anything. I can always return a shipment and cancel at any time. My free books and gifts are mine to keep no matter what I decide.

☐ 262 HCN 5576   ☐ 462 HCN 6676

Name (please print)

Address   Apt. #

City   State/Province   Zip/Postal Code

Mail to the Harlequin Reader Service:
IN U.S.A.: P.O. Box 1341, Buffalo, NY 14240-8531
IN CANADA: P.O. Box 603, Fort Erie, Ontario L2A 5X3

50BOOKHS22R

COMING NEXT MONTH FROM

ⓗ HARLEQUIN
HEARTWARMING

#383 BUILDING A SURPRISE FAMILY
Butterfly Harbor Stories • by Anna J. Stewart

Being nicknamed Butterfly Harbor's most eligible bachelor has taken Ozzy Lakeman by surprise! But he's more surprised by the town newcomer and single mom-to-be, Jo Bertoletti, a woman he can't get off his mind...or out of his heart.

#384 THE SECRET SANTA PROJECT
Seasons of Alaska • by Carol Ross

Travel blogger Hazel James has scheduled her holiday at an unexpected but much-needed locale—home. Major disruption to her peaceful Christmas: Cricket Blackburn, her brother's best friend and the love of her life she can't quite seem to get over.

#385 STEALING HER BEST FRIEND'S HEART
The Golden Matchmakers Club • by Tara Randel

Heidi Welch wants the house Reid Masterson intends to flip for a profit, which puts it out of her price range. Will they make a deal or take a chance on a friendship that has grown into love?

#386 A COWBOY'S HOMECOMING
Kansas Cowboys • by Leigh Riker

Rancher and widowed single mother Kate Lancaster needed help. But she'd never accept it from Noah Bodine—the man she was drawn to...and the man she blames for her husband's death.

YOU CAN FIND MORE INFORMATION ON UPCOMING HARLEQUIN TITLES, FREE EXCERPTS AND MORE AT HARLEQUIN.COM.

HWCNM0721

Visit
ReaderService.com
Today!

As a valued member of the Harlequin Reader Service, you'll find these benefits and more at ReaderService.com:

- Try 2 free books from any series
- Access risk-free special offers
- View your account history & manage payments
- Browse the latest Bonus Bucks catalog

Don't miss out!

If you want to stay up-to-date on the latest at the Harlequin Reader Service and enjoy more content, make sure you've signed up for our monthly News & Notes email newsletter. Sign up online at ReaderService.com or by calling Customer Service at 1-800-873-8635.